I0761865

FASHION GOES TO THE DOGS

Other Books by Peggy Gaffney

The Crafty Samoyed Knits
The Crafty Labrador Retriever Knits
The Crafty Golden Retriever Knits
The Crafty Bernese Mt. Dog Knits
The Crafty Newfoundland Knits
The Crafty Welsh Corgi Knits
The Crafty Poodle Knits
The Crafty Cat Knits
The Crafty Llama and Alpaca Knits
Knit a Kitten, Purl a Puppy
Do It Yourself Publishing Nonfiction in Your Spare Time

FASHION GOES TO THE DOGS

a kate killoy mystery

Suspense for the Dog Lover

PEGGY GAFFNEY

KANINE BOOKS

This is a work of fiction. Names, characters, places, and incidents either are the product of the author's imagination or are used fictitiously, and any resemblance to actual persons, living or dead, business establishments, events, or locales is entirely coincidental. The publisher does not have any control over and does not assume any responsibility for author or third-party websites or their content.

Kanine Books is a division of Kanine Knits Books and Patterns,
877 Marion Road, Cheshire, Connecticut 06410

ISBN 978-0-9964531-5-8

Acknowledgements

I'd like to thank my team of editors, my friends and mentors in Sisters in Crime, my son Sean who keeps me on task and of course my wonderful Samoyeds who have filled my life with joy for years and without whom this book would not have happened.

CHAPTER ONE

"Kate, we need to leave now." My cousin Agnes charged past me out of the pre-dawn darkness grabbed my shoes from the shelf where they lived safely out of puppy reach and tossed them at me. While I was still struggling to tie my shoes, she pulled my coat off the rack shoving me out the door and into Henry, her Ford Explorer. Before I could even ask where we were going, we were headed south on the Yankee Expressway known to the locals as Connecticut Route 6, toward the interstate. She reached between the seats and grabbed a large Dunkin' Donuts bag which she plopped onto my lap.

"There's two cups of tea and croissants with orange marmalade. It was the best I could do on short notice."

Having grown up with four brothers, my first instinct was to argue, but the smell of those buttery croissants on my still sleep befuddled brain was too tempting to ignore. In half the time it normally took, we turned up the ramp onto I-84 and were heading west.

Once the bag's contents, including both cups of tea, were history, I felt awake enough to speak. "Where the hell are we going?"

"Into the city."

"I hate to inform you, Rambo, but taking someone across state lines against their will is kidnapping, a federal offense. I've got two businesses to run in Connecticut and don't have time to watch the sunrise over the Hudson with you."

"It's all taken care of. Sal is getting coverage. You were smart to bring him on as kennel manager. He told me he could manage without you in the boarding kennel this weekend. This week's numbers are low because, next week, everyone and his brother will be boarding their dogs, when they go away for the long Thanksgiving weekend. Since it's Saturday you're not scheduled to teach training classes. Also, I checked, and you don't have any entries in the dog show at the Big E this weekend so that's not an issue. Lastly, according to Ellen Martin, you could take the month off from your knitting studio and still submit the number of new designs you've created for the business since summer. Your studio manager is about to start kicking your butt."

I stared ahead, silent. I had to admit, I'd hit a dry spell. Following the second funeral, I'd just stopped, thinking, doing or caring. If it didn't happen by rote, it didn't get done.

In the Killoy family, I was not only the sole girl of the five children, but the only offspring who possessed a passion for the world of dog breeding and showing, especially Samoyeds. My mother and all four of my brothers lived and breathed mathematics. That was Dad's and Gramps' field too, but their true passion was the dogs. I, meanwhile, showed no aptitude, let alone genius, for numbers and it absolutely appalled everyone when I snubbed MIT to study fashion design. But Dad and Gramps stepped up to the plate and supported me, turning the second floor of the dog-training barn into a design studio for my business. The fact that my designs were aimed at people who showed dogs, also helped.

Losing Gramps to cancer had been heartbreaking, but I'd seen it coming and I still had Dad. Sharing our love of dogs, the three of us had been a team all my life. Since I was seven, we'd spent weekends together at dog shows. They had taught me my craft the way no one else ever could. Always together, we became "The Three Amigos" of the dog-show world. With Gramps gone, Dad and I had just begun to build a new connection, working as a pair. We had begun taking an interest in the new litter of puppies and their show potential. We'd actually been in the puppy pen, laughing at their antics, when the aneurysm hit him. They told me later there was nothing I could have done. Dad was dead before he reached the hospital. My world caved in as though the ground had been cut out from under me. I stood at his graveside, oblivious of the crowds that had gathered. I was alone and, after that, nothing seemed worth the effort.

We'd driven for about half an hour when I finally I roused myself. "Why?"

Agnes didn't take her eyes off the road. "So I can help a friend. As for why you're going, I need someone who looks like you."

"Looks like me how?"

"I need someone who looks like a kid. You've got to pretend to be a kid who likes dogs but knows nothing about them. Act like you're very shy so you won't have to talk, your voice would give you away." Her eyes were glancing at the clock every few minutes.

"I'm twenty-four."

"You look twelve."

"Bitch."

"Agreed. Though I think I qualify as veteran bitch. Look Kate, you've been trading on that 'little-girl' look in the ring for years. I just thought I'd take advantage of it for once. You run around the ring with your braid flying and your cute innocent expression and all the judges think it cool to put up the young handler with the great dog. Tell the truth. Don't you think it's about time to start playing on a level field with the grown-ups?"

"Any more advice, Dear Abby? What else can't you stand?"

"Well someone's got to tell you this stuff. Your mother doesn't notice you exist, Grace is too sweet to criticize her granddaughter, and everyone else thinks it but likes you too much to say anything. It needed saying. You adored your dad and granddad, but they kept you frozen in amber and didn't let you grow up. If they'd tried this type of control with your brothers, there would have been war, but you were their sweet little girl. They could keep you young and play with you in the dog show world forever."

"They didn't..." I began what I knew was a flimsy protest.

"You haven't changed a thing about yourself since you were twelve. Even in design school, people thought you were some young kid in a special program. People didn't take you seriously."

I moved as far from her as possible. Pressing up against the door I stared out the window. I wanted to scream and shout that she was wrong. She wasn't. What's more I'd known it for a long time but just didn't want to admit it because the thought of change scared the hell out of me.

With work everything was fine. I could run the kennel and teach the classes, no problem. And my design business was done online. No challenge there. No, I knew she meant that I should have a social life as a woman. Truth was that terrified me. The world of sex, drugs and rock n' roll was not even in my solar system. I glanced at her determined expression and knew I was about to be ripped from my protective cocoon and thrown into the cold cruel world. After more miles of silence, Agnes sighed and glanced my way.

"Remember when we were kids and I'd ask you to do things and not ask why?" I nodded. "This operation is like that. I'm involved in something I can't discuss, but I need your help."

The words "Go to hell," popped into my head, but "fine," came out of my mouth.

We were making excellent time. She crossed onto I -684 heading into White Plains. It was good we'd gotten this far so early because the sun was coming up–and that meant a gazillion cars would be flooding the highway any minute traveling the same direction we were. I twisted in my seat to look at Agnes. She was biting her lower lip as her thumb twisted the Claddagh ring she always wore. She was nervous which was unheard of for her. She could handle any situation with style and aplomb. Hell, her photo was on a billboard in Time Square. I'd never seen her stressed. I went back to staring out the window. We ate up the miles as we transitioned from the Saw Mill River Parkway to the Henry Hudson Parkway which ran along the Hudson River as both the city and the sun rose before us.

Before I knew it, we were swinging into the parking garage of Agnes' condo. I headed toward the elevator, but she yelled, "Come on," and ran for the street.

Five minutes later we slowed to a stop at the entrance to Central Park nearest Strawberry Fields, an area named in memory of John Lennon. Agnes grabbed a gaudy scarf from her pocket tying it around her head like a turban, and turned her reversible white coat inside out so, the white fake-fur collar stood out against a now bright-purple coat. Then she put on the ugliest pair of glasses ever designed and slipped the strap of a camera over her head.

We'd barely gone forty feet into the park when I noticed a group of men moving toward us. "Don't speak and follow my lead," she whispered. Then in a voice that dripped of a supposed Georgia birth, she ordered me to pose in front of a statue as she morphed into the quintessential obnoxious touristzilla. My eyes focused immediately on a gorgeous Afghan Hound walking at the side of Bill Trumbull, a handler I'd known all my life. "Oh my God, darlin', will you look at that pretty doggie!" Agnes gushed. "Oh I've got to get a photo of that. People back home won't believe that you can see something that beautiful just walkin' in the park."

The men had all stopped because we were blocking the walkway. I automatically moved toward the dog which was an exceptional blue-gray color with a white blaze. "I just know that you gentlemen won't mind if my baby sister poses for a picture with your magnificent doggie. Step a little closer sweetie. Stand right behind the—excuse me, what kind of dog is this?" Agnes raised her camera and waved me into position. I stood beside Bill, but he didn't show any recognition.

"It's an Afghan Hound, madam. You may touch the coat young lady." He reached out to stroke the dog. "Feel how sleek it is—like your own beautiful long hair." He reached out and stroked my hair, giving it a slight yank partway down.

"Oh, thank you so much." Agnes gushed. "Come on, darlin' we don't want to be late meeting Cheryl for breakfast." I turned and waved shyly at Bill then hurried to join Agnes. As soon as we were out of sight, we exited the park. She waved down a cab and gave the cabbie an address I didn't know. As we started forward, she looked back to make sure we hadn't been observed. Once we were in traffic, Agnes grabbed my shoulders.

"Turn around and let me see your braid." Her hands worked their way down to the spot where Bill had yanked it.

"Ouch."

She pulled something out of the braid along with a clump of hair that had recently been attached to my head. Turning, I saw her slip a mini memory card into her bag.

"What the hell is going on?" I was now getting worried. "Bill acted as if he'd never seen me."

Agnes didn't answer; she just looked out the window.

We pulled up in front of a brownstone building with a plaque on the door that read Marcel. As we got out of the cab, I looked at her. "Those men with Bill were not the kind I'd like to meet in a dark alley. Are they a danger to Bill or to us?"

"Neither they're bodyguards."

I looked at her in surprise as we climbed the front steps, but her frown told me the subject was off limits. When we neared the top, she turned to me, grasping my shoulders to hold my attention. "Since you were twelve years old, what has been your one goal in life?"

I laughed because this had been the family joke forever. "You mean my fantasy, to have my own fashion show here in the city during Fashion Week?"

"Well, what if it weren't a fantasy? What if it were a challenge? What if I told you that since we were coming into the city today, I thought it might be a good time to kill two birds with… well, you get the picture? Kate, it's about time you show the world that you really are a serious designer. Fashion Week is in February right before the Westerland Kennel Club show. I pulled some strings—well a lot of strings—and you'd better be ready to put your ass on the line, kiddo, because your fashion show is in the works. I suggested it at the board meeting of the Canine Genetics Foundation. They were looking for something to use as charity event to raise research money during show week. It will happen the last evening of Fashion Week. You'll meet with the sponsors later today to finalize the plans and sign the contracts."

My foot slipped on the top step and I grabbed the

railing to keep from falling flat on my butt. Her words slowly sank in and began to have meaning. "I get a fashion show of my designs...here?"

"Actually, I think Marcel might object to that use of his front steps, but the ballroom of the host hotel should do. It's scheduled for the Saturday of their show week, which, as I said, happens to be the last day of Fashion Week so all the buyers will still be in town. You'd better close your mouth or Marcel will think you're an idiot."

"Marcel who?"

"There is only one Marcel. He's my step one in the plan to pull you out of your cocoon and turn you from a frumpy, dog-enrapture child into a sophisticated fashion designer. That has got to happen before you sit at the grown-up table today to sign the contracts for the show."

Agnes pulled me inside to meet Marcel and in a flurry of activity my transformation began.

Like Alice after falling down the rabbit hole, I felt disoriented. Each successive change was tearing me farther away from the only Kate Killoy I had ever known. Saying goodbye to my braid broke my heart since my hair had never been cut. The resulting stylish hair-do, clothes, and make-up created an entirely new person. As she stared back at me from the mirror, I didn't recognize her. She was beautiful. She scared me to death.

Agnes and her agent, Arden, supervised all the contracts for my show. The deal guaranteed a winning result for all. The Agnes & Arden show took over the room, charming everyone while they pointed to the many places I, and everyone else involved should sign. Once the stack of contracts was complete, they left, pulling me in their wake. Each gave me a high-five and welcomed me to the world of high fashion. I had ceased thinking hours ago and was running on autopilot. All I could do was smile and mutter my thanks. Reality began forcing its nasty way into my brain and I questioned whether thanks were premature. Had I just signed contracts that could sound the death knell for my career?

We'd spent so much time today in Agnes' fairytale world that I was surprised when we arrived at a place I actually recognized.

Reilly's was my great-aunt and -uncle's favorite pub. We pushed open the door, and there they were. I was so happy to see familiar faces I almost burst into tears trying to hug them both.

Maeve, held me at arms length, just staring at me, but Padraig leaned over me to whisper in my ear. "You are the spitting image of Maeve the day I fell in love with her. John and Tom would be thrilled speechless if they could see you now. In fact they're probably doing a jig up in heaven now, knowing their little girl has grown up."

I wanted to cry but was afraid the tears would turn my newly applied makeup into a horror mask.

Supper turned out to be a noisy affair with friends of Maeve and Padraig coming over to our table to be introduced to Agnes and me. For some reason, many thought I was a model too. Only their oldest friends recognized me right off.

Reilly's attracted mostly retired members of what I called 'The long arm of the law club.' Patrons tended to be both active and retired NYPD, FBI, CIA and MI-5. Maeve had been working for MI-5 when she met Padraig. They moved to New York where Padraig's family business was, but Maeve had kept her hand in, on an informal basis.

Partway through dinner, a man whose name wasn't mentioned joined us at the table pulling up a chair next to Agnes. As I watched, she slipped him the memory card. He apparently knew everyone there, because he jumped right into the conversation. After about five minutes he said his goodbyes and disappeared. Agnes leaned back, relaxed and ordered a cocktail, the signal, I guess, for a job done.

I wasn't sure if I was just overly conscious of my new appearance, but I was aware that we were being watched. The watchers sat at a table to our left. At first I didn't pay much attention. I know the effect Agnes has on the world's male population. However, as one hour passed into two, this began to feel creepy. The younger one, who was dressed much more formally than any of the other men in the place, neither spoke nor ate. Every time I glanced in his direction, his eyes—his beautiful green eyes, I noticed—were focused on me. He didn't look like the men shadowing Bill, but...

When we stood to leave, I took Agnes' arm. "Those two guys at the table on the left have been watching us since we arrived. The guy in the double breasted suit hasn't taken his eyes off me since we came in. Could he have recognized us from the park? Should we be worried?"

She glanced casually in their direction. "No, you needn't worry. Nobody could recognize you as that little girl in the park this morning." She grinned at me. "Brace yourself, Kate, I'd say it's a case of you having your first admirer."

When we turned to go out, I frowned and glanced back at the table. Both men were still watching. From where I stood, I couldn't read the expression on the younger guy's face, but when I looked at his older friend who had focused all evening entirely on Agnes, what I saw wasn't admiration. His look was pure, unmistakable hatred.

CHAPTER TWO

When I awoke the next morning, it was to full panic. What had I done? I had signed legal contracts stating I would have a complete line of fashions, not just ready to show, but in production and ready to supply to stores in only two months. Impossible! The high yips from the puppies' room that connected my house to the kennel were the only thing that kept me from crawling back under the covers and hiding for a year—or maybe two. I'd gotten in so late last night I hadn't had a chance to call Ellen. I'd see her at morning Mass. I considered offering up a special prayer that she wouldn't kill me.

My feet hit the cold floor and I reminded myself for the hundredth time that I really needed to get a rug for this room.

I had moved into the tiny kennel manager's house which backed up on the kennel, the week after my father's death. I needed my own space, even if it measured less than eight-hundred square feet and was two-thirds unfurnished. My bedroom set plus a table and two chairs in the kitchen were as far as I had gotten. My Grandma Grace had made sure I had dishes, cutlery, pots and pans, and I often found casseroles mysteriously appearing in the freezer. However, I hadn't had any enthusiasm so far for making the house a home. Mostly, it was a place to be alone.

I hurried through the puppy routine and then hopped into the shower. It suddenly dawned on me I could wash my hair and have it dry before I was dressed. Maybe this new look wasn't so bad. My head felt light and naked, but the thought of not having to go around for hours with wet hair down to my waist every time I washed it, had me smiling as I began throwing on my usual Sunday clothes. Then I stopped.

I took them off and put on one of the outfits that Agnes had had me get yesterday. I slid my feet into the stylish boots, put on a little blush and lipstick, and I was ready. It was time to go or I'd be late, and Father Joseph would give me the evil eye as he watched me sneak into my seat. Then I looked in the mirror and laughed. Father Joseph might not even recognize me.

Rather than sitting with my family, I slipped into the pew next to Ellen. She moved to let me in. I waited.

My watch told me that fifty-three seconds had passed before I saw her back go ramrod straight and her head turn. I gave her a sheepish grin and she reached out to hug me only letting go when Mass began. I made her sit in the pew after everyone left, so, I could make my confession in a place where her religion might keep her from killing me. I told her the whole story of the makeover and the fashion show and the contracts.

"This means we've got two months to do everything, the line, the models, the samples, finding someone to produce the designs in volume for the shops—and more that I haven't even thought of yet."

"Well, it looks like all that research I've been doing to keep from getting bored will pay off," Ellen quipped as she smiled at me. "If we have to go with large production numbers, I've got mill sources and I think we would best try the one in New York that specializes in intarsia with Stoll machines. However, even they would only be good for the dogs with limited color changes."

Ellen got more comfortable in her seat as she warmed to the topic. "I think we should begin small by selling only through certain exclusive boutiques. I've been running training classes, in cooperation with a state sponsored adult education program for single mothers and women returning to the workplace. I've got four production knitters trained and ready to begin work immediately, and two more who just need more practice on intarsia. They can start at minimum wage plus two dollars an hour. As their skills increase, their pay can grow. We can do flexible hours, and I think if we wall off the corner where you've been storing extra dog equipment, we can then have a nursery area, for the moms with babies. I've got a source for used Studio/Silver Reed 860 intarsia machines. I'll send him an order for a rush shipment. She stopped and took my face in her hands. "Thank God, my Katie, you're back!"

When we left church, I saw my twin brothers, Tim and Seamus standing by my truck. They looked right past me when Ellen and I approached. Seamus finally recognizing me, whooped and swung me off the ground. What followed was a recitation of what Agnes had done from makeover to fashion show.

Grandma Grace required attendance at Sunday dinner. She had always done the cooking for our family. My mother, though a brilliant mathematician, could burn water. Though invited to join us, Ellen begged off attending to spend the day with her husband and grandchildren. She said it might be the last time she'd see them in the next two months.

The next day, Ellen and I took a drive to northeastern Connecticut to visit a mill and arrange for yarns of the proper weight, texture and colors to set off our designs. It meant several hours on the road and three more hours haggling with their technicians but we came back with yarn cones that could get the new employees started. It was a beautiful fall day, and both Ellen and I decided that we deserved a drive through what remained of the fall color before we disappeared into our killer work schedules.

The studio wasn't a hard place to work. Built on the second floor of a barn, it was a huge open space. Gramps had read that designers needed lots of light so, skylights dotted the ceiling and a large picture window looked out onto the woods and trails behind the barn. As fall drifted into winter, the view would lose its color, but stay beautiful. The women we hired appreciated the fact that the break area was set in front of that window.

For the next few weeks, we worked flat out and barely had time to draw a breath. While Ellen handled the production end, I spent many sleepless nights producing twenty new styles that would be popular both with boutique buyers and the dog public. We agreed that limiting distribution to a few boutiques and specialty outlets for the first two seasons would give us the ability to handle production without getting overextended. This way we could train new people without having to subcontract the labor. Since Ellen and I were both control freaks, this plan worked well. I kept Agnes in the loop and she arranged for buyers who specialized in small, exclusive-client shops to get invitations to the show.

Limiting the number of sizes available also helped. Our yarn supplier came through with out initial order and soon the new design shapes were on display.

It fell to me to get models for the show. I was worrying how I could afford models with so much of my money tied up in equipment, supplies, and salaries. Then I remembered my senior-year project for which I had created a fashion line, actually the precursor to what I was now doing. For that event, I had brought in my dog-show friends and their dogs to model the fashions. Of course it didn't hurt to have Agnes Forester, the top model in the country, strutting down the runway with her pair of greyhounds. Needless to say, I got an A and graduated with honors.

This is how I found myself on the phone inviting twenty of my closest dog-breeding friends, to be part of my first New York fashion show. Much to my amazement, everyone said yes! I sent out instructions explaining how they should measure themselves and told them to return the forms with a recent dog-show win photo.

Days flew by in a whirlwind of activity. Even Christmas was a blur—I did all my shopping in one afternoon at one store in less than three hours. The day itself came with early Mass and the traditional dinner. But after the presents were exchanged, I disappeared back to my little house to work.

Day and night, my phone buzzed.

"I've got you Andy Sibowitz to do your photography. You may kiss my feet later. He'll be exhausted from doing Fashion Week, but apparently he knows you from school." Disconnect. Agnes.

"Kate, Carolyn said you should handle Ajax at the show. She's bringing people to look at him for stud. I'm going to be visiting Bunny that week in the city but she'd love to have Ajax stay as well." Disconnect. Sarah Mondigliani, Sal's daughter-in-law, whose German Shepherd Ajax, I'd trained.

Three nights later, another call from Agnes roused me from sleep.

"I've got you Ulysses Jones to do your show. Luckily since it's happening on Saturday night, he can fit you in. He apparently knows you from school as well." Disconnect.

For all the chance I got to speak on these calls, I should have let them go to voicemail.

Sal was a blessing. He covered the bookings for the boarding kennel and found me two high school girls to take my place doing grooming. I still taught my classes, plus did the demos we'd set up with the police departments in Connecticut and neighboring states. Dillon and I worked together, shocking most of the police-dog handlers that this fuzzy, show-dog Samoyed could match their guys one for one going through the course. Also Wednesday nights, I worked with my dog dancing team to perfect the routine that we'd been booked to perform as part of the Westerland week.

I know I must have slept some time, and even eaten, but it came under the heading of little and not much. Finally, Grace stepped in, forcing me to stop and eat supper with her each night. Since I usually ate my breakfast when the dogs ate theirs, that guaranteed I ate at least two meals a day. As we hit the second week in January, with styles and intarsia designs completed, I began to get my second wind.

On Friday, with only two weeks 'til the eve of the show, Agnes suddenly appeared in the studio. All my knitters were thrilled that a famous celebrity had come to visit them, even more so when she sat and chatted as they ate their lunches. Now, I know Agnes and her taking a drive to Connecticut when she's involved in the chaos of posing for magazines layouts for Fashion Week was unheard of.

I let her do her meet-and-greet, and then asked her to take a walk with me. "Okay, what's going on? You're up to your ears with work and you're sitting chatting with my staff. You need something. What is it?"

"I need you to add someone to the fashion show. I know it's late and it's going to throw your schedule into the toilet, but I need you to do it anyway."

I stopped and looked at her. "Is this a favor for your friend who joined us at Reilly's?"

"Who says you're just another pretty face? You can't tell anyone. Bill needs to be in the show with Ashraf. As soon as the prince heard about the show, it became a deal breaker."

"My fashion show is that big a deal?"

"Haven't you been reading all the publicity clippings I've been sending you?"

"I haven't really had time."

"Kate, your show has sold out. There's a waiting list for tickets. I've got six buyers already on board and several others talking to their clients. So yes, it is a big deal."

"I'll need Bill's measurements and a show photo of the Afghan."

"I've got them with me. I called Ellen before I came to ask what you required of the models."

"You knew I'd say yes." I looked up from the papers and photo and smiled.

"Kate, when someone needs your help, you always say yes. You don't have a selfish chromosome in your body. Someday I'm going to have to teach you to think of yourself first, but not today, thank heaven."

"I *am* going to be a bit selfish. There's no way I'm putting up with those bodyguards Huey, Dewey and Louie hanging around and throwing a scare into the proceedings. I'll take this on but I want to keep it low key and friendly."

"I'll tell them they need to come up with someone who will blend in. Thanks, Kate." With a hug, she hopped into Henry and was gone.

I stared at the photo of the dog. He really was magnificent. My mind was already creating the design before my feet hit the stairs to the studio. I'd have to capture all that majesty.

"Yipes!" It suddenly dawned on me how much work Agnes had added. This was going to be tight. I giggled at the thought of my working with the State Department this way. 'They also serve who only design and knit.'

With a laugh I ran the rest of the way upstairs to show Ellen what we needed and to get the design done. With less than two weeks before everything had to be in New York City, it was going to be insane.

Agnes was wrong about one thing. Before I began on the design, I selfishly sat down, had a cup of tea and read every one of those press clippings. Sold out, indeed!

CHAPTER THREE

"I still can't believe we got everything done for this week of madness. It feels like I just signed those contracts yesterday. I have never worked so hard in my life. Designing and making twenty-one new outfits as well as all the prep to launch the ready-to-wear line has left me feeling like the favorite toy in the puppy pen, chewed to bits with my squeaker gone," I ranted at Sal Mondigliani who was driving me to the show hotel.

This morning I'd rolled out early, looking forward to The Day. Now panic was taking over. I glared at the man with the all-too-huge, all-too-solid presence, sitting behind the steering wheel. Sporting a smug grin he inched his way the last few feet down Seventh Avenue to the curb in front of the hotel.

"This is insane you know. What do I think I'm doing? I can't run a New York fashion show. It's all Agnes' fault. I belong in the dog-show ring not on the runways." My arm automatically reached between the seats, my fingers pushing through the wire grid to scratch the excited dog pressed against the crate wall behind me.

"Well, I'm not going to argue with you." Sal, the world's best kennel manager, didn't even look my way. "I don't know how to run a fashion show either. But I didn't go and promise Agnes and twenty-one of my favorite dog-loving friends, plus the hundreds of people who bought tickets that I would. So I'd say you've got two choices. Do it or do it."

"Damn it. Why doesn't Agnes answer? I've left her a ton of voicemails and a dozen texts in the last forty-eight hours, and there's not been a peep out of her. She knows I can't do this alone. It's almost as though she's hiding. Though, how, I ask you, when you're the most recognizable face in the country, can you disappear?" Typing one more text, I hit send. "Hell Agnes, answer me," I growled in frustration as I shook the phone. In defeat, I stuffed it back in the pocket of my parka and stared straight ahead.

Through the windshield, the familiar marquee of the Garden announced the dog show. The sight killed my temper as the many memories of Dad and Gramps and the past seventeen years filled me. They'd always been here for these frozen arrivals. Now for the first time in my life, I was on my own.

I shoved open the van door, the cold biting my cheeks and eyes. Sounds of traffic, the vibrations of trains and the chatter of crowds hit me. Feelings of déjà vu ran through me and I straightened my shoulders. "I'm an idiot." The admission slipped out of my mouth as I jumped from the van and slid open the side door.

"I never argue with a lady when she's right." Sal muttered to himself just loud enough for me to hear. He slid from behind the wheel and waved to a pair of bellhops with luggage carts. They got to work emptying the van as I grabbed my purse and a briefcase. I tossed their straps over my head and grabbed a lead that was clipped to the now-rocking travel crate. With deafening barks and the banging of paws on crate walls, the Samoyed tried to exit through steel mesh.

"Wait!"

At my command, Dillon froze, a coiled spring, poised for release. I unlatched the crate door, snapped on the lead, and waited. He knew better than to move a muscle. His dark brown eyes stared, linked with mine.

"Out!"

The dog shot straight to the sidewalk and shook until he disappeared into a white blur of hair, legs and ears. Finally, with a whirl, he sat perfectly straight facing me with a killer grin on his face. I looked down and grinned back.

"Good boy, Dillon. Heel." His body shot into the air and spun into heel position landing perfectly at my side. I laughed as we walked around to the back of the van and smack into the brick wall that was Sal. My feet left the ground as massive hands lifted me by the elbows and deposited me out of the way.

"Just take the fuzz-ball and stand aside, Kate. We can unload faster without you."

I didn't argue. If I'd learned one thing in the six months since Sal had retired from his job as a police chief in Massachusetts and come to work for me, it was never to argue with a man when he's right.

"Ya know, I've learned a lot about dogs since working for you, Kate." He looked around at the dozens of dogs that crowded the sidewalk. His tough old face finally split with a grin at the sight before him. "This, however, is just ridiculous. Are you sure all of these things are really dogs?"

I watched as three Welsh Corgis, five Westies, and two Chinese Crested mingled with a Newf, two Shar Peis, a Golden and a Komondor. "They're dogs all right and each comes with an owner who will tell you their puppy is the best breed in the world; they wouldn't own any other."

"Like you and Mr. Dillon."

"Damn straight," I reached to scratch the white head beside me. Sal had become my anchor. He kept me focused and concentrating on what really needed my attention. When the death of my dad had made me owner of Shannon Samoyeds Breeding and Boarding Kennel on top of my knitting design business, I refused to tell anyone how scared I was that I'd fail at both businesses. But since Sal arrived, I'd not only survived, but thrived. "My reason for being here early is I've got a knitting design of each and every one of these dogs and this fashion show will let their owners know that." I looked at the crowd. "That's why I let Agnes talk me into this insanity."

"So you admit that it's your own fault." He grinned down at me using his massive hand to ruffle my short curls. "Look Kate, I've watched you work for six months. You've got more guts than ninety percent of the youngsters I trained to be cops and you don't run away from a challenge. You and I both know you're too stubborn not to nail both the fashion thing and the dog show. For you, it will be a piece o' cake. By the way, Miss Glamorous, you look great in all of the new duds your cousin forced you to wear instead of your usual outfit of grubbies and muck boots. Hell, you look almost grown up."

Pausing, he glared at the bellhops, "Move it, people. You're done." As the bellhops slammed all the van doors, I hopped back to let them roll the carts toward the lobby.

He hugged me, his smile returning. "So go get 'em, tiger. Just be packed and ready when I come to get you on Wednesday, so I don't have to wait."

My grip tightened on Dillon's lead and I leaned into the hug. "Thanks, Sal. Take care of everything for me."

"Kate, I know you're worried about Agnes, but she'll turn up. If there are any problems at all, just press pound three on your cell. I'm now on speed dial." I could only nod, the lump in my throat making speech impossible. "Give my love to Sarah, and make sure she takes care of herself and that grandchild of mine she's carrying."

He folded himself into the van, slammed the door and, with a wave, merged back into the busy Manhattan traffic for the drive back to Connecticut.

I let Sal's words wrap around me like a security blanket. He was right. Too many people were counting on me to get all chicken hearted now. *Show some Irish backbone Killoy and just get on with it. After all, it's going to be a piece o' cake.*

I straightened my shoulders, told Dillon to heel, and stepped out, ready to take on the world or at least the dog world. I'd just turned toward the door and taken one step when, out of nowhere, I was body slammed. Instantly, Dillon reacted, shoving his own body against my thighs and keeping me from landing face down. My hands dug into his coat, holding on for balance. "Thank God. Good boy Dillon. You really saved my chops this time."

"Oh my God, I am so sorry. I'm such an ass, just a clumsy lout. It is entirely my fault. Are you hurt? I was looking at that van moving into traffic and stupidly didn't see you there." Her assailant's thick Boston baritone poured out his apology. "I spotted someone I thought I knew driving off, and like the complete imbecile I am, wasn't looking where I was going. Please tell me you are unhurt."

The expletive that came to mind died before it reached my lips. I froze and looked up at the creature before me. Suddenly I was in 1930 and the world became that of high style and civility. From the top of his fedora to his Harris Tweed belted double-breasted overcoat, to the inch-high pant cuffs resting on the toes of his wingtips, he was the living breathing incarnation of my dream man come to life. I was caught by a pair of bright green vaguely familiar eyes behind wire-rim glasses, and a face robbed of being handsome only by its sharp angles. My mouth had lost all connection to my brain. "No. Really, I'm fine. No damage." I was able to sputter my response.

"Oh super. So glad you are unscathed." He turned again to look down the street.

Rather than stand there with my tongue hanging out embarrassing myself, I slunk off toward the entrance. *Focus you idiot. You've got work to do. But God, he's the hero you've fallen in love with over and over, in every black-and-white movie you watched. In those movies you enchant him with your quick wit and charm. To bad this is reality.*

I hurried through the lobby door, headed up the steps, and then froze, testing even Dillon's skill at the instant automatic sit. There, displayed at the entrance to the lobby of the hotel, was a poster of me. It had to be at least ten feet high. Humanity slid all around me but I couldn't move. It was a gorgeous shot showing the woods behind my house in their full fall glory as I strode along behind a pair of greyhounds. Whoops, wrong breed.

Damn, I don't know how she did it, but Agnes had been at my home last fall undetected. The me in the poster was wearing a sweater I remembered knitting for Agnes one similar to the one I had on. It was knit of the same Plymouth worsted weight yarn in navy blue. Except across the front of this sweater was a design of a pair of racing greyhounds knit in Highland Heather yarn, the subtle shades of gray and white mixed to catch the highlights of their coats. The one I was wearing now showed a litter of Samoyed puppies.

The two greyhound grand champions leading her down the path were from a litter I'd whelped four years ago when Agnes was on a photo shoot in Greece. I'd even handled Twisp, the bitch on the left, to her final championship points. It was creepy that the smiling face that now stared down at me was the same one I'd seen in the mirror that very morning. Short golden curls framed the head and bright blue eyes looked right back at mine. The resemblance was complete down to the matching silk turtleneck, coordinated slim jeans and the tall boots I'd put on only hours ago. Agnes had nailed it. Across the top of the poster was lettered *Kate Killoy's Fancier Fashions, Saturday Night Fashion Show.* All I wanted to know was, what in hell is going on?

"You look gorgeous Kate, great photo."

"Looking good there, girl!"

"Hey, beautiful!"

Fellow dog nuts I knew were calling out to me as they pushed past. I had just opened my mouth to argue when a voice from behind me spoke. "Agnes Forester, I believe."

I turned slowly and saw a man in a dark suit, with short hair and an official looking presence, standing behind me.

I was yanked back to reality. "Kate Killoy, actually,"

He reached into his pocket and pulled out his ID. "Whitford Donner, FBI. Miss Forester. I must say you've been leading the Bureau on a merry chase. However it's time you came with me."

I hadn't a clue what this bozo with a badge wanted, but it was an obvious case of mistaken identity. "Agent Donner, you have confused me with my cousin Agnes, though why the FBI would want to talk to a supermodel is beyond me. As I told you, my name is Kate Killoy." I mirrored his move, reaching into my purse to pull out my ID. "You can check my driver's license, my room confirmation, or you can just look behind me, see?" I smiled pointing to the poster. "There I am advertising my fashion show on Saturday." The lie rolled off my lips. What in God's blue earth had Agnes gotten herself into with the FBI?

"You carry off a disguise very well, Miss Forester. But our agents have been following you all week and we've seen you enter this hotel looking like a model and leave looking like you do now. It took us a while to spot to the disguise, especially with these posters all over the hotel. But the merry-go-round has stopped, and it's time for you to get off. You are a material witness in an ongoing investigation and as such are compelled to come with me now. Some very important people need to talk with you." He reached for my arm but pulled back when a low growl from Dillon gave him second thoughts.

Shaken, I prepared to argue again when I heard a familiar Boston accent. "Pardon my rudeness for interrupting, Miss Killoy, but you seem to have incurred a spot of bother. The man who'd bumped me on the sidewalk now appeared beside me. Those beautiful green eyes locked on mine and my breathing stopped. I shook myself and was about to answer when he rounded on Agent Donner. "Have you been driven to harassing innocent young ladies now, Donner?"

"What the hell are you doing here?" Donner screamed, furious at him. "You're not an agent any more, Foyle. You're not part of this, so move on. We don't need freaks like you butting in."

I saw Foyle grin. "All evidence to the contrary my good chap. Apparently, since I left the Bureau, there's been a staggering decrease in the application of fact, logic and reasoning when working investigations. Please forgive my rudeness Miss Killoy. I couldn't help overhearing your conversation. Agent Donner was addressing you as Agnes Forester. I assume that he meant to refer to New York's most popular model. I further hypothesized he would like to speak with Miss Forester and she is resisting his charming requests. Your solution to the quandary Donner seems to be to approach random women, address them as Agnes Forester and then with your usual charm, entreat them to join you on a stroll to 26 Federal Plaza without even offering tea and scones. I am left agog at the thought of the ensuing lawsuits." He shook his head. "It's so embarrassing. The cost to the Bureau in legal fees and payouts alone must be a fortune to say nothing of the public's good will. It boggles the mind. Let me just solve this problem and tell you the beautiful and oh-so-charming Miss Kate Killoy standing before us here is not Miss Agnes Forester and I can prove it."

"Don't try to pull that hocus pocus crap you used at the Bureau on me, Foyle. You can't possibly know this isn't Agnes Forester in disguise." Donner reached for me, but pulled back when Dillon moved between us. "I'll tell you right now this lady is good at changing her looks."

"Correct. A change in appearance, eyes, hair and clothing is easily accomplished, even by amateurs."

I watched in silence, sensing he was setting Donner up.

"However, you are overlooking one vital factor. Agnes Forester, the lady you so desperately seek, is a fashion model, a profession that by its very nature, requires height. I happened to have noticed that on the billboard in Times Square, Miss Forester is standing next to a stockade fence which measures typically 183 centimeters. In the picture, she is wearing boots with high heels possibly adding eight centimeters to her height."

Spotting the mathematical prize at the end of the road, I smiled as Foyle continued, "The photo, which was taken at eye level, shows the top of her head to be at least three centimeters higher than the top of the fence, making her height to measure 178 centimeters. As even you can see, the very charming Miss Killoy here, though statuesque and quite beautiful in her own right, stands before you measuring a mere 168 centimeters. So you have absolute proof that she is not Agnes Forester."

I felt a laugh bubbling up ready to burst free. I'd grown up surrounded by this kind of reasoning. I happily was now on familiar ground. Feeling once more secure, I smiled up at my mathematical knight-in-shining-armor, then transferred my smile to meet Donner's glare as I slipped my arm through Foyle's.

"What Mr. Foyle explained so beautifully is that Agnes Forester may be capable of changing her appearance in many ways, but becoming four inches shorter is not one of them. So, as I told you earlier, Agent Donner, my name really is Kate Killoy." I pointed to the poster. "If the fashion show hadn't been completely sold out for weeks, I'd invite you to come and watch. Now if there is nothing else, please excuse me. I really have a lot of work to do." Donner scowled and stomped off through a door he would have slammed had it not been revolving.

"Thank you so much, Mr. Foyle." I pushed out my hand to shake.

"The pleasure was all mine." He bowed slightly then reached down to scratch Dillon's ears. "Allow me the favor of a formal introduction. I'm Harry Foyle at your service."

"It's a pleasure to make your acquaintance Mr. Foyle."

"It is an absolute delight to know you Miss Killoy. I do wonder though, if you would be gracious enough to satisfy my curiosity?"

"Of course, if I can."

"Could you explain to me why, in this poster advertising your fashion show, Agnes Forester is pretending to be you?"

CHAPTER FOUR

"Katie? Katie, there you are, dear. Oh, look at you. So grown up, I can't believe it. That short hair is really flattering. Who would have known what was lurking under that mile-long braid. But you've got to come now, Katie. We're all waiting, dying to see what you've got us wearing in the show. Please excuse us young man." Alice Simmons' gray curls bounced as she pushed her solid body between us and grabbed my arm pulling me across the lobby. Dillon moved into position alongside Alice's Golden Retriever, Lucky. "We're all waiting for you over at that last banquette on the other side of the elevators."

I looked back over my shoulder. *Saved by the bell I might have told him everything. How had he recognized Agnes in the photo? And why didn't he tell Agent Donner?* Mr. Harry Foyle of the beautiful green eyes was still standing by the poster watching me. He turned slightly and I froze. It was him!

My poor excuse for a brain hadn't made the connection up close. This was the guy from Reilly's. What was he doing here? Was he following me? I needed to talk to Agnes.

"Alice," I dug in my heels halting all forward progress. "Give me a minute to check in, please, and then I'll be right over to see everyone, I promise."

"Okay, but hurry." Alice was reluctant to let me go. "We're waiting. This is just the most exciting thing that has happened to me in years. I can't wait to tell my students how Lucky and I got to be fashion models in New York City. They'll never believe it. We'll need pictures."

I turned toward the check-in line at the desk only to run, literally, into another friend. "Kate darling, easy does it. Spike and I are waiting with bated breath to see what you've designed for us. We're going to be stars!" The dapper six-foot two-inch Richard Carsley, clutched his tiny Chihuahua under one arm and reached with the other to hug me. Richard always looked as though he had just stepped from the pages of GQ which is not surprising because he had graced its cover more than once. "My goodness!" Richard held me at arm's length and tilted his head to get the full picture. "Well, aren't we looking all gorgeous and grown up. It seems like just yesterday you were running around the ring barely as tall as your dog. Here you are about to become a famous fashion designer. Tom and your dad would have been so proud of you."

"Thanks Richard." My heart gave a little lurch at the thought that my Amigos wouldn't be here with me. "It's about time Spike let you share some of the limelight." Spike was the number one Chihuahua and number three toy dog in country, according to the standings. He and Richard attended my advanced obedience class. Spike was the latest in a long line of these tiny giants Richard had bred and shown with his husband lawyer Brandon Morton. Richard, whose family owned a bank in the city, was the third generation to serve as its president. However, though both he and Brandon worked in the city, their home was only a mile from mine in Sterling, Connecticut. "You will both look marvelous, never fear."

I smiled as I reached the long marble check-in desk. Dillon pressed against Richard as he gazed up at his tiny friend. I flicked Dillon's lead making him step back. "If you don't want to be wearing Armani with Samoyed accents today, Richard, you should put Spike down and let Dillon say hello."

"Your Sams are always so very generous in sharing their undercoat, Kate." Richard laughed as he put Spike on the floor.

"Sammy hair is everywhere!" I waved my hand and smiled. Stepping up to the desk and reaching into my briefcase, I pulled out my email confirmation, driver's license and credit card. "Kate Killoy, I've reserved a room that's set for dogs with two queen-sized beds."

"Yes, Miss Killoy you're right here," the desk clerk said as he consulted his computer, "and the concierge is holding something for you. I'll get it if you'll just wait one minute." My hand slid over the marble desk, enjoying its feel as I waited. I'd always loved that smoothness when I came here as a child. The only other thing I'd ever felt that was as smooth were the dolphins we got to pet when my middle school took us to Mystic Aquarium for a field trip. Few hotels attached to dog shows these days could boast marble floors, walls and ceiling. The rows of mirrors on pillars that extended the length of the room simply heightened the grandeur. I always felt I should be more dressed up when I entered this lobby.

The clerk returned with two large brown envelopes and a smaller white one. I recognizing the two large brown ones as the schedules Ellen had mailed to the hotel so I'd stop altering them. Apparently my nerves had begun getting on her nerves. In spite of—or maybe because of—her bossiness, she was still the best thing that had ever happened to my design business.

The third envelope had my name written in block printing, but with no return address. Frowning, I was about to open it when Dillon pulled on the lead, trying to follow Spike across the lobby. With a sigh, I jammed all three envelopes into my briefcase. Telling Dillon to heel, I asked the clerk to have my luggage delivered to my room. I pointed to the two carts at the left of the line. He called the bellboys and I passed each a tip. Turning toward the banquette, I relaxed and headed toward the crowd of eager faces watching my approach.

I squeezed myself onto the banquette next to Richard. Questions flew rapid fire until I held up my hand. The crowd of dogs milling about at our feet just added to the general chaos so I decided to establish some order.

"Down your dogs." At my command, everyone's hand shot out and canine butts hit the floor in unison. "Good dogs." I used my praise voice. "Good handlers." Everyone laughed.

"Let's have a drum roll please, Richard." He beat one out on the back of the banquette 'til I signaled him to stop. I pulled stacks of different-colored papers from my briefcase. "I give you the schedules, ladies and gentlemen. We're going to be very busy." As eager hands grabbed the sheets, I explained what they included. "First, we have the fashion show. You need to be in the Grand Ballroom on the 18th floor at ten o'clock tomorrow morning. We will be meeting photographer Andy Sibowitz. For those of you not aware, he is the best fashion photographer on the planet. Just ask him and he'll tell you. He has agreed to take portraits of you dressed in the outfits you'll be modeling, posing with your dogs. Any fitting adjustments will be made at that time. Then, Saturday morning, same time, same station, we'll have the dress rehearsal, with all the lighting and special effects. Any of you who think there may be a problem pronouncing either your name or that of your dog, please check with Denise Simpson, the mistress of ceremonies, at that time. She'll have the script and will mark any changes then. Ladies, at both of these practices, you should be in full makeup because you will be caught on camera. May I suggest dog baths be taken care of today so the coats, especially the double coats, will be ring ready. Remember—and this is important—wear comfortable shoes. You'll do a lot of strutting around on a raised runway and climbing up and down stairs. We don't want any turned ankles before you go in the ring next week. None of the outfits are formal, so low-heeled shoes are definitely the order of the day. Any questions?"

"What are the other sheets?" Susan pointed as she patted her Welsh Corgi, Angus.

"On the purple sheets, for those of you performing as dog dancers, you will see the schedule for your appearances. Tomorrow afternoon, up in Central Park, we will be performing for all the media. Then at the indicated times and locations through Sunday, dog dancers will provide interviews to go with the filmed footage. Lucy, Ralph, Agnes and Richard are doing those. Ralph, is in charge of the music. Lucy, do you have the banner and press releases?"

"We are ready, oh fearless leader," a voice piped up from the edge of the group and everyone chuckled. "We will get some TV exposure but I'm not sure when it will be broadcast. You're going to have to call people to record it when we find out. I've got requests in for copies of any tapings but who know when we'll get them."

"Can we have a peek at the designs, Kate?" Alice was trying to peek into my bag.

"All I have with me are sketches." I pulled my design book from my briefcase, slid out the rod that supported it for viewing then balanced it on the back of the banquette so the group could see. Slowly I flipped the pages. The accompanying squeals and cheers were music to my designer ears.

"Will Agnes be at the rehearsal to show us how it's done?" Kathy King asked as she stepped back to give her Newfoundland, Tenney, room to stand.

I paused for a moment. "I don't know if she'll have time. Her schedule is really busy." It could possibly be true rather than a lie. "Don't worry. It's easy. Everyone's going to be looking at the dogs anyway. The people running the show are friends of mine from college. They'll make sure you look great."

Dillon poked me. "Mr. Dillon is telling me it was a long drive and he needs to go, so I'll see you all in the morning. You have my cell number if there are any problems. If you see Jimmy, Bill or Ralph, who aren't here, please pass the word."

I stood and gathered my stuff, let Dillon move into heel position, then headed for the stairs down to the green room. That was an area set up to cater entirely to the dogs' comfort. Alice, Susan and Cora decided to tag along.

"Alice, how did you get time away from school to come?" I looked at her and she grinned.

"I gave a free seminar to the entire town-wide faculty in trade for being allowed to use my accumulated personal days all at once. The superintendent was required by law to have the in-service on this new testing topic and I'm the only one in town certified to teach it...He and I played *Let's Make a Deal*." We all laughed.

"I need to double check Hugo's grooming time." Cora headed for the grooming area. Dillon and I walked into what felt like a sea of wood shavings. Then I saw Cora do a quick about face back toward where we were standing, as a stunning woman in a groomer's smock strode in. "I think I'll wait and check Hugo's time when that person leaves." Cora scowled.

"Wow. Who is that?" I looked at the groomer as she disappeared into the back.

"She's Sonja Kunar, Bill's new groomer. She's gorgeous enough to have every Y chromosome's attention but has all the charm of a pit viper," Susan said. "When Cora was telling Mrs. Oliver about the fashion show, she thought the malicious Sonja was going to hit her, the woman was so nasty. She treats those of us who are in the show like we're the enemy. I thought I saw you arguing with her in the lobby early this morning."

I had opened my mouth to deny it when the thought of Agnes in the poster hit me. Could Agnes be in the hotel disguised as me? "Right, but I didn't know who she was, just that she was rude." My rapid cover slipped out. "She should be nice to her handler's potential clients or she'll be out on her butt." *Why in the world was Agnes arguing with this girl? For that matter, how can there be two of me wandering the hotel?* I checked my phone. Nothing.

Susan stepped over her Corgi and grabbed Cora's arm. "She's leaving. Quick. Go check on your grooming appointment and make sure she isn't scheduled at the same time." Cora and her Bernese Mountain Dog scurried into the bathing area.

"Has anyone talked to Bill about this?"

"I haven't seen him. He's got a new dog."

"Well, I'll try to talk to him about her attitude at the photo shoot tomorrow."

Once I reached my room, I let Dillon explore while I collapsed onto the bed, trying not to let the panic grab hold again. I was in so far over my head. All I needed was a problem with this groomer of Bill's. Wait, could this be the replacement for Huey, Dewey and Louie? I glanced at the other bed. Agnes should be sitting there making fun of me and my panic instead of creeping around the hotel wearing a Kate Killoy disguise. I grabbed my phone. *No calls.* I desperately scrolled through my contacts. *Arden. Of course! I'll call Agnes' agent.* I hit dial. Arden picked up on the second ring.

"Hi there, Kate. Are you all set for your show?"

I ignored her question. "Arden, have you heard from Agnes today?"

"No. She told me she was going to be out of touch until all this dog stuff is done. Isn't she with you?"

"No, I haven't heard from her since Tuesday and I'm beginning to panic."

"She probably got tied up with a bunch of last-minute details. You know Agnes. She likes every I dotted and every T crossed."

"You're probably right. If she calls you, tell her I need to hear from her."

"I will. I'll see you Saturday night. This is a new kind of fashion show for me. Who knows what marketable talent might be lurking there? Don't worry. You'll do a great job."

"Thanks, Arden." I rang off and stared at the phone. Arden hadn't mentioned that the FBI was looking for Agnes, so I guess she didn't know. I tried to remember why Agent Donner had said they wanted her, but the morning was becoming a blur. Could it be something to do with the memory card shed gotten from Bill? I texted Agnes: *Why r u hiding from FBI? Why disguised as me? Agent tried to take me in. Rescued by a geek in shining armor. What's with poster? Contact me, dammit.*

I wish Dad were here now telling me I was being an idiot. Just eight months ago we'd been sitting together on overturned milk cartons watching the antics of Kelly's puppies, and laughing as they romped through their food. I wanted to freeze that moment forever and be able to erase the rest of that day from my memory, but it still haunted me. How, without any warning, he had gripped his head, screamed in pain, struggled to stand, then bent forward and vomited. How he had collapsed unconscious pulling me down. How I had rolled over to grab my phone and dial 911 then crawled to the desk and slapped the intercom screaming for help.

Before I could stand, people rushed into the room. Soon I heard the ambulance screeching to a stop. They'd come in less than five minutes. I was shoved aside and Dad was loaded and gone before I could get to him. I ran for my car, but my brother Seamus grabbed the keys and drove. The doctors said the aneurysm had been so severe, it was over before they could do anything.

At the flood of memories, I felt helplessness and tears taking hold of me again.

The hit came out of nowhere, knocking me off the bed. It was followed by licking and poking and pulling of shoelaces 'til I was laughing so hard I had to roll into a ball to stop. Then Dillon looked at me and barked once.

"If I didn't know better, you mangy cur, I'd say you were channeling Dad. He taught you to do this. He hated pity parties." I got to my feet, depression gone, and began setting up the room. "I need to train you to unpack suitcases," I told Dillon as I repeated the routine I'd done hundreds of times. Five minutes later, everything was in place, I'd filled the water bucket, and Dillon was sprawled in his crate chewing on his Kong.

I pulled the photo of Gramps, Dad and me from my briefcase and, smiling stood it on the desk. "Thanks Dad for training him to keep me on track." The folder of schedules was on the desk next to the heavy tote bag with everything needed to run the *Kate Killoy Fancier Fashions* booth at the dog show. Heather Miller and Jennifer Santos would be running it for me.

The beauty of coming into New York City, for me, was seeing the women who ran Tail of the Dog. On top of the basic necessities for dog owners, the shop carried all sorts of arts and craft, jewelry and specialty items for pampered pets. It wasn't the shop but the women running it who made the difference. Jennifer Santos and Heather Miller had worked there since high school. Jen's mother Cathy owned it and was a good friend. Tail of the Dog was one of only three, non-knitting stores, that carried my line of patterns and kits, and they sold well. I had even conducted a few workshops on picture knitting for them and the crowds had filled the shop.

I was reaching for my phone to call them when it buzzed with a text.

Lunch, 20 min. Chinese restaurant 2 doors down from shop. Heather.

I'd have to run. I closed the crate door, and grabbed everything I needed including the ten-ton tote. My briefcase tipped over when I moved the tote. The envelopes I'd received when I checked in tumbled onto the desk including the hand lettered one. I reached for it but stopped when I saw the time. I was going to be late. I slapped the 'Do Not Disturb' sign on the door, and ran for the elevator. Whatever was in that envelope had waited this long. It could just wait just a little longer.

CHAPTER FIVE

In the elevator, my phone rang again. I checked the screen and sighed.

"Hi Sarah,"

"Kate, I am so excited. You do remember that I'm staying with Bunny Robinson, don't you? Being at Bunny's this week has been wonderful and no problem for Ajax. But guess what? Bunny's planned a trip with a bunch of our sorority sisters to go to Atlantic City. It's going to be fabulous. I'm getting so big with the baby this may be my last chance to go out and have fun. With Pete on deployment, I never get out, and this trip is strictly for girls. So I'll stop by the hotel sometime tonight to leave Ajax with you. This will give you more time with him before you take him into the ring on Monday. I think it's a perfect arrangement. It'll be great. I'll see you then. Bye."

I smiled and disconnected the call as the elevator reached the lobby. The beauty of talking with Sarah Mondigliani whether on the phone or in life, was you never had to say a word.

My stomach growled as I crossed the lobby reminding me it had been seven hours since breakfast. I was starved, and ready to pig out on Chinese food

When I was a block away, my nose told me the restaurant was near. The aroma had me almost drooling.

"Kate, over here." Cathy, Jen, and Heather jumped up for a hug as I entered the restaurant. I crossed the room to join them.

"Way to go Kate. You look hot, girl!" Heather pronounced giving me a thumbs up. "Braid is gone, stylish clothes, boots with actual heels; I spot your cousin's magic touch. You look gorgeous, lady."

Cathy hopped on the bandwagon. "Heather's right. You've needed this for a long time. You actually look like a fashion designer."

I grinned and slid onto the bench. "I *am* twenty-four. Agnes thought I should look it."

Heather was quick to point out, "It's not everyone, though, who can go from looking twelve to looking twenty-four overnight."

The waiter came and we ordered everybody's favorites to share.

"Just make sure there are plenty of egg rolls." I sat back in the booth and relaxed. "Lunch is my treat, gals since you're doing so much to help me out with the show. We can go over the paperwork, IDs and whatnot as we eat. Wow, the food must be good, because this place is jammed."

"You even need a reservation, thanks to a *Times* review in the food section last Sunday." Cathy pointed to a copy of the review framed above the booth.

While we waited, I hefted the tote onto the bench beside me and dug out my master sales book, which held photos and information on everything in the booth. "You'll have the original kit collection along with these eight new ones including the mitten and scarf paw combo pattern. I made sure you'd have enough so our regular customers have first crack at the new patterns and kits, but you'll also have extras for the walk-in trade. The cartons are numbered and labeled with a content list that matches your master list in this blue notebook. The credit card thingy, phones, and wireless receipt printer are all in the big envelope along with the codes and passwords. I need you to print a duplicate of each receipt to keep in the cash box. The credit-card company will email daily tallies to Ellen at my studio. Ellen Martin's contacts are in there as well. Any questions—no matter how trivial, call her. In fact, think up some piddling questions. She's furious that after all the work she put into it this week, a sprained ankle is keeping her from coming out to play."

Jen circled Ellen's contact information. "I love talking with Ellen. I'll call her with a blow by blow. Two to one she'll come up with some ideas off the cuff that'll double sales."

I grinned. "She walks on water as far as I'm concerned. She drove my mother to the hospital when I was born because Dad and Gramps were at a conference. She still brags that she was the first person I ever met. You don't know how great it was the day she showed up at the door of my studio, two weeks after retiring from Killoy & Killoy, and told me she was my new manager."

As the waiter filled the table with their choices, talk switched to the girl's majors at NYU and the guy Cathy was now dating. She'd been a widow for four years and was just starting to date. She seemed to have found someone she really liked. I envied her.

As a noisy group of men and women headed toward the large corner booth next to us, I happened to look up and spotted a familiar fedora and topcoat. I felt his eyes on me and froze with my chopsticks half way to my mouth, only to feel heat turning my face (and probably the rest of me) red. Looking down didn't help as a pair of wingtips came into view.

"Hello, Kate." The soft Boston accent made me look up. He held his hat in his hand and was showing off his winning smile. "We meet again."

He started to say something else when someone called, "Hurry up Foyle. We're starving."

I looked up into those force-ten green eyes. "Hello." He smiled and nodded then joined the others at their table.

I turned back to the girls only to be pinned down

by three pairs of curious eyes. "He's just someone I met."

The women grinned and Jen pointed out the obvious. "Well, that certainly never happened when you looked twelve."

I quickly wracked my brain for a way to change the subject. "The weather predictions for Monday and Tuesday are for lots of snow, but I don't know how this will affect the show."

"Jen's boyfriend has a Jeep with snow tires and four-wheel drive, so they'll be there."

With the subject of the weather covered, we spent the rest of the meal catching up on everything in the girl's lives and mine including my hopes for the dog show. It was great just to relax and chat. Cathy finally checked the time.

"Rats, I've got to leave."

Standing, she gave me a hug and was about to race off. Heather and Jen stood too, stuffing the notebooks and copious paperwork back into the massive tote.

"Hold it a minute." I pulled an envelope from my purse. "Here are three passes to the fashion show. You are part of Kate Killoy Fancier Fashions this weekend so you should enjoy the whole shebang to quote my dad."

"We can't wait." Heather hugged her. "Thanks, Kate. See you Saturday." They dashed out the door, and I waved for the check. Leaning back, I smiled, relaxed and sipped my tea.

"Anyone got leads on Agnes Forester?" a loud voice from the next booth asked.

I stiffened and ducked down in the booth, glad that Harry Foyle was the only one who could see me.

"Donner's gotten so that he'll grab anyone," chuckled Harry as he grinned at the man.

"I still think that was the Forester dame in disguise," grumbled Donner.

"Not Forester," Harry scoffed at the man. "I can absolutely positively guarantee it."

"Our source told us somebody slipped her classified information at the Zanifra consulate. We need to know from whom she got it, what it is and where it is now. The talks between Zanifra and Naro are only a week away."

"Actually, I think it's just a publicity stunt this model is pulling." The comments flew around the table.

I froze. *Agnes is being hunted? It must have had something to do with Bill and that memory card. I need to get out of here and find her.* I slid on my coat, pulled up the hood, paid the waiter, and headed for the door. As I wove my way through the crowd, I heard Harry Foyle excuse himself from his friends. I pushed open the door and started downtown at a trot.

"Kate, wait." I heard him yell. Glancing back, I saw him stuffing his hat on his head and yanking on his coat as he came out the door. I had half a block head start but lost it when the light changed. I had just reached the corner when I heard him almost catch up. He was right behind me when he yelped in pain. As I started to turn, a blow between my shoulders knocked the wind out of me and sent me flying forward into moving traffic. The street sped toward my face as brakes screeched deafeningly in my ears. A yank that was as hard as the first blow followed, pulling me back to the curb and safety away from spinning wheels and death. I landed hard and hurt everywhere. But hurt was good. Hurt beat dead.

"Kate." I felt myself being scooped up "Kate, say something."

"I'm okay. Help me stand up." I struggled to sit, but lifting my head was a mistake and I barely managed to roll over when I lost my lunch. "Give me a minute."

"What's going on here?" My eyes barely two inches from the pavement, registered cop shoes. Turning to look up at him was too much effort. Everyone in the gathering crowd wanted to tell him what had happened which was excellent, as I didn't have a clue. A warm hand stroked my head. I didn't want it to stop or the arm holding me close to a warm body ever to let go. I could have stayed like this for a year, maybe two. Large police hands were now pushing and prodding and the officer's clipped questions seemed to expect answers. "You're absolutely sure nothing is broken?" Both the cop and the one holding me carefully eased me to my feet. I was finally able to move my head to see who was holding me so firmly against his lovely warm body. Concerned green eyes frowned into mine.

"Nothing is broken. I'm just bruised. Please. I need to get back to the hotel." I turned, saw the walk sign flash and took a step. "Argh." Pain shot up my leg and I reached for Harry's supporting arm.

Gentle hands pulled me back. I winced when an earsplitting whistle pierced the air, bringing a cab to a halt in front of us. Harry lifted me gently into the cab and gave the driver the address of the hotel. I started to say something only to have shivers jerk my body making my teeth chatter. Harry rubbed my arms, stopping every so often to check my eyes. "It's shock and it will pass. You were lucky. That guy who shoved you into traffic tried to kill you Kate. You're in no shape to answer questions, but when you can, you'll need to tell me why someone wants a fashion designer who trains dogs dead."

I looked at Harry Foyle and knew he must have seen only confusion and fear in my eyes. "I'll be happy to tell you—as soon as I find out."

CHAPTER SIX

"Kate, go easy now." Harry gently lifted me from the cab, slowly walking me inside. By the time we reached my room, I felt like I'd been trampled by every dog in my kennel and I was shaking so hard I couldn't hold the room key. "You don't know me, but I swear I only want to help, Kate." Harry took the key from my trembling hand and pressed his business card into it. "You can call the FBI to check my references."

I looked down at the card in my shaking hand and read, 'Harry Foyle, Private Corporate Security'. Another wave of shivering shook me as Harry opened the door. Barking and banging filled the room. I reached to open the crate door and, with my arms around Dillon, I broke into sobs and fell to the floor.

Harry lifted me onto the bed, pulling the straps of my bags from over my head. Dillon quickly followed.

"Dog not allowed on beds," I sputtered trying to talk between shivers and tears. But I couldn't force myself to let go of my hairy security blanket and I buried my face in his thick ruff. My purse suddenly began to bark and hands and paws dove toward it. Dillon almost had the phone, but Harry, a second faster, snatched it out of his reach and hit speaker.

"Kate, are you there?" came a shout and Dillon barked at the sound.

"Quiet, Dillon. I'm here Sal." I couldn't keep the shaking out of my voice.

"Kate, I was just calling to check on you. Hey girl, you sound funny. Are you crying? What's wrong? What's happened?"

"I'm okay." I took a breath to calm down and control the shakes. "There was an accident on my way back from lunch with Jen and Heather. At an intersection I got knocked into traffic, but luckily I was pulled to safety." I gave a quick, grateful glance up at Harry's tranquil green eyes. "It was scary but probably just an accident."

"Someone pushed you into traffic? Tell me exactly what happened or you are going to see me there in two hours. I'm not kidding Kate."

"I should just have been paying better attention. As traffic began to move, someone bumped me from behind. I lost my balance and pitched headfirst into traffic. Luckily a man grabbed the strap of my briefcase and swung me to safety on the curb. I'm shaken and bruised, but he brought me back to the hotel."

"Are you sure he didn't push you and stage a fake rescue just to get at you? What do you know about him? What's his name? Who is he? Where is he now?"

"I'm right here, Sal. It's Harry Foyle." Harry moved closer to the phone.

I turned to stare at him. *How does he know Sal? What iss going on here?*

"Harry, what the hell are you doing in New York? Wait a second. How did you happen to meet up with Kate?"

"I'm on vacation. One reason I came into the city was to visit Bill Hendrix. We had lunch today with a bunch from the Bureau's New York office. It turns out it was the same restaurant where Kate was eating with her friends. I had literally bumped into her earlier in the day when I spotted your van leaving after you dropped her at the hotel. I wasn't sure it was you then. What are you doing with her?"

"I work for her. I aged out of the department and moved to Connecticut to be near Pete and Sarah since the baby's coming. I went to work for Kate six months ago. Enough of this small talk. Tell me what really happened to her."

"You're right to assume it wasn't an accident. The guy who pushed her knocked me out of the way to get at her. He wore a black hoodie which kept anyone from seeing his face, but the traffic cameras may have caught something. Kate is feeling the aftereffects of shock and has scratches on her hands. I imagine she's got bruises on her hip and knee from the way she landed and she twisted her ankle but there's not much swelling. Other than that she should be fine. Do you have any contacts at the fourteenth precinct I could call about the traffic-camera coverage?"

"Yeah, but I'll make the call and have him call you. In the meantime, I need you to keep an eye on my girl. I want her protected."

I had sat and listened to this without objecting, but now this was too much. "Sal, don't be ridiculous. You're overreacting. I'm sure it was an accident. I don't need a babysitter." I scowled at this man who was upsetting Sal.

"If Harry says it wasn't an accident, Katie, it wasn't. He knows his stuff. I don't know why someone tried to kill you, but if someone wants you dead, you need protection and that's what Harry does. Look, you're not stupid. You've got two choices here. You can either let Harry protect you until I come get you on Wednesday or I'll be there in two hours and won't leave your side 'til we're back home. You choose."

Now I was getting pissed. "Wait a second. Don't I get a say in this?"

"No," both men said and Harry scowled at me letting me know they were serious.

I didn't know this man from Adam, but Sal seemed to think he was safe. Serious emerald-green eyes stared back at me causing other feelings I didn't quite understand. Then, to make it worse, one eyebrow lifted. *How does he do that?* I knew Sal wouldn't back down. It would be like walking around with a sign that said VICTIM if he came here. I had no choice.

Harry scratched Dillon's head. I watched my standoffish Samoyed who never warmed to strangers, snuggle him. If Dillon trusted him…. "Okay, if I must choose. Harry."

"Fine, but that means you do everything he says. Don't leave her side Foyle for a minute until I come get her on Wednesday. If that messes up your vacation I'm sorry. And don't let her argue with you. She loves to argue but she's also the best boss I've ever worked for. Plus her family would kill me if I let anything happen to her. Kate, talk to Agnes. Find out if she knows anything about why you're in danger. It seems ridiculous anybody would want to hurt you. She set up this show. She must know what's going on. Call me as soon as you know something. I'm counting on you Harry." Sal rang off.

I slid off the bed and limped to the desk to plug the phone into the charger. The white envelope I hadn't opened still sat there. Maybe it held some answers about what was happening and why. I glanced over my shoulder at Harry, slid it into my pocket, and moving to the bureau, grabbed some clothes. "I'm going to take a bath and get rid of this blood if that's okay."

"Good idea. Dillon and I will just work on our male bonding skills." He rubbed the belly of my once-loyal sidekick. Fickle. All males were fickle.

I limped into the bathroom, latched the door and began filling the tub. Lowering myself gently onto the commode, I pulled out the envelope. Inside was a letter which, except for the greeting, 'Wendy,' and the signature, 'Peter,' was entirely in code. *Oh shit. I haven't worked one of these in years. Now isn't the time for these games. What does she have to tell me that she can't put into a text, a phone call or a normal letter? Damn it, Agnes, what in hell is going on?*

When I emerged, all pink and puckered from the bath, Harry was on the phone and had his back to me. He'd taken off his suit jacket and I got my first view of the broad shoulders and narrow waist that somehow managed to hide underneath that well-tailored suit. "Thanks," he told whoever was on the other end of the call, "we'll see you around four-thirty then. Great."

Ending the call, he turned and grabbed his suit jacket slipping back into it and straightening his tie. "How do you feel?" he asked, taking a step closer. "You look stunning. I mean you seem to have recovered."

I smiled, feeling shy and awkward. I picked up Dillon's lead. "I'm much better. I've got to take Dillon downstairs to pee. We can talk when I get back."

"I'm sorry Kate. I realize this is not what you want but I promised Sal to protect you and I always keep my promises. That means I'm with you twenty-four seven. This is not a game."

"Fine," I sighed. "Let's go." I headed for the door. He reached for the lead and before I could argue, his hand rubbed Dillon's ears and my traitorous dog moved to his left side. I watched in shock as Dillon leaned into Harry's leg. That had never happened with anybody but my father or grandfather.

As we left the elevator, I spotted Sonja Kunar, the woman everyone was avoiding. She had the Afghan Hound Bill had been walking in the park, on the treadmill. She scowled as she watched the room and seemed to be checking to see who was there. This was not a happy person.

As I walked Dillon to the wood shavings she stiffened. Obviously I wasn't on her Christmas card list. She glanced at the poster on the wall, then back at me and her scowl looked more like worry. I grabbed the pooper scooper, and Harry took Dillon's lead while I cleaned up. As we walked to the exit, I felt people staring. I knew they had questions about my being with a man. This was going to be a problem. Embarrassed I ducked, and felt the now-familiar heat rising up my cheeks. Harry went to take my hand, but I froze, and he pulled back. I looked at him feeling guilty, then stared at the floor until we reached my room.

"I get the feeling you don't enjoy being the center of attention because of the fashion show?" He stood until I sat on the bed and then took the chair.

"That's not why people were staring at me." I didn't elaborate but just stroked Dillon's ruff not looking at the man.

After a few minutes, I gave Dillon a biscuit and began to rearrange the room. I started moving the crate and equipment boxes in order to leave space for a second crate by the door. Silently, Harry's hands grabbed each item from me and placed it where I wanted. When we finished, I crawled onto the bed by the far wall and leaned against the headboard. Grabbing a huge pillow to hug, I stared at Harry. He'd unbuttoned his suit jacket. "May I…?" he asked permission to remove his jacket.

"Make yourself at home."

As I watched, he hung up the jacket, unbuttoned his vest, and folded himself into the overstuffed chair against the wall, toeing off his shoes, and using the bed as a footrest. I watched this process. With his height, he seemed to go on forever. Finally, he slumped down and relaxed. I wished I could.

Suddenly I found tears spilling uncontrollably down my cheeks. I ached for the security Dad and Gramps had always given me. They were both gone now. I was totally alone. Harry pressed a large white handkerchief into my hand, I buried my face in it and letting the tears flow. Finally they ended. My pity party seemed done. I felt Harry's eyes on me and winced at the thought of his pity. I didn't want to explain the flood that just happened.

"Why did you run out of the restaurant at lunch?" he asked, concern in his eyes when I looked up. "You were having fun with your friends, but something happened right after they left. I saw it in your face. What was it?"

I looked at him. Sal trusted him, but…. After a minute I came to a decision. "I couldn't help overhearing your friends, whom I assume are agents, talking about Agnes. They're hunting her."

"Agnes Forester? The model who was posing as you in the poster? You told Donner she was your cousin."

"Well, second cousin actually, but we're as close as sisters." Kate lowered the pillow to her lap. "She arranged all this for me. The fashion show was her idea. With her connections, she got the ballroom, the sponsors, the charity affiliation, the photographer, the show manager; she even had her assistant handle the ticket sales. All I had to do was show up with the sweaters and other pieces, arrange for the models and be there and take the bows."

"So where is Agnes now? Isn't she part of the show?"

"That's the ten million dollar question. Too bad I don't have an answer. I expected her to be here when I arrived. I haven't heard from her since Tuesday which is not like her at all. She normally would be calling and texting me every ten minutes now that we're down to the wire." Suddenly I needed to know. "Now I've got a question for you. How did you know it was Agnes in the poster?"

Harry looked at his hands and shrugged. "The eyes were different and her shoulders are straight out, whereas yours slope a little. Plus she was looking at those greyhounds the way you look at Dillon. They're hers, I take it."

"You only looked at the poster for a second and you'd only just met me a few minutes before. How...?"

"I notice things can't help it. I see anomalies in

things or people or posters. It's who I am. Tends to bug the hell out of everybody, and completely freaks out people like Donner. Occasionally it comes in handy. Plus I'd seen you together a while ago." He smiled.

"It was you at Reilly's last November. I knew it."

"You recognized me?"

"How could I not? You stared at me the whole evening." Now it was Harry's turn to blush.

CHAPTER SEVEN

"How does a private security business work?"

Harry sat up straighter and pushed up his glasses. I saw him study my face to see if I was humoring him. I must have passed. "Each assignment is assessed as a unique entity. The risks are evaluated, options weighed, consequences appraised, results projected and plans formulated. The development of each plan is highly influenced by the specific number of factors that could constitute a perceived threat. A probability factor is assigned based A, on whether these factors are approached separately or B, on whether they could be handled as a whole. Each possible threat is assigned a mathematical value. When the data collection is complete, I create a set of algorithms. These help me assign threat levels, calculate probabilities and institute plans based on the projected results which appropriately control each level."

"Okay, I get that." I told him. A look of shock passed quickly over Harry's face. "But, how can you calculate an algorithm when the threat is unknown, and the victim is a person? Is it possible to create a workable algorithm in that case?"

Harry stared at me in silence to the point where I was ready to squirm. Then suddenly his expression changed. It was like watching the sun come out. A grin spread across his face. "Ah yes, now we come to the incongruity of our specific situation. In the interest of full disclosure, I should inform you that 'Harry Foyle, Private Corporate Security' has an extremely limited amount of experience with this particular scenario."

"None?"

"That would be correct."

"So why did you agree to do it?"

"Two reasons. First, I owe Sal my life, so if he asked me to walk through fire, I'd rent asbestos long johns, but I'd be there."

"You said two reasons."

"Yes, well." Now Harry gazed down at his hands. "As part of that full-disclosure thing, when I...umm...met you this morning, and I started to explain why you were not Agnes, you smiled. In fact, your eyes lit up and you grinned. You got what I was saying. That has never happened before when I talked to a beautiful woman. In fact, I don't remember connecting this quickly with anyone ever. Add to that the fact that you hypnotized me at Reilly's last November and I must confess that I'm smitten. I should apologize for being so forward. I have a bad habit of saying what I think. Tact and I are practically strangers. You should probably ignore my ridiculous ramblings and consider me just another guard dog. Since Sal wants you covered twenty-four seven until he picks you up, you are my number one security job."

I watched Harry rest his hand on Dillon's head. He slouched into the chair while his body stretched seemingly half way across the room. Slowly he raised his eyes until they met mine. My cheeks—even the tops of my ears—were growing warm. Looking away, I fished out my phone and checked for messages. There weren't any.

He went for his phone as well. "What we need are facts. We must identify the threat. That way, we can develop an appropriate plan to neutralize it."

Hitting speed dial, he said, "Sadie, love of my life, how is my darling girl? Look, Sal has given me a project and I need some quick research. Of course, sweetie, what I need is for you to get me any and all information on Agnes Forester; yes the supermodel, but she has become of vital interest to our old friends. Oh and fashion designer Kate Killoy as well. Feel free to browse wherever you want, but since we're trying to avoid a potential killer, speed and extreme stealth are vital. As you get details, pass them on. Yes, my love, give my best to the monsters." He closed the phone and looked up, startled.

All the blood seemed to have drained from my face, which I'm sure had now turned dead white. He looked at what I hoped was my blank expression and cleared his throat. "While Sadie is doing research on you, your cousin Agnes and any FBI operations where Agnes is involved, we've got to come up with a plan of action explaining my presence so I can keep you from harm."

"May I ask you a question?"

"Of course."

"How do you know Sal?" I waited, watching him study me.

"He saved my life." Harry sat up as though that was the end of the discussion, but as our eyes met, he seemed to change his mind. "I was in my fifth year at the Bureau last spring. I specialized in data analysis. I took information collected by field agents, decoded it and analyzed it. I'd calculate the probability of success, depending on each possible scenario. Nine months ago, I spotted discrepancies in data all coming from an operation in Springfield, Massachusetts. My boss decided I should check it out personally. I went undercover in Sal's police department because they were linked as local contacts to the operation. The agents under surveillance somehow found out about my investigation. Two nights into the operation, I got caught in the crossfire during a stakeout gone wrong. Sal took out one of the shooters using his dog to attack and pin him down and then carried me to safety. It took three surgeries to put this particular Humpty Dumpty back together again." He paused and looked at the ceiling. "Sal came to see me every day I was in the hospital. I never found out who betrayed me. Analysis of the bullets in me identified two of the shooters as agents. Everything was swept under the rug. So I quit and set up on my own."

I realized that somewhere during Harry's story, I'd stopped breathing. I listened to his calm explanation, but found my mind struggling to imagine the amount of pain and suffering he'd been through.

Harry squirmed. "I thought you were going to ask me about Sadie."

I now straightened and turned to stare coolly toward the window. "Your private life is your own business. I wouldn't dream of intruding."

"Sadie is the smartest and most wonderful woman in world. She is a former analyst with the Bureau who retired to take care of all her boys. That would include yours truly whose business she runs as well as her five grandsons. We all adore her."

I turned back toward him, scowling, but then grinned. "You strung me along on purpose."

"Perhaps I did, a little. You've had two questions. Now it's my turn. Why did your cousin pretend to be you in the poster?"

"I have no idea. I was stunned when I saw it this morning. She hadn't said a word about it to me. What's your other question?"

"What's in the letter you're holding that's got you so nervous."

I froze. I'd been trying to figure how I could get enough privacy to decode Agnes' message since codes weren't my thing and always took me forever.

"I can't answer that."

"Can't or won't?" We locked eyes and I blinked first. This man saw too much. I grabbed my phone, excused myself and ducked into the bathroom. Then I hit pound three. *He isn't the only one who can check up on things.*

"Well, it took you long enough," Sal bellowed.

"You don't even know what I want."

"You want to know if you can trust Foyle."

"Right, but how did..."

"Kate, you've always had your dad and granddad for backup. Today someone tried to kill you. If you aren't scared shitless, you should be. Now you've been told to believe that some guy, someone you don't know from Adam, will keep you safe from threats. I'll make this simple. If I didn't trust Harry Foyle to do as good a job taking care of you as I would, you'd be hearing me banging on your door this minute. I'd trust him with my life, Kate and furthermore, I trust him with yours."

"But this involves Agnes too."

"Doesn't matter. Same speech."

She sighed, "Okay. But, Sal, I'm so..."

"I know kiddo. I wish I could give you a hug but take my word for it, Harry is your best hope."

"This isn't easy."

"It never is, kid."

"Okay, thanks, Sal." I put the phone away and washed my face, which was definitely showing the strain of the day. With a laugh, I suddenly realized that with all this madness, any panic I'd had about the fashion show was gone. I straightened my shoulders and opened the door.

Harry stood and looked at me. "What did Sal say?"

"Oh, you know—faster than a speeding bullet, walks on water, moves mountains—the usual."

"His standards are high. I'm going to have to hustle. And moving right along, let me remind you that we have a movie date at the Fourteenth Precinct in an hour."

"Great. Hope they have popcorn."

I grabbed my Kindle and walked to the desk then sat looking at Harry. "When Agnes and I were young, we did everything together, including showing dogs. Often those weekends were long and for kids, could be boring. Agnes and Gramps used to create complex numerical puzzles for each other to solve. I wasn't the super math nerd they all were. She and I did create our own code and when we didn't want other kids at the show to read our notes, we'd use that. When I checked in this morning, several envelopes were being held for me, including one from Agnes that contained a coded message. Now, understand, the last time we used this code I was twelve and we had had to hide something scary that had happened. For her to use it now…" I shook my head. "I haven't had time to decode it yet." I pulled the paper from my pocket and spread it out, turning on my Kindle where I'd stored Agnes' key to the code as a note so I could begin working. Harry shifted to look over my shoulder.

"Wendy and Peter?"

"Our last play for the family was *Peter Pan.* Agnes, of course, played Peter. My brothers got drafted to be the lost boys and I got stuck playing Wendy."

"Stuck?"

"I always thought she was a little silly and helpless. Face it, she was a wimp. I wanted to fight with a sword." I admit I felt a smidgen gratified when Harry laughed.

"Anyway, I don't know what this says yet." I grabbed pencil and paper then began decoding...slowly.

"This is a basic alpha-numeric substitution code with one for e and two for f and so on. I don't want to offend you, but it might speed things up if I just read it." Harry waited for my nod then picked it up and adjusted his glasses.

Wendy,

I've done something dangerously stupid. Last November I dragged you into the city early and took you to the park so Bill could use you to pass information. That was the first of a series of stupid and dangerous things I did. It was all for good reasons but now I wonder if the price was too high. Bill had been secretly getting information to our State Department about a plan to overthrow Zanifra's monarchy. His daughter met a Zanifran while she was there with the Peace Corps. They married and had a daughter. Her husband was murdered last year and Bill has been trying to get his daughter and granddaughter out. He has been handling the prince's Afghan in hopes of finding someone within the royal household who could help him. He did. I got involved when Bill approached me at a show last fall. He'd used me several times without a problem. I thought the one in the park would be the last.

Then last week at a Zanifra fundraiser where I was doing the celebrity guest thing, I got a text I thought was from him asking if I could smuggle another piece of information to the State Department. Later in the evening as arranged, I accidentally dropped my bag. A waiter picked it up and handed it to me. I felt something had been added and when I checked my makeup, I found a thumb drive. On the way home from the event, someone tried to run my companion and me down.

Bill's rule had always been that the person contacting me would appear within the hour. To prove he's genuine, he'd tell me the name of the second dog whose championship I finished, except when another arrangement was made such as the one that day in the park. When I wasn't contacted after three hours, I copied the files to an old laptop that's not connected to the internet. I glanced at the information when I uploaded it and noticed enough to see it was coded and had to do with Zanifra. However, I didn't have time to figure it out without a key. I printed out the files, put the laptop in a box with summer clothes and gave it to my doorman to mail to M. for me. Then I hid the drive.

The next morning, a man claiming to be an agent from the FBI knocked on my door and demanded the package that had been given to me last night. I told him I didn't have any package and didn't know what he was talking about. Luckily, Sean came by. We'd been arranging a surprise anniversary party for his parents. He was in uni-

form and went all state trooper on the agent. The guy left. I know I've seen him before, but lacking your memory, I don't recall where. After he left, I remembered he didn't give his name, which we know isn't SOP. Later that day, someone tried to push me in front of a subway train. When I got back to my apartment, it had been trashed and the drive was gone. I thought once they had the drive, I'd be safe, but someone driving by took a shot at me as I left my building. I decided I had to disappear. I left everything behind including my phone and disguised myself as you so I could finish working on the show. I worry that I wasn't able to pass on the information for Bill. I spotted the agent who'd come to my apartment, following me into the host hotel, and I realized he was onto that disguise. I'm now in complete hiding while I try to find out who at State is the right person to contact before it's too late. Be careful and don't trust the FBI. I'm sorry I got you involved. If anything happens to me Nana holds the answer.

Peter

Harry looked over his glasses at me. "I don't think your cousin is a fan of the Bureau."

"Which is a surprise since Killoy & Killoy has done contract work for them for years, and Agnes has been involved, albeit anonymously."

"Well, now we know why someone is trying to kill you, though we don't know who." Harry stood and began to pace. "At lunch, the agents were talking about Agnes. They said she'd gotten involved in something questionable and needed to be brought in. It seems to me that whoever wants to stop the information getting to State needs to kill Agnes. They may know she hasn't been able to pass the information on. Since they realize she's been disguising herself as you, whoever it is is willing to kill you just in case you're Agnes in disguise."

I let what he had said sink in before I spoke. "So they want me dead because Agnes *might* know something?"

I felt Harry's eyes on me, waiting for me to freak, probably. This was real. Dead meant dead. I had a sudden vision of home, me in bed with the covers pulled over my head and all the dogs, including the puppies, snuggled around me. That image transformed into home with some faceless person killing me and my dogs. Fear grabbed me, but the thought of anyone harming my pups made me see red. My phone buzzed and I jumped.

A picture of Ralph Gorbensko's Borzoi, Wolfgang, popped up on the screen. "Hi Ralph," I said.

"Kate, I got a late start and wasn't able to make the meeting. I need a schedule."

"Not a problem, Ralph. Just be at the Grand Ballroom on the 18th floor tomorrow for the photo shoot at ten o'clock and we'll take it from there."

"Thanks, Kate."

I rang off and looked at Harry. "Ralph's breed is Borzoi," I laughed. "Sal was right. I've got two choices; do it or do it." I took Agnes' letter, put it in a baggie, sealed it, and shoved it to the bottom of the bag of dog food.

"By the way, Foyle, I want you to know I really hate you. Do you have any idea how long it would have taken me to decode that? I know Agnes said it was easy so I could work it, but that performance was disgusting." I glared at him, hands on hips, fighting a smile.

"Sorry about that. I've been decoding things since I was four." Harry held up his hands in mock defense. "I don't try; the pieces just fall into logical patterns that are easy to read."

"My grandfather would have loved you. God, wait 'til my mother meets you. She'll want to dump me and adopt you. You're as bad as Agnes. She does that, too. I thought she was unique. This proves how mathematically feather-brained I am."

"Don't you use a ton of math in fashion design?" he argued.

I began to split hairs about the levels of math when Harry placed his hands on my shoulders. "As much fun as this is, we're getting away from the point. Someone really wants the two of you dead."

He sent a quick text to Sadie to add Naro and Zanifra to her research then handed me my boots. "We've got a movie date, remember? So don't dawdle. I promise we'll talk about the information in the letter and what it means later." He held my coat for me to slip on, turning me around to zip it up. I met his eyes as he did. Those green eyes made me want to step forward into his grasp. I didn't know what was happening to me with all these new feelings, but suddenly I found curiosity beating out fear in my mind.

Harry turned and smoothly slipped on his coat, buckled the belt, grabbed his hat, and took Dillon's lead.

Reaching for the door, he looked at me. “Are you okay for now?”

I gazed up as he took my arm and slipped it through his. Letting out the breath I didn’t know I was holding, I said, “For now.”

CHAPTER EIGHT

It looked like an old Charlie Chaplin film. The sped-up black-and-white footage scrolled by, its choppiness forcing me to smile. "Wait. Stop." Harry said, standing behind me as he stared at the screen. "Move it at normal speed. See, there you are coming out of the restaurant, and here I am, trying to catch up. The black-hoodie guy comes out of that doorway. Here's where I catch up and he collides with me. Look, his hands are already on your back. He shoves and then melts back into the crowd while everyone is watching you."

"God, it's worse, watching." On the screen, the black hoodie guy's hands, in black mittens, were flat in the center of my back. They were so low I couldn't have gained my balance. The shove was hard, aiming me to land right under those tires. There was no way I could have stopped myself from pitching forward. In my head, I heard again the blaring horns. Again I felt the bumper as it slammed into my shoulder and then suddenly, I was on the curb. Shaking off the vivid memories, I turned to tell Harry, "I didn't feel you grab me. I expected to die, and I didn't even have time to pray." I turned back, unable to take my eyes off the screen. Dillon pressed his body against me and put his head in my lap.

"Kate, you're safe." Harry placed his hands on my shoulders. Their warmth helped me shed my new case of the shakes.

"You grabbed my strap so fast!" I leaned back, tilting my head to rest on his hand. "'Thanks' doesn't seem enough for saving a life."

He stepped to the side, gave her a salute and clicked his heels. "Nothing at all, Miss. It's just part of the service." I smiled and focused again on the screen.

"Watch how he keeps his head down and turned so we can't get him on camera. He knew exactly how to escape being recognized. We never see a face." Harry's frustration seemed to be getting to him.

"We're not done yet. We've now got a time code." Sergeant Sanchez finally spoke. He seemed to realize we needed to work through the experience. He typed in some numbers and a new scene appeared with the same man walking toward the camera this time. He turned up Fifth Avenue and with a few clicks on the keys, the scene shifted again. A short, heavyset man stepped from a doorway. Spotting the attacker, he waved. As our man approached him, he pushed back the hood. Sanchez hit a few more keys and a different angle appeared. Another adjustment and the screen froze on a close-up of the man who tried to kill me.

"I've never seen him before," I muttered.

"We'll circulate his photo and see what we get." Sanchez switched back to the last angle. The man from the doorway was now center screen. His collar was up, a scarf covered most of his face and the brim of his hat secured his anonymity. He passed an envelope to my attacker, who took off. Then he waved down a black Gypsy cab and was gone. Sanchez froze the footage on the cab and zoomed in to get its plate number. "We'll see if we can find out where he went."

Harry asked him, "Could I get a copy of the guy's head shot? My people might be able to trace it."

Sanchez looked at the card Harry had handed him when they arrived. "I'll send it to your phone," Sanchez told him. He turned and I felt his eyes on me. "Sal speaks very highly of you. He made it clear you should be high priority. He had a word or two to say about you too, Foyle. Not with the Bureau anymore, I understand."

Harry shrugged, reaching down to scratch Dillon as Sanchez continued.

"Once we have something....By the way, how'd you get this guy—he motioned at the dog—past the desk? Rogers never allows non-cop dogs into the station." I smiled, pulled a laminated card from my bag, and handed it to him. He whistled. "Damn. He's got more clearance than I do."

"He's very good at undercover work since he looks like the sweetie he really is until I, as his partner, am threatened. Sal and I use him in the police-dog training program."

"Right. Speak softly, but carry a big fluffy dog with sharp teeth. Well, don't go anywhere without him from now on."

I smiled at Harry and Dillon. "Hopefully, two guard dogs will be enough." I shook his hand, noticing that like Harry, Sanchez realized clothes say a lot about a man. He stood an inch taller than I, his stylish gray suit, maroon-striped silk tie, and neatly trimmed, black, curly hair communicating authority without a word. "Thanks for your help".

"Anything for Sal. He's the best."

***

At the hotel, I shifted my gear to extend the plastic tarp covering the carpet. This made room for a second crate. "I've got another dog coming in later, so could you move that food bag over onto the end of the bureau?"

"Okay, but before we go much further, we've got to build a cover story. I'm going to need an excuse to be with you all the time. How well do these dog people know your family?"

"Very well. My family has cheered on all my big wins, even though they don't handle the dogs. Plus we're a distinctive-looking lot, all with sandy hair and blue eyes."

"How about a boyfriend?"

"A boyfriend might come to some events with me, but he wouldn't be around all the time."

"Meaning that your boyfriends haven't been following you around?" he asked.

"Meaning..." I stopped, sighed and walked to the window. "I haven't had any boyfriends."

Startled Harry asked, "Are you surrounded by blind men? Unless, umm, I mean it's perfectly okay..."

"I'm not a lesbian either." I grabbed an album from the oversized L.L. Bean paw print tote bag on the back of the crate. Flipping to the final two pages, I turned it so he could see the last photo. It showed Agnes with her arm around a cute young girl. Each was grinning and waving rosette ribbons while standing behind a greyhound and a Samoyed respectively.

"That's Agnes Forester and the girl looks something like you." Harry flipped through some of the other photos, all showing the young girl winning.

"It *is* me." I turned back to the shot of both of us. "That's the day Dillon finished his grand championship."

"But Dillon's only.... When was this taken?"

"At this show last year."

The shock on Harry's face would have been funny if it didn't hurt so much that I had an overwhelming urge to cry. I turned back to the window. "Go ahead. Get it out of your system and laugh."

"Why?"

"Look, Dad and Gramps loved my hair long. And the dogs didn't care. My social life was totally in the ring. Time passed and, well nobody noticed that my appearance hadn't changed."

"What about your mom?"

I laughed a snort. "Mom is a mathematician and since I'm not, I barely register on her radar. Let's just say conversation over Cheerios in the morning were more likely about differential calculus than fashion or makeup. She never wears makeup herself, so I don't think it ever occurred to her that her daughter might need to know this stuff. I managed my own homework and taught myself to cook with help from my grandmother. Mom and I have no idea how to talk to each other, so I usually take the coward's way out and avoid conversations. To my father and grandfather, I was always beautiful. I don't think they noticed I never seemed to grow up. Though we were close and talked constantly, it was always about the dogs. Agnes has been so involved in her career for the last few years she didn't have much time for girl chats, either.

"After the funerals last spring, I sort of buried myself in kennel work. I had been playing with a ready-to-wear line to market in boutiques before my dad died, but I hadn't done anything with it after that. I found out recently Ellen Martin, my office manager, had called Agnes and ordered her to do something. No one says no to Ellen. So the weekend before Thanksgiving, Agnes showed up early one morning, shoved me into her car and took me into the city for a makeover. I went through the day in a haze of losing pounds of hair, buying clothes that fit and made me look feminine and, finally learning makeup from the people who do hers for the photo shoots.

"We ate dinner that evening at Reilly's with my great -aunt Maeve and Uncle Padraig, who live on the upper west side. I cried when Padraig told me I now look the way Maeve did when he fell in love with her. That was the night you stared at me all evening. I couldn't figure out why. By the way, who was that man you were with? He looked at Agnes all evening; though that's normal.

"Oh, that was Hendrix, an old friend from the Bureau." I filed the information away. I wouldn't forget Agent Hendrix.

"Agnes wasn't done. Ellen had told her about the line of ready-to-wear clothing I'd created, so she arranged for me to have a fashion show of my designs on the final Saturday of Fashion Week in February to be held here at the dog show hotel. She said that it was time to show people what I could do. She also pointed out that my new look was necessary. To quote Agnes, 'a designer dressed in baggy jeans, a frumpy oversized sweatshirt and muck boots does not get a New York City fashion show.'"

"That explains why the ten-foot posters all over the hotel disconcert you."

"I still haven't gotten used to the new Kate Killoy," I admitted.

Silence settled on us. Harry had stretched out on the second bed, staring at the ceiling and petting Dillon, who had somehow managed to work his way up onto that bed without my noticing.

Rolling over to face me, he announced, "Okay, Cinderella. There's only one thing missing from your new style. That would be a man dogging—pardon the expression, Dillon—your footsteps. How do you think I'd work as Prince Charming, your fiancé, who has just proposed?"

"Fiancé?"

"Don't you remember? We met the weekend of your makeover. That way people won't think I'm a pervert. I was immediately smitten and couldn't stop thinking about you. I'd gotten your number and we've been carrying on a secret courtship with calls, emails, texts and Skype as well as meeting on dog show weekends. I finally came into the city today to pop the question. You said yes, and we're going to try to fit in the time to go ring shopping in between the events."

"Fiancé? I can't have a fiancé. I've never even had a boyfriend. I've never even had a date. I don't know how to be a fiancée. Everyone will know."

"Kate, believe me. Everyone will assume you're just living the life you deserve. I will be the envy of every man at the show. Don't worry about your lack of experience. This is an engagement in name only. I would never ever do anything to hurt you or embarrass you," Harry said as he pulled me down to sit by him and wrapped his arms around me. "I will be your Professor Higgins, teaching you Engagement

101. In fact, I will teach you so well, even you will be completely fooled."

That's what I'm afraid of. But the arm wrapped around me felt so good, I smiled up at him. "You do know you're crazy."

"Crazy, mad, demented, bonkers, deranged, actually all of the above, but I'm also right. Just think about it. I would be able to guard you twenty-four seven and no one would be the wiser."

He suddenly got serious. He lifted his hands and held my face, "Kate, you're twenty-four years old and the most beautiful woman I've even known, inside and out."

I looked at him and felt suddenly shy. No one had ever looked at me that way. I blinked, and when he smiled, the tension in my shoulders finally let go. Harry wrapped his other arm around me and I found myself wanting him to keep doing this forever. He tipped up my chin and looked directly into my eyes. Then he slid to the floor on one knee, wrapped an arm around Dillon and reached for my hand, "I've asked Dillon's permission and he said yes. Miss Kate Killoy, it would gladden my heart if you would agree to becoming engaged to me."

I looked into his face and saw something more than whimsy and it set my heart fluttering. Fighting to catch a breath, I softly answered. "Mr. Harry Foyle, it would be my honor to become engaged to you."

A small kiss followed this exchange, one with training wheels on it. He was so careful not to scare me that it worked. I couldn't stop myself from responding and when it ended, I felt myself smiling all the way to my heart.

We fed Dillon his nightly treat and headed down to the restaurant to get dinner. As we entered, my phone buzzed with a text. "It's from my friend Sarah. She wants to know when she can leave Ajax. He's to stay with me until Saturday. Her friends want to take her to Atlantic City to meet up with some sorority sisters."

After we were seated and had placed our orders, I watched as Harry unfolded and refolded his napkin. "Kate, umm remember when you asked me how I knew Sal? Well, I only told you half the story. The other half is that his son Pete is married to my sister." Harry looked down at the table.

"Your sister? Sarah? You're Sarah's brother? Sarah has a brother? I've know her for two years and thought she was an only child."

"She'd prefer it if she were an only child. One of the reasons I'm here is my mother wants us to try to make peace. Sarah doesn't. She has no idea I'm here and she won't like it."

"Then she's really going to be surprised when she learns you're engaged to her friend and handler."

"Look, Kate, if this is going to create a problem…."

I gazed at him and began to laugh and kept laughing until I could barely stop.

Harry asked, "You want to share the joke?"

I gasped, holding my now sore stomach and struggling to get my laughter under control. I noticed people at other tables were giving us strange looks. "This is perfect, absolutely perfect. You can't imagine how good. Your sister, New England's top-rated dating evangelist, has spent every waking minute since we met two years ago, bugging me over not having a boyfriend. I'm almost afraid to attend any event where she might be because I know she'll have a minimum of three guys lined up primed for dating. Agnes' makeover sent her into overdrive; she must have introduced me to every single man in the state of Connecticut under the age of fifty." I took one look at Harry and gave in to another fit of laughter; only this time, Harry joined me. Grinning, I texted Sarah that she could come at eight.

CHAPTER NINE

Harry had grabbed his suitcase from the checked-bag storage on the way back from dinner and unpacked. Collapsing onto the bed, he propped his phone on Dillon, who was draped across his legs. He'd just finished texting updates to Sal about the police video and our cover story, and was chuckling over Sal's response to the latter, when the knock sounded. I raised my eyebrows at Harry before I answered. Smiling, I took a breath, put my hand on the door and braced myself with the positive attitude I always bring to competition in the ring. I threw back my shoulders and swung opened the door. Ajax pushed by me and, spotting Dillon, jumped onto the bed.

"Hey Sarah." I smiled as I grabbed one end of her luggage cart. "I imagine you can't wait to get started on this trip to Atlantic City." Backing carefully, I eased the cart loaded with gear into the room.

"Absolutely. This is going to be—" She stopped dead. "Harry? What in hell are *you* doing here?"

"Sarah," he said smiling, "Sal told me you'd be here."

I interrupted. "God, Sarah, I couldn't believe it when Sal told me you were Harry's sister. I didn't even know you had a brother."

"Well, that makes two of us," Sarah spat. "He hasn't been much of a brother since he took off for college right out of grade school. Mr. Mathematical Genius was too good to associate with us peons and go to regular school. No, he had to run off to Cal Tech to live with the other freaks."

"Mathematicians are freaks?" I asked quietly, but Sarah was oblivious to the insult she'd just delivered to my entire family.

"God, Kate, what's he doing in *your* room?"

I bit my tongue, ignoring her severe case of foot-in-mouth disease, and said, "He's staying with me until Wednesday. Then he has to go back to Boston. This is the longest stretch we've had together so far. We're enjoying taking advantage of not having to rush off. We're going to try to go ring shopping in amidst all the hoopla of public appearances, the fashion show, and the dog show."

"Ring shopping?"

"Congratulate me, Sarah. Kate said yes," Harry piped up as he took my hand.

"Yes to what? I don't understand."

I smiled at Harry as I slid onto the bed his arm circled my waist. "Sarah, we're engaged."

"I don't believe it. I would have known."

"Really, Sarah? You know everything that's going on in my life—and in Kate's?" Harry raised a single eyebrow expressing his doubt.

"When did it happen? Who knows about it?"

"Maeve introduced me to a bunch of guys the weekend Agnes did my makeover. I told you about that. Harry was with one of her friends from the FBI. We ended up talking all evening, which I didn't tell you. He emailed me the next day and we've been emailing, talking on the phone and Skyping ever since. We spent time together at Eastern and the January shows. Then Harry surprised me when he showed up at lunch today. He popped the question and I said yes. You're the only one who knows besides Sal and my Aunt Maeve. We had to tell her because, of course, she introduced us. Harry's coming down the weekend after the show so we can tell my family together, and then I'm going up to meet your mom."

By now, Dillon and Ajax had moved to the floor where they were now contentedly gnawing on matching chewies. Harry shifted me so I was sitting in front of him and wrapped both his arms around me, which made me lean back into him without thinking.

"Sal knew and he didn't tell me?"

"I asked him not to. You're not exactly known for your ability to keep secrets. I didn't want a lot of interference from friends and family." I folded my arms and frowned. "I didn't need my brothers trying to bully Harry."

"Well I guess with your family, you marrying a math freak would be considered a good thing. But Kate, are you sure? I mean you don't even have any dating experience; you're a virgin, for heaven's sake. Harry is...well, just look at him."

I turned and stared over my shoulder, smiling. "I am."

Sarah's snort drew our attention back to her. "Congratulations, I guess. Look, Bunny is waiting downstairs and we leave in the morning. I might be back for the fashion show, but if they have other plans, I'll see you Sunday evening."

"Enjoy your reunion and have a great time in Atlantic City. Sal said to remind you to take your vitamins, get plenty of sleep and take care of that grandchild of his you're carrying."

After she left, Harry's arms stayed wrapped around me. Neither of us moved nor spoke for several minutes. Finally, I stood and began adding Sarah's gear to the stack on the crates.

"You are incredible," Harry said, putting the second crate into the space I'd made earlier along the wall. "You had me believing every word. Now I only have one regret."

"What would that be?"

He turned and placed a finger under my chin. "That I didn't get to live it." I looked into those warm green eyes, and we both smiled.

Heading down to the green room, we were both lost in thought. I had to admit to myself that Sarah was right. I knew nothing about having a relationship with a guy. In high school, when Friday came, all my classmates gathered in the hall by the lockers making arrangements for parties, dates, and football games while flirting with one another. I remember feeling at the time like a visitor from another planet as I grabbed my things from my locker and made my usual dash to the van that would be pulled up near the gate. That van, loaded with dogs plus two men, would whisk me off to another world. It was a world of dogs and competition, wins and losses, joy and sometimes sadness, but a world where I knew I belonged. That world of dating and crushes and first loves was completely foreign to me. For the first time, I felt, that perhaps my perfect life growing up might not have been as sublime as I had always believed it to be.

The green room was jammed. Much to my dismay, I found myself the center of attention, fielding comments on my looks, questions about the fashion show and curious stares at the tall man beside me. Richard and Brandon were there with Spike, so I introduced Harry.

My friends seemed both surprised and delighted to learn of the engagement. Standing nearby, Alice heard and squealed, "Little Katie Killoy engaged? It's about time someone realized what a catch you are." She gave Harry a thorough going over. "He's cute too, and knows how to dress like a gentleman."

Richard stepped up to Harry. "I know Ajax isn't yours."

"No, he belongs to my sister and her husband."

"Ah, she's the pregnant one who never stops talking. So you, yourself, don't have dogs?"

"No, my life up to now hasn't let me have a dog, but I love them and Kate is going to change that."

"Right answer." He looked hard at Harry, trying to read his intentions. "I've known her since she was seven. She had a different style of growing up and doesn't know how to play games. Any man would be lucky to have such a woman. We tend to think of her as a child, but she's not. However, she's still quite vulnerable and I for one wouldn't like to see anyone take advantage of her innocence." He studied Harry for a minute. Brandon came up to stand beside him. "Take care of her because she's the best."

Harry looked at me surrounded by my friends. "I agree."

A silence suddenly spread across the crowd and I looked up to see Sonja Kunar come into the room with the Afghan. I watched as she took care of the dog's needs then turned to leave. I don't know what I had in mind, but I stepped forward.

"I love this Afghan. He's exceptional. I'm Kate Killoy, and you are?" I held my hand out to her. From her expression I half expected her to step on me and keep going; but instead she stopped and, after a minute, took my hand.

"Kunar, Sonja Kunar. You're the girl in the poster. I checked you out online. Your designs are good. I understand Bill is going to be in your fashion show with Ashraf. This is a very valuable dog. I must be with them to make sure that he is safe."

"Understood. Then I'll see you with Bill at ten o'clock tomorrow morning up in the eighteenth floor ballroom for the photo shoot. The photographer will enjoy taking pictures of this beauty."

"Ten o'clock. We will be there." We shook hands again and she left.

I turned back only to find everyone staring.

The silence stretched until Richard waved his hand. "That, ladies and gentlemen, is how Kate Killoy wins in the ring." he tipped an invisible hat in my direction. "She charms everyone until even the competition wants her to win." Laughter broke the tension.

"What is her problem?" Harry asked as we made our way back to the room.

"It's just a guess, but I think she's not just the dog's groomer; she's also his body guard. She'll be there with Bill tomorrow." Where she fit into this whole cloak-and-dagger game I couldn't guess. "If I'd known earlier they were sending her, I could have worked her into the show. She really is stunning," I sighed. "Is it still Thursday? It seems like a week has passed since Sal dropped me off this morning."

"Yeah...about that—Sorry again about plowing into you. I spotted Sal and wasn't looking. If I'd arrived a moment earlier we could have been formally introduced."

"You certainly know how to get a girl's attention—and you did win points by vanquishing Agent Donner. The Bureau is treating Agnes like a criminal. I know after this morning's episode, my willingness to help the Bureau in any way whatsoever is nil. You also get bonus points for saving my life. You seem determined to earn your Hero Dog Excellent title."

"Woof." He returned my grin. "It was my unqualified pleasure. I think I might have lost some points on the latter episode, though, due to lack of finesse."

"Have you been reading my obedience manuals on the sly?"

On our way back to the room, we crossed the lobby, pushed through the doors and stood outside on the sidewalk. I took a deep breath of the frigid air. Even at this time of night, the city was alive and in constant motion. "I've been coming here since I was little and I've never been afraid. I know it's a big city, but the people are nice once you understand them. Plus it's easy to find your way around. This is why I chose to go to college here; that and the fact I could get my degree in fashion design and still be home to show dogs on the weekends. The thought of someone hunting Agnes here—and the idea that whoever it is wants to kill us because of something we might know—is disgusting. I don't like being frightened to walk in this city I love."

Harry put his hands on my shoulders and pulled me back against him. "I will not let anyone hurt you, Kate."

I turned and looked up at him. "You can't stop him until we know who he is. Harry, I know the police will try, and even the FBI might make an effort, but to them it's a job. I'm not sure how, but we've got to find out who's doing this, both for Agnes and for me. It's life or death. I've got you to protect me, but she's out there hiding with no one there for her. We've got to make her secure too."

Harry squeezed my hand. "Then we've got work to do. We'd better get some sleep so we're ready."

Once we got the dogs settled for the night, we sat in companionable silence for a few minutes. Neither of us seemed inclined to fill the stillness with chatter. Finally Harry asked, "Can you explain the references Agnes made in her letter?"

I looked at him and asked, "How tied are you to the FBI?"

"Why?"

"Because you might not want to hear what my take is on her letter."

"It was an FBI mole and two agents that put me in surgery for three months."

I stared at him. Then taking a breath, I nodded. "I'll tell you what I can, provided it doesn't endanger Agnes. First of all, you've got to understand that, as part of her job, she's in demand to make appearances at events and parties so being invited to the fundraiser for Zanifra would be normal. I'm sure, considering her public image, when they used Agnes to transport the information, they didn't expect her to read it. However, if she hadn't read it, she wouldn't have realized she was in danger."

"You said she read it. If it were in code and she translated it that quickly, the code must have been pretty simple. It usually requires some training in the field. I mean, she's a fashion model and playing with codes growing up doesn't really qualify you to …"

"Stop talking before you embarrass yourself." I put up a hand in front of his mouth, pulled out my phone and pushed pound three. "Sal, Harry thinks Agnes is an airhead because she's a model and could never handle anything as complicated as decoding something. You didn't tell me he was a chauvinist. You need to talk to him."

Harry took the phone. "Sal, all I said is that it must have been a simple code for someone not trained in the field…Oh. She worked as a consultant for Killoy & Killoy? She specialized in the ability to decode with speed. I've got it. Yes a complete horse's… Thanks, Sal." He rang off and handed back the phone. "So when you say that she read the files you mean …?"

"Like you, when you grabbed the letter and read it."

"Okay, she reads some of the files. Then…?" He prompted.

"She realizes what she's looking at, and when she's not contacted right away, the way it was handled in the past, she finds a way to hide the information as well as create a security copy and get it to a safe place. The agent comes to her apartment and tells her to hand over the package. He doesn't use the proper password, so she goes into dumb-model mode."

"Now here is where we have a problem." Harry put up his hand to stop her. "When I was at lunch, they said she had taken something that was vital to the talks concerning the Principalities of Naro and Zanifra. That's why they've been searching for her."

"Yet in her letter she said she was contacted by the FBI, but the person didn't have the right code words, didn't really know what he was looking for and, more to the point, didn't give his name. Even I know that's not standard operating procedure."

"Kate, I know she's your cousin, but—"

"Harry, are you implying all FBI agents are pure as the driven snow and would never lie?"

"No."

"Have you ever approached someone in your role as an agent and not identified yourself?"

"You're right. That is suspicious."

"I've never known Agnes to fudge the truth except when flattering the elderly."

Again silence descended. Harry stood up and began to pace. I left him in his own world and walked over to look out the window. The view of the Empire State Building all lit up was fantastic, but the ring around the moon told me there was bad weather on the way. I wondered when it would arrive. I heard Harry drop back into his chair.

"Harry, you can not tell the Bureau that you know for sure that Agnes has read the information. If you do, her life—and mine—will be over."

"You're sure this is the reason behind the attack?"

"Attacks, plural. If you remember from the letter, someone tried to run her down and push her in front of a subway train as well as shooting at her and ransacking her apartment."

Harry pulled out his phone and asked Sadie to check for reports of a problem at Agnes Forester's apartment. He was startled to learn she already had the information and the police were investigating. Harry sent a text to Sergeant Sanchez, asking about the destruction at Agnes Forester's place. Harry told the policeman about the possible connection between the attacks on Agnes Forester that were on record and the attack on Kate, mentioning that they were cousins. He asked again about suspects or videos.

I grabbed my things and went to take a shower before bed. I stood under the spray, willing away the anger I'd been holding in check. Agnes had worked so hard to make this week fantastic for me. She knew how hard it was for me without Dad and Gramps, so she'd created an experience to keep me busy and to make me happy. I needed for her to be safe.

Feeling warm and sleepy, I crawled into the far bed and snuggled down after making sure the dogs had water and a bedtime treat. Harry ducked into the bathroom, dousing the room lights. I lay on my side, exhausted but too wired to close my eyes. Later, when the bathroom door opened, Harry stood in the doorway, wearing just boxers. Having four brothers, I'd seen guys in just boxers often—but not like this. I stopped breathing and stared. He was Zeus descended from Olympus. How had I not noticed all those muscles under his dapper suit? I couldn't look away. The scars from his wounds still blazed red across his chest and shoulder. He looked my way, and, for a moment, we locked eyes. Then he shut off the light and slid into the other bed.

I lay, not able to sleep, wondering what tomorrow would bring.

"Go to sleep, Kate. Your whirling brain is keeping me awake."

I smiled and sighed. "Goodnight, Harry."

"Goodnight, Kate."

CHAPTER TEN

"Whoa mama! Agnes said you'd changed and I saw your posters but, oh my, if you were a few inches taller, girl, you could be walking the runway for big bucks. Yes sir!" Ulysses Jones, all six-foot four inches of solid black badass, waved a clipboard in my direction. "If I hadn't seen it with my own eyes...Who'd have thought that that little girl would turn out looking this hot? Amen! Good to see you, honey, but back to business. Do you have the lists with the number of models and the order? There are boxes in the corner with your logo, but I haven't checked them yet and Andy has parked his carcass over there." He waved toward the corner. Ulysses should have been exhausted from working so hard on Fashion Week, but thanks to Agnes, he was here and ready to go. "You may not quote me, darling, but give me a professional model any day over amateurs. Dogs, Kate? Really? Dogs? Give me a break!"

I laughed and hugged my old friend. Then I introduced him to Harry, Dillon, and Ajax. Ulysses and I had been classmates. He wasn't anyone's idea of what a fashion-show coordinator should look or act like. He scared the life out of almost everyone in the business but he had proven over and over that he was the best. I'd known him for years; he was the sweetest man on the planet. He and his wife had been the only married couple in my class. Shaniqua had been pregnant then with the first of his two beautiful little girls, whom he adored. I knew I could count on Ulysses to make my show perfect.

"Don't worry about the dogs, big guy. They're show dogs. They hit their mark and never talk back. Now the owners are perhaps not so easy. I'm counting on you to charm the ladies and scare the shit out of the guys." His laugh shook the room. I quickly went over the paperwork, reviewing the order in which each owner and dog would appear. I listened to him outline the lighting, agreed on his seating chart, and checked off the other details on my list. Ulysses then gathered his crew together and began to make magic.

Harry and I headed toward the boxes stacked at the back of the room. Andy Sibowitz, also an old classmate, was relaxing, stretched out on a couple of chairs, eyes closed. I knew he wasn't sleeping, but rather mentally lining up each shot he would be taking.

"Got the whole shoot figured out yet, Sibowitz?" I yelled as I pulled Harry across to him.

"No problem, Irish. This is a piece of cake." Slowly opening his eyes, he rose, then fell back onto his seat. "I thought Agnes was crazy when she told me what the new you looked like, but...Oh my God. Kate, my sweet darlin', you've got to give in to this obvious attraction between us and run off with me." He grabbed all his equipment and stood, in a single motion, sweeping me up in a hug at the same time. Andy was my height but was built like a longshoreman.

"Not this week, Andy, I've got too much to do. Plus, you're a little late."

Harry stuck a hand out, looking Andy up and down. "Harry Foyle. I'm Kate's fiancé." Andy raised both eyebrows. "Engaged? Well, I guess if you've managed to catch this dog-loving sprite, more power to you, Foyle." He thumped Harry hard on the back and was shocked when Harry didn't flinch.

I turned at the sound of people and dogs suddenly filling the room. Alice came in squealing. "Kate, I can't believe this is really happening. I'm so excited." At her side Lucky, her Golden, was definitely the calmer of the two

"Really, Alice, I hadn't noticed. Okay, everyone. Thanks for showing up on time. Andy is on a really tight schedule to get all these photos done for tomorrow night's show. In the boxes behind me are your outfits, each marked with your name and breed. Tomorrow night you'll be dressing behind a screen to the right of the runway. For now though, get into your outfits and let me know if any alterations are needed. They should fit according to the measurements you sent. I hope none of you shaved a few pounds off for ego, but luckily, knits are forgiving. Once you're dressed, gather over at the side of the runway and I'll show you what we're going to do." Grabbing my clipboard, I called out names and checked them off the list. "Jimmy? Has anyone seen Jimmy?"

"Sorry Kate I don't think he's going to make it. He's trapped in Chicago along with Roger and a couple of other handlers. Apparently the storm we're supposed to get on Sunday has canceled flights out of O'Hare. It's one of those slow-moving deals that's dropping a ton of snow. Roger's call said if it's not done by tomorrow, they're going to rent a truck with chains and drive."

"So, no Shepherd." I frowned and then smiled. Turning, I looked at Harry.

"Why don't I like that smile?" He backed away as I grabbed the last garment bag and walked slowly toward him, my smile growing.

"Please? You and Jimmy are almost the same size and you have Ajax. Pretty please?"

With a snort and a scowl, Harry grabbed the bag and headed across the room.

"What's she doing here?" Cora asked, pointing to the figure standing next to Bill, holding the lead of the Afghan.

"She's here because I told her she could be," I answered in a voice that didn't invite argument. "She's here to watch. So let's get started."

Cora and some of the others gave the woman a wide berth, but Bill came over and thanked me. "Sonja needs to stay and guard us, and the prince wants the dog in the show."

"Bill, have you heard anything from Agnes?"

He shook his head as Sonja approached with the dog. I turned toward the improvised runway that now took up the entire center of the room. This setup was good in that it would let everyone get the full effect of both the outfits and the dogs. I walked over to where Andy was standing with Ulysses and gave him the heads up to begin.

"Okay guys, Kate's going to go first with Dillon just to show you how it's done. Irish, up you go." Andy grabbed my waist and swung me up. "Let's make this happen."

I got right into the fun of the day, and began strutting down the runway, imitating the many models I had worked with at the School of Design. Dillon was excited and doing his 'electric Samoyed' thing the whole time ears pricked and tail curled firmly over his back. I strolled the length of the runway, paused, and turned, looking first out at the crowd, and then down at my dog. When I reached the end of the runway again, I laughed and clapped, while Dillon jumped up to lick my face. I hopped down and moved to Andy's side.

Richard was the next up and looked like he'd just stepped off the cover of GQ. He and Spike went through their paces by having Spike dash through his legs as he did a model stroll. At the end of the runway, Richard clapped and caught the jumping Chihuahua, raising him in one hand, waiter style, high above his head and grinning at everyone's applause.

Alice and Lucky were up next. The Golden was focused tightly on Alice, matching her moves exactly and I noticed why when they reached the end of the runway. Alice suddenly pulled a training wing from under her sweater and Lucky froze into a point. Two seconds later, he had snatched the wing from her hand and bounded around her, only to sit in front to present *the bird* proudly.

Cora and her Bernese, Hugo, were next and I really wished we had room for a cart to match the one pictured with Hugo on Cora's swinging red cape, but the pair managed to look wonderful without it. Susan followed in a plaid shawl containing a head study of Angus, her Pembroke Welsh Corgi. Then came Ralph, all in black with a formal knit jacket showing his equally distinguished Borzoi, Wolfgang.

Lucy, wearing a vest with a design of a Poodle soaring over the high jump, appeared with Chance, her big black Poodle who was both a breed and obedience champion. At the end of the runway, Lucy gestured for a short recall, bringing Chance to sit in front of her.

I heard the shutter click on Andy's camera. Knowing what would happen next, I signaled Andy to get ready and then nodded at Lucy. At a slight move of Lucy's hand, Chance flew straight up into the air, spun around and landed in a perfect sit in heel position. Everyone cheered and Andy whispered, "Thanks."

Byron and Winston, his Bulldog, were the perfect example of an owner who ends up looking like his dog. They hammed it up. Immediately afterward, Maria with Bitsy, her Cavalier, swirled down the runway in a full skirt with the puppy's image on it. The imposing Landseer Newfoundland, Tenney, then filled the runway, his owner, Kathy, following in a sweater that showed him performing a rescue at sea. Next came Barbara with her Cairn Toto. She wore a sweater that showed Toto hopping over a pair of ruby red slippers. Each model stepped onto the runway fully prepared to do a grand gesture, and Andy just kept snapping away. I noticed the frown of concentration he'd worn at the beginning had turned into a wide grin.

With each model's strut, my spirits rose. This was going to be great! Everyone was giving one-hundred fifty percent. Enthralled by Andy's sweet-talking chatter and Ulysses' directions, they strode and stopped when I whistled to alert their dogs. Each pair enchanted the group with a unique performance. Bill was second to last and was wearing a sweater depicting a group of Afghans racing across the desert with the stunning gray in the lead.

When Ajax stepped onto the runway, Harry right behind, I froze. Harry looked me in the eye, gave me that half smile that brought out his dimple and started forward with Ajax glued to his side, only to have the dog freeze into a Shepherd's characteristic sloping stance at his command. Harry stepped forward and turned, looking over his shoulder, to show the exact pose pictured on the sweater.

"Great. He's a natural," yelled Ulysses.

Andy yelled, "Hey, Irish, true love can wait. Do your dog ear thing if you want to finish on time."

Startled and fighting the heat of a blush that traveled up my neck to my face, I took a breath and whistled. As expected, Ajax cocked his ears perfectly as the camera caught the series of images.

Andy shouted, "We are done, ladies and gents. It has been a pleasure. Kate will get the copies of your shots to you. Please make sure she has your waivers so she can use the photos in her ads."

He started packing his equipment as I hopped up onto the runway followed by Dillon who greeted Ajax. Harry grabbed my hand as the dogs crowded against us. I couldn't tear my gaze from his face. "Thanks," I finally murmured as a series of flashes went off.

"Best shots of the day. See you, Kate," Andy shouted as he headed slowly toward the door, in full pack-mule mode.

Startled, I turned to wave, only to be distracted as the workers hauled a ten-foot high poster into place.

"Sibowitz!" I yelled.

Andy did a one-eighty, and headed back toward me.

"You took that!" I pointed at the poster.

"You've got a good eye, darlin'. Of course I did."

"Those are my dogs. That's Ryan, Dillon's grandfather and Liam, his father."

"I know." He answered. "Agnes said these dogs meant a lot to you and, therefore, should be honored."

"But how did you do it without my knowing?"

"All I know is Agnes called me the Sunday before Thanksgiving to do a photo shoot. She said I should be there on Monday between two and two-thirty and dressed for the woods. When I got there, she was coming out of this little house with those dogs on lead, wearing the Samoyed sweater and pardon—me for saying this now that I see the real thing—looking the spitting image of your beautiful self. We walked into the woods quite a ways, even though I told her the light would be better closer to the edge. When we reached this spot, she looked around at the backdrop then gave me the go ahead, and we quickly did the shoot. She told me exactly what she wanted with the scrim, and that was what you got. Then she put the Sams back in the little house, pulled on the other sweater and got the greyhounds out of her car. The light was just filtering through the trees at the beginning of the path so we did the shot that's in the lobby."

I just stared at the wall and the image staring back. I felt tears filling my eyes and a lump growing in my throat.

"I take it she didn't tell you," Andy continued, reaching over to grasp my shoulder. "You two really need to talk. Nevertheless, take it from me, this is a money shot. It tells the story of you and your line. Having that barn, with the double-S showing through the trees, is a great setting too."

"I know. It's my home. You're right. It is a fabulous shot. I just wasn't expecting it. Thank you so much."

"It was a pleasure. Now I've got to go. I've got a lot to get done if you want those projections finished in time for the show. I'll ship everything else to your studio after the show is over. Take care, Irish. Nice meeting you Foyle."

I stared at the scrim for a few more minutes then took my phone and photographed it. Harry moved up behind me. "I think she really wanted it to be a happy surprise, Kate."

"You're right. It's a beautiful present." I cocked my head to the side. "It makes me look pretty."

Harry whirled me around to face him, "Kate, you're beautiful, and I think that's what Agnes wanted to show you." My tears were falling in earnest now, but a yell interrupted the moment.

Taking Harry's proffered handkerchief to dry my eyes, I headed toward the escalating shouts.

Bill was trying to make peace as Sonja was yelling that nobody could ride in the elevator with the prince's dog.

Alice and Cora were standing with their hands on their hips, ready for a fight, so I stepped in quickly. "Bill, Sonja, could you please wait just a minute? I have to check on the arrangements with you for the royal party's attendance." I had them step back into the room and then I turned to the crowd by the elevator. "I'll see most of you later in Central Park."

"Bitch," Cora muttered to Sonja's retreating back. Then she turned and disappeared into the elevator.

Harry slid his arms around me from behind and pulled me against him. "You did a good job managing that mob, Kate. How did you get that tough?"

I looked over my shoulder, enjoying the feel of his arms, and grinned. "Four brothers. This was just a skirmish, not a real battle. If you want to draw blood, you should try pitting my brothers against my cousins from Framingham on the subject of Yankees versus Red Sox."

"You're a Yankees fan?" Harry whirled me around, held me at arm's length and frowned. "I don't know about this engagement, Kate; that may be too great a deal breaker."

"Suck it up, Boston; you've got your World Series now. We can probably let you have a Series or two more in the next fifty years." Patting his cheek, I laughed and headed back into the ballroom to talk with Bill and Sonja.

Sonja had been carrying on with much waving of arms, but when I shouted, "Stop," she froze. "Sonja, this is how it is going to be. You will behave in a courteous manner to the people who are involved in this show. The prince politely asked, and I happily agreed to have me include his dog because he is justly proud of his fabulous Afghan. I do not think he would be happy to hear that the person he put in charge of his beloved dog's safety was going out of her way to make enemies for herself which would reflect back on both the dog and the prince. As a gentleman, Bill hasn't told you off when you needed it. I have no problem doing so. This is my fashion show and, therefore, everyone will behave by my rules. If, because of your behavior, the prince's dog is removed from the show…."

"No, no. That cannot happen. You must not take the dog out of the show."

"Then we will proceed as follows. If you can't say something nice to one of the other people present, you will not say anything. Understood?"

She looked at me for a moment, obviously debating whether to keep arguing. "Yes."

I waved at Bill and Harry to give us a minute. Facing her, I asked about why she was angry. After a moment she told me her family—her father and her brother—had always guarded the royal family. "What do I get? They assign me to guard a dog."

I looked her in the eye. "They assigned you to guard the prince's most treasured possession. They assumed you could blend into the background like a covert operator. This is a job they couldn't give to one of the usual guards. Are you up to the challenge?"

"You think this is so, that they really respect me?"

"I know it is so."

For the first time since we met, I saw her smile. She

truly was a stunningly beautiful woman.

When we returned, Bill waved her toward the elevator, mouthing the words, *thank you*, over his shoulder.

Still waiting for me by the elevator, Harry smiled, and Dillon barked, which reminded me we still had a lot of ground to cover today. "Let's take these pups down to relieve themselves and then you can grab us some hot dogs from Nathan's while I do my first scheduled PR interview in the lobby. After that we can head uptown."

"Yes ma'am. Remind me never to get on your bad side."

I laughed. "I raise dogs, remember. I've had many generations of bitches to teach me how to keep unruly litters and recalcitrant puppies in line. They were all were lucky I didn't bite."

CHAPTER ELEVEN

We stuffed our faces with hot dogs and fries as we walked over to Eighth Avenue, to grab a cab then headed up Central Park West to 72nd Street and the famous Strawberry Fields. As we strolled through the park, I had a knee-jerk urge to look for gray Afghans and Bill surrounded by body guards, but instead, we'd arrived at the place where our demonstration would be. I spotted Cora and the others gathered together near what looked like a good-sized crowd of spectators. Cold doesn't stop New Yorkers. There were also three camera men, two broadcast trucks, a dozen reporters, and, I suspected, a partridge in a pear tree. As PR person for the club, Kathy was in the middle of the group of media, but she spotted us and waved. "You're right on time, Kate. It's cold, so let's get this demo into action. Brian has cued up the music."

I reached into my backpack to pull out a short jacket in royal blue, emblazoned with our logo and saw that everyone else was already suited up. Harry grabbed my pack, coat and leads. Handing Dillon back to me, he took Ajax and wished me luck. I unhooked Dillon's lead, tossing it to Harry, and took a tightly rolled bundle. Finally, I signaled Dillon to heel. We headed across the lawn to where the others were lined up, stopping only to whisper something to a small boy standing with his parents in the front row. Richard stepped forward to give his introduction, which included laughs when Spike kept sticking his head out of the top his jacket, apparently without Richard noticing. When he began to look for his dog, everyone roared 'til the inevitable child told him Spike was hiding in his jacket.

Grabbing Spike and setting him on the ground in heel position, he moved into line next to the gigantic Newfoundland, Tenney. I nodded and the music played. Reporters scurried to get out of the way as the group of fourteen handlers and their dogs marched forward to the music. Without missing a beat, the group began to create intricate weaves, spirals, a cross-over, twists and a grand right and left, plus every possible formation imaginable. It didn't matter the size of the dog, which is why we always paired Spike with Kathy's Tenney. People loved watching the Chihuahua taking about twenty steps to the Newf taking one as the handlers managed to stay in perfect unison in the line. The finale brought us back to our original line, only to have Dillon break ranks and, weave at a run, through the line to the end, circle the group and then fly into the audience to grab a flag from the hand of one very thrilled child. Then as the music reached a crescendo, he raced around t he edge of the crowd with the flag flying, sprinted up the line and swung about until he sat facing me. Then, as one, all the dogs sat back on their haunches, paws raised in a salute to the flag, their actions timed to the final flourish of the music. The crowd cheered and the children rushed forward to hug the dogs and get photo ops with their favorites. Ten more minutes of reporters' questions and TV people doing their lead-ins with the dogs in the background, and we were done. The group broke up with promises to get together at the party that evening.

I hurried over to return to Harry and switched to my warm winter coat and scarf.

He reached out to rub my hands, holding me until I was warm. "That was incredible," he raved.

"It only took ten months of weekly practices and excellent dogs to make it look easy. The trick is moving evenly when you have both big and small dogs. We purposely put Spike next to Tenney for contrast. Since both handlers are in perfect step, the anomalies don't show up. It also makes the training for high scores in obedience competition a piece of cake. The dogs learn to focus to the point where they are riveted, waiting for your command. Turning to the dogs, I smiled and reached into my pocket for doggie snacks. "Okay boys, here's a treat for Dillon for being a super showman and for Ajax for sitting quietly and watching like a grown-up puppy."

"What's next?"

"Next, you get to go thank Maeve for introducing us. I called Niall this morning to see if he could find a tux in your size."

"So I'm meeting the family?"

"She's my great aunt. You'll love her. She's your kind of people."

We grabbed a cab for the ten-block trip further up Central Park West to the front of a brownstone, still bathed in its original beauty.

"This brownstone has been in Donovan's family since it was first built," I told Harry, my voice spilling excitement all over the cab. "He brought Maeve here right from their honeymoon and they've lived here ever since."

Dashing up the stairs, I twisted the brass ringer set in a beautifully carved rosette. Then I reached back to pull Harry up beside me. I pointed up at the tall home rising above me. "I've spent some of the happiest times of my life here. Wait 'til you meet Maeve."

A middle-aged man opened the door, and his formal expression transformed from dour to delight.

"Hello, Niall, how are you doing in this cold weather?" I jumped forward and hugged him.

"Ah, Miss Kathleen, 'tis good to see your lovely self today. You look more like Herself every day."

"It's in my daily prayers that I'll ever be half that beautiful, but thank you for saying so, Niall. You know Dillon, and this is Ajax. I'll be showing him on Monday. And this," I said slipping my arm into my betrothed's, "is Harry Foyle."

Niall nodded, but the smile had left his face and he gave Harry a good long stare before turning back to me.

"I know The Woman has planned to fix something special to eat. She loves spoiling all of you. Herself is waiting for you in the library. Go on in." He took our coats while shooting another look at Harry.

I led the way as Harry stared around at the hall with its cream plaster walls rising above the dark oak wainscoting. Then he said, "I suspect my wardrobe is highly suited here to the times when gracious living really meant grace and not ostentation. I don't know why, but I suddenly feel relaxed; this feels like a home."

We walked past an open double doorway on the left. I stopped and pointed out the massive yet graceful drawing room whose one-of-a-kind hand-carved fireplace was centered on one wall. I loved this room with its comfortable sofa facing a pair of overstuffed chairs. As was common in this wintery weather, a fire warmed the hearth. This was where the Killoy and Donovan clans would all would gather to open presents every Christmas.

Harry reached for my shoulder when he saw the painting above the mantel. I smiled and pulled him forward to get a good look. "That's you," he gasped as he gazed up at the image that looked exactly like me. Now that I thought about it, this might have been Agnes' inspiration for the posters. In the painting, a woman stood, relaxed, in a period dress the color of her blue eyes beside a handsome man, their hands entwined. Harry looked from the painting back to me. His smile had disappeared and he had let go of my hand.

"Who's the man?"

"Handsome, isn't he?"

I walked back to the hall. He followed me, our footsteps hushed by the worn Persian runner. It glowed in colors of red, gold, white and a rich royal blue, worked in a paisley pattern. The rug ran from the entry door to the staircases, one leading up, the other down. Both staircases were decorated with carved newel posts, intricate balusters and shiny banisters. Then the runner widened into a full carpet that filled an open area, where Niall stood tucking our coats into a closet.

"Harry liked my portrait in the living room." I smiled as I crossed the room listening to the snort that came from behind me.

"Did he now?" Niall raised an eyebrow and glanced at Harry's scowl as I headed toward the doorway ahead.

Before me, extending up to the ceiling, stood a massive pair of oak pocket doors. I threw them open to reveal what I have always thought of as the quintessential gentleman's library. Harry walked beside me staring in obvious amazement at the twelve-foot bookshelves that lined the walls. These massive floor-to-ceiling shelves were filled, not with neat rows of matched book spines, but with volumes jammed into every crevice of their imposing oak mass. The shelves bowed slightly under the weight of the thousands of books housed there for many, many years. A fire crackled in a smaller fireplace obviously carved by the same hand as had done the one in the drawing room, and Harry's face showed pure delight at the thought of spending any time here. He turned slowly and then stopped to look up at yet another painting. In this one, the woman was standing, wearing an outfit from the nineteen sixties, with Dillon at her side. Though the room was beautiful, Harry couldn't seem to tear his eyes from the painting.

"Kate, you're here!" At that shout I saw Harry look up to see a woman rushing down the circular library stairs from the balcony and dashing forward to hug me.

"Maeve!" I returned the hug of the person I considered the most strikingly beautiful woman in the world. Glancing back at Harry, I smiled, watching his face as the truth slowly dawned on him. He now understood that Maeve was the woman in the paintings and at one time she'd been the spitting image of me.

"My darling Kathleen, I haven't seen you since November. How are your mother and grandmother and those gloriously handsome brothers of yours?" Maeve held me back after the hug, the soft brogue gentle on her lips. Dressed in jeans, boots, a sky-blue turtleneck and an Aran sweater and with her curls drawn up and piled on top of her head, the resemblance between us was amazing. Her smile and eyes swiftly focused on Harry.

"Everyone is fine, Maeve. I'm sorry that Grace's illness and the twins' hockey tournament kept us from making it in for Christmas." I stepped back to remove the dog's leads.

"Ah, you've brought my wonderful Dillon, along with two strangers."

"The handsome young Shepherd is Ajax. He belongs to a friend. I'll be showing him on Monday. The equally handsome man is my friend, bodyguard and temporary fiancé, Harry Foyle."

Harry must have caught the mischief in my eyes because he suddenly grinned. "Your niece has been having me on with the painting in the living room."

"Ah, yes, she loves to do that and it looks much more like her now with her hair short. Delighted to be meeting you, Mr. Foyle." Maeve's smile for Harry was warm, but slightly curious as she reached for his hand. "Actually, I'm Kathleen's great aunt, Maeve Killoy Donovan," she explained pulling his arm through hers. "I suspect there's a story behind your introduction."

"Actually, Maeve, you introduced us last November when I had my makeover, which ended up with dinner at Reilly's. We gradually fell in love over the winter and just got engaged yesterday. That's our story and we're sticking to it for my safety and also for the safety of Agnes. By the way, only you and Sal know the real story."

"As you say and I'll be interested in hearing more of these exploits. I guess congratulations are in order, both to the two of you and to myself for my matchmaking talents. You'll have to regale me with all the romantic details at lunch but you're not the only one with a surprise."

Harry turned to where Maeve was looking and I saw his surprised expression as he gazed over my shoulder and then back at me. I glanced in the big mirror on the wall over his head and saw two of me reflected in the glass.

"It's about time!" I shrieked as whirling, I ran forward to hug Agnes. Looking up, I saw from Harry's expression he'd figured it out. I jumped back and stood, glaring at her. "How could you? I have been so worried. You didn't answer any of my texts or my calls. Then the FBI came after me. People were telling me they'd seen me in the hotel when I was still in Connecticut. Trying to maneuver the minefield you left wasn't fun. So, out with it. What's going on?"

Maeve interrupted. "Now I don't want to keep Sally's wonderful lunch waiting, so we'll eat before we talk. Let's move to the dining room, and you can tell me everything. Dillon's and his friend can stay here with his grandmother." The dogs had moved to greet the older Samoyed bitch who'd been snoozing comfortably in front of the fire. Maeve took both my arm and Agnes'.

A voice boomed as a tall man walked into the room. "Now if that isn't the most beautiful sight in the world! I do believe my eyes are seeing triplets."

"Donovan, you're just in time to eat. Isn't it a joy to have our two girls with us today and they've brought a guest. Padraig Donovan, meet Harry Foyle, Kate's fiancé."

Harry straightened up as his hand was taken in a grip of steel and piercing blue eyes looked him over. He recognized the handsome man from the portrait in the living room, changed little physically except that his still-thick hair was now pure white.

"Fiancé, is it? I don't recall giving my approval. I don't let just anyone court my girls."

"Relax, Donovan. He's protecting Kate this weekend. That's his cover. Now, let's not be keeping Sally waiting. She'll not be thanking you for the meal getting cold."

We settled at the table and dug into a main course of shepherd's pie along with individual loaves of soda bread. The men and Maeve had hard cider while Agnes drank wine and I had water. The conversation turned quickly to the fashion show.

"Now about those posters...." I looked across at the mirror image staring back.

"I wanted to surprise you. I guess I did," Agnes began cautiously. "While you were getting your makeover, I decided to have Andy take those photos for the event. I hoped you understood the surprise. I just wanted to show you how the beauty we always saw in you could now be visible to the world. Once I saw the photos, I couldn't resist using them in our ads. They told the story of the show. I might point out that, as soon as they appeared, we sold out.

To tell the truth, I've always been slightly jealous. Here I work so hard at this modeling career with an army of people around me to remove any flaw and make me look perfect. You, on the other hand, can appear dressed in your brother's hand-me-downs, muck boots and no makeup, having spent hours cleaning kennels and scooping poop and look absolutely lovely." My face must have reflected my shock and disbelief.

"She doesn't believe you. She's the most beautiful woman I've ever met, and yet she has no clue." Harry reached across the table and squeezed my hand.

I turned to stare at him only just remembering to close my shocked mouth. I shook myself, heat creeping up my neck to my cheeks. I lowered my eyes, cleared my throat and told him, "You're full of it Foyle, but I thank you for the kind thought, fiction though it may be."

As we finished our delicious dessert of bread pudding, I turned to Agnes. "Could we now talk about all this cloak-and-dagger stuff? And can you explain about your hiding out—disguised as me—from both would-be murderers and the FBI?"

"I'm not able to tell you what was on the thumb drive. Maeve and I have been working on the code, but since we don't have the key, it's been slow going. Maeve helped me locate my old contact at State, but their key doesn't work. They told me that nobody was expecting any information on Zanifra after what we brought them in November. The question is if State isn't involved, why was I given the drive and why is someone trying to kill me?"

"And Kate." Harry wasn't smiling when he dropped in that information and Agnes blanched.

"It seems there's also a problem with a mole in the Bureau. The man who approached me seemed to be an agent, but he refused to give his name, which I found strange," Agnes elaborated with a look of annoyance.

"Well, Agnes, you're going to remain here until we have this figured out. I'll check with some of my old friends at the Bureau." Maeve was frowning as she looked around the table.

"If you're checking on Bureau people, Agent Bill Hendrix might help. He had the office next to mine for years and was really conscientious," Harry offered not wanting to be left out. "When I had lunch with him yesterday, though, he said he was one of the agents assigned to find Agnes."

I stood and laid my napkin on the table beside my empty dessert plate. "I hate to eat and run, but we've got a lot to do today that won't wait for bad guys or government agents. Thank you so much, Maeve, Padraig. Stay safe, Agnes. Don't worry about the show. Things are going along perfectly."

When we got into our coats and took the dogs' leads, Niall approached carrying a garment bag. "I think this will do, Mr. Foyle."

Harry thanked him and we headed out. As we settled into the cab we'd flagged down, Harry looked at me. "Thanks for letting me meet your family. They're great."

"I know. I'm so lucky." My hand automatically sought Dillon's head to stroke. "And, really, except for this clandestine stuff, this week is going great. I expected we might have a few more problems with the show, but so far it's been a breeze. I guess I'm truly lucky."

Harry looked at me and frowned. "I pray you're right but, I've never been a great believer in luck."

CHAPTER TWELVE

The scene at the hotel was like a fifty-percent-off sale at Saks. We pushed through the crowds of humans and canines and the mountains of luggage, working our way slowly in the direction of the elevators. We hadn't gone more than a few steps when I spotted Bill standing with the prince's Afghan at the concierge's desk. What struck me as strange was that Sonja was nowhere to be seen. Grabbing Harry's arm, I turned in Bill's direction. "Bill's alone. This might give us a chance to get some information from him before his watchdog shows up." I wove like a good quarterback over to the concierge desk.

"Hi Bill," I greeted him as casually as I could manage. "Can we talk to you for a second?"

"God, Kate. This might not be a good time to talk, though I'd welcome your just standing here until security arrives from the consulate. I feel as though I'm holding the Hope Diamond at a jewelry conference."

"Where's Sonja? She's never been more than two inches from Ashraf since I arrived."

"That's the problem. When we got back from the photo shoot, I lay down to take a snooze. I'm not as young as I used to be. Sometime after that, Sonja opened the door between our rooms and told me she'd had a call and needed to take care of something. She sent Ashraf into my room and left." Bill stroked the dog, which leaned into him, displaying the bond between them. "When we woke, I realized hours had gone by and Sonja still hadn't returned. I tried calling her cell, but it went immediately to voice mail. We checked all the places she might be and then I had to call the consulate because Ashraf is never supposed to be without a guard. Ah, thank God! Here they are." I looked up to see the familiar trio of black-suited men I remembered from the park.

"Will we see you at the party tonight?" I probed, trying to find a time to talk as Bill began to head out with his guards.

"I don't know. It depends on what's happening with Sonja. Anyway, thanks for the moral support, Kate. Good to see you again Harry."

"Curiouser and curiouser." I quoted *Alice* as this situation was getting as weird as *Wonderland.*

We resumed our slog through the mass of bodies—human and canine. Not only were folks trying to check in for the dog show, and for the many specialty shows at hotels around the city, but also for both the Master Agility Trials and the AKC Meet the Breed event. The latter two would be held over at the pier tomorrow during the day. For a number of years as part of the activities that the Minuteman Samoyed Club did representing the Samoyed Club of America, I had participated in the Meet the Breeds when it was held in the fall. The booth would display the ancient lineage of the breed and some of the members would bring in dogs and puppies for the public to see. This year, though, it had been moved to Pier 92 to coordinate with the agility trials. This was a wonderful chance for the public to learn about all the American Kennel Club's recognized breeds, and for breeders to engage in a massive brag fest. However, with everything else going on, I'd had to beg off this year. By the time we reached the stairs to take the dogs down to the green room, Harry looked like he was drowning in canines.

The exercise area was jammed. I trotted both dogs to the shavings, trading dog leads for the pooper scooper with Harry when they finished.

"Kate, there you are. I've been telling some of the Chihuahua Club members about the fantastic photo shoot this morning," Richard bragged, breaking from a group of friends.

"It really went well, Richard. Andy does a fantastic job. Wait 'til you see the results."

"How are you holding up, Harry? Are you suffering canine overwhelm yet?"

"Pretty close. I had no idea there were this many different breeds of dog, all of which seem to come in huge numbers."

"Well, this weekend is the biggest deal of the year. Just think of it as basic training for your life with this dog nut." He smiled at Kate.

I laughed. "He's tough. He can take it. By the way, Richard, have you seen Sonja around? I've got a question for her."

"Nope. It's been quiet since we got back from the park. I've been in a Chihuahua Club meeting for most of the afternoon."

Harry reached out to scratch Spike's head then nodded toward the elevators. "We'd better get a move on it. We wanted to grab an early supper so we wouldn't be showing up at the party hungry. It will be our first chance to dance."

His smile made my heart speed up and my mind conjured a picture of my being in his arms. He flashed that half smile and I knew he could read my thoughts.

Back in the room, the dogs ate their dinners, and Harry stretched out on his bed while I answered all the texts and emails about the show.. Then hit pound three on my phone.

Sal answered immediately. "Sal, I just wanted to update you on the situation here. I talked with Agnes. We are no closer to finding out who's behind the attacks and we've only have a slightly better idea about the reason behind it. Harry's Sadie is working on it. Yes, I've heard she's something special. How is everyone there? Have you been checking Siobhan's temperature? I know she's not due to deliver the puppies for a week, but better safe than sorry. If it drops, call Sybil immediately. Agnes' grandmother has whelped more litters than I can count and she's only twenty minutes away. I don't want to take any chances with this litter. I've got a waiting list for them since it will be Siobhan's last litter. My fiancé? Yes, he's sleeping on the job. I'll wake him." I tossed the phone to Harry, who caught it one handed and swung himself into a sitting position.

"Hi Sal, yeah, she's doing great. She's tough. Right, I've noticed. It's been relatively quiet. The only strange thing is that the guard on the Zanifra prince's Afghan Hound has gone AWOL. They took Bill and the hound back to the consulate for safety. Considering she's been glued to that dog, it's suspicious. I think they're hoping she'll show up with a viable explanation. Right I will. Dogs are doing great. We've bonded. Dillon has given me permission to court his owner. Yeah, right. Take care. I'll keep you posted." He tossed the phone back to me, which required a two-handed catch on my part. I organized all the papers I would need tomorrow on the desk and stood.

"Let's go eat before the place fills up." I grabbed a couple of small biscuits and signaled the dogs to go into their crates. Harry slid on his shoes, picked up his suit jacket and tightened his tie. I wanted to reach out and adjust the tie myself, just to be close.

When dinner arrived I dug right in. I had the swordfish with teriyaki rice and Harry ordered a steak with a massive baked potato. We were both hungry in spite of the good lunch we'd had just hours ago. Stress had ramped up our need for calories. Finally coming up for air, I decided more tea and no dessert was what I needed most and Harry signaled the waiter. He felt that he could squeeze in a piece of cherry pie along with more tea. I leaned back and scanned the room looking for familiar faces amongst the other diners. I'd met many of the people over the years, but some were new to me—either from the other side of the country or abroad. I imagined every hotel in the garment district was as jammed as this one. A waving hand caught my eye. The woman looked vaguely familiar, but the kind of familiar you get from seeing a picture rather than from a face-to-face meeting. I waved back and she headed our way."

"Kate, it's so good to get a chance to have a word with you before the show. I'm Lily Peters. I know we've spoken but we've never formally met. I wanted to get here early enough to go to the fashion show. Katja is up in the room, but I'm sure you're busy and would rather wait to see her in the ring. You said you liked the pedigree, so if it turns out you like her as well, we can talk. She has all her clearances and she'll be in season next at the beginning of April."

"It's good to finally meet you face to face. To tell the truth, I'm working on overload right now and wouldn't be able to give Katja the attention she needs. Why don't we get together after the judging on Tuesday and I can go over her.

We can chat then."

Harry reached out to shake her hand when she turned to him. "Hi, I'm Harry Foyle, Kate's fiancé."

"Oh, congratulations." She smiled at Kate. "I'll plan on talking with you next on Tuesday, if I don't get a chance at the fashion show."

As we left the restaurant, Harry chuckled. "I guess my friend Dillon is a hot-shot stud."

"Yeah, he'd be happy to please all the ladies, but as his doting mother, I'm very fussy about the girls he dates."

CHAPTER THIRTEEN

I stared at the garment bag hanging on the back of the bathroom door and wished I were back in Connecticut cleaning kennels. I wasn't sure about this. This dress was a racing bike where I was barely ready for a bike with training wheels. I reached out to touch the soft, silky fabric and sighed. This wasn't even on the same planet with my comfort zone. I'm not glamorous like Agnes. I'm just plain Kate. I sighed, looked at my watch and finished unzipping the bag. Reaching into the bottom, I pulled out the slinky bra and panties and put them on. When I turned to the mirror, I noticed I suddenly had breasts, the kind in the ads in fashion magazines. I'd never even noticed them when wearing my cotton sports bra. I reached in again and grabbed the shoes, delicate, lacy sandals with high pointy heels. This was going to be so bad. I just knew I was going to fall flat on my face trying to walk on these stilts.

I slid my feet in and buckled the straps. Holding on to the edge of the sink, I stood up. One step, two and then I walked back and forth across the room. Maybe these weren't so bad. They certainly felt a lot more comfortable than they looked. Reaching for the dress, I pulled it from the bag. It was like holding water. Agnes had chosen it because she said it really brought out the blue of my eyes, but I hadn't noticed at the time how the fabric imitated flowing water as the light hit it with my every move. I unhooked it from its hanger carefully and, taking a deep breath and holding it, slid the dress over my head. It flowed down my body and I felt as though I were standing in a waterfall. In the full-length mirror, I saw it travel all the way to the floor. Even as I breathed, the highlights within the fabric gave the appearance of an icy stream cascading down my body. I'd been so tired the day Agnes had chosen it. I'd barely looked at it, agreeing just to get the shopping finished. I turned to look at the back and saw why the clasp of the bra was situated so low. Where the front of the dress descended from my collarbone to my toes, the back didn't begin until slightly above the waist. I revolved to get the full effect of this stranger reflected in the mirror. I was still gazing at that unrecognizable woman when Harry tapped at the door. "Don't dawdle in there."

"Just a minute," I said and dove into the bag to get my makeup and earrings. With my hands shaking only slightly, I brushed on some blush and put on lipstick. Attaching the dangling earrings, I gave one quick look, ran my hands through my curls, walked out of the bathroom and gasped.

Harry in a tux made James Bond look frumpy. I smiled, thinking what a pleasure it was going to have the handsomest man at the ball be my escort. I started to tell him how great he looked in my grandfather's tux when I realized he was standing frozen, staring at me. He didn't even blink. I took a step forward and touched his arm. Suddenly shaking himself, his eyelids fluttered, he took a breath and a smile broke across his face. He stepped forward, taking my hand and lifting my fingers to give them gentle kiss. A thrill of warmth shot from my fingers down to pool between my legs. Only slightly out of breath, I smiled up at him. Suddenly he was holding my face. With incredible gentleness, he leaned in and kissed my lips. I reached my hands up to hold his shoulders; my body felt suddenly weak, and the world tilted. I needed to cling to him and, perhaps, never let go.

With a sigh of regret, he ended the kiss. He gently steadied me and drew away. "You look exquisite," he whispered as he pulled back.

"Thank you." I could feel a blush spread to my cheeks and who knew where else?

His hand gently played with my earring while he looked at me and I felt curious sensations building. I was filled with a need I didn't understand, but I was sure of two things; the need had to be satisfied, and only Harry could do it. I never wanted these feelings to stop. I leaned forward, resting a hand on his chest, and could feel his heart pounding beneath it.

Harry shook his head and, with a sigh of immeasurable regret, stepped back. "We'd better go or I'll be having Donovan after me with a shotgun."

I felt bereft and confused when he let me go. Turning away to check on the dogs, I disguised the regret that must have showed on my face. Both were sleeping.

When we reached the elevator, a group was already waiting to go up to the party. I knew Ulysses would have redecorated the room so it fit the fundraiser ball tonight. As we walked in, I saw that hints of tomorrow's fashion show still lingered. The entire length of the runway was draped with a curtain that matched the apron. Spotlights were pointed to emphasize the chandeliers and I noticed the poster of Agnes as me was subtlety lit. I moved closer to Harry. Nerves were starting to make me feel exposed and vulnerable.

He looked down and whispered, "You win dog shows, escape from bad guys and stop fights without raising your voice. As Sal would tell you, tonight's a piece o' cake. Just smile and they'll all love you."

Richard swooped in. "Kate, you're the most beautiful creature in New York City in that dress."

"Richard is right Kate. You're lovely." Brandon echoed coming up behind.

"Thank you. You both are quite handsome yourselves."

"Kate, you look wonderful." Cora gushed as she, Alice, Susan and Ralph all crowded around, full of good cheer. Excitement filled the group as they talked about what fun they'd had posing for their photos.

"I emailed all my friends," Cora said, "that I was just photographed by the famous fashion photographer, Andy Sibowitz. What a coup. Everyone's green with envy. Hugo looked great. Most of his win photos don't do him justice, so this will be perfect, showing us both at our best. I noticed the nasty groomer isn't here tonight. I couldn't believe that scene she caused after the shoot."

"She is very protective of the prince's dog, and she isn't used to being around dog people. I'd like you guys to cut her some slack for Bill's sake. I spoke to her, and I don't think we'll be getting any rudeness from her again." I told the crowd, trying to pacify them.

Harry took advantage of the group's trying to decide whether Sonja was worthy of a little slack. He slid his hand through my arm and, making our excuses, led me toward the dance floor.

I knew how to dance because all my brothers had drafted me as a practice partner by when they were learning. However, there was a world of difference between being pushed around the floor by my siblings and being held in Harry's arms as we floated around the room. Harry was a magnificent dancer. I found his shoulder was at the perfect height for me to rest my head. His hand, resting against the bare skin of my back affected me in ways that had nothing to do with the room's ambient temperature. I was now beginning to realize I might enjoy having someone think I was beautiful as long as that someone was Harry. I heard him humming quietly as we moved together to the music. Harry's chin rested lightly on the top of my head. I sighed and leaned closer. Tonight, I was certain, was absolutely perfect. This was an evening I would never forget.

A scream ripped through the ballroom, then absolute silence. The music ceased along with every conversation. As one, people turned toward the runway. Lucy stood near the stage, white faced and in a panic. The curtain on the stage had been pushed to one side and I could see a hand and part of a sweater-covered arm sticking out from under the bottom edge. Someone yelled for a doctor and another voice said, "Call the police."

Harrison Coulter picked up the microphone he'd so recently abandoned after welcoming everyone to the event and implored everyone to remain calm. As president of the Westerland Kennel Club, he had the clout to make people do as he asked. Everyone gathered into small, quiet groups. "You will all have to remain here until the police arrive," he announced while nodding to the ticket collectors to close the doors. "I am sorry that your evening has been disturbed, but please be patient."

The crowd had drawn back. Lucy was left standing alone. Nobody wanted to be involved. Glancing up at Harry, I walked over to stand with my friend. I pulled Lucy away to sit on the edge of the runway, a few feet from what was obviously a dead body. Harry stood in front of us, blocking people's view to give us a bit of privacy.

What was probably only a few minutes but seemed like hours passed before I heard movement at the entrance and looked up to see a familiar face. Sergeant Sanchez was striding in our direction alongside a distinguished older black man, no taller than I wearing a well cut suit and rimless glasses. "Miss Killoy, Foyle, can you tell us what happened here?"

Harry quickly filled them in. "The party was in full swing when we heard a scream. It looks like Kate's friend, Lucy, found the body. We don't have an ID yet because I've been keeping people back, though, from the look of the hand and arm sticking out from under the curtain, I'd say the deceased is female." Harry stepped to one side to reveal what was visible. Sanchez fished a pen out of his pocket and gently lifted back the curtain. Lucy and I gasped. We had found Sonja Kunar.

Harry took my hand and we guided Lucy to a small table to wait. Sanchez climbed onto the runway to examine the body. A police photographer moved in and began taking both stills and video of the corpse and the area around her. When the photographer was done Sanchez reached over to examine Sonja, rolling her over onto her back and revealing a thin metal rod sticking out of her neck. As I recognized the protruding object, my hands, hidden in Harry's, fisted—as if that could keep the horror away.

Sanchez jumped down from the runway and turned

to speak quietly to the man at his side. After a few minutes, they walked over, and the sergeant introduced his companion to us. "This is Detective Harrison Williams. He will be supervising this case. Sir, this is Kate Killoy and her fiancé Harry Foyle. They're friends of Mondigliani from Connecticut."

The detective nodded in our direction and stepped forward to talk to Lucy. "And you would be…?" he asked, looking past me.

"Lucy Nicolette. I was just showing a friend the stage where we'll be doing the fashion show tomorrow and I reached out to straighten the curtain that was crooked and the hand fell down. It was awful, so white and lifeless. It didn't look real. I guess I screamed. I'm a little vague after that."

Turning back to me, he pointed to the body. "Do you have any idea who the woman is?"

"Her name is Sonja Kunar."

"How did you know her?"

"I just met her yesterday. She's a groomer who works with Bill Trumbull. I haven't seen him this evening. He told me earlier he wasn't sure he would make the party."

"So you've just met the victim. How would you describe her?"

"Sonja was an abrasive person. She often was rude to people, especially those involved with the fashion show. She had a knack for starting arguments."

"Right. So we've got a woman people didn't like

who has been found dead onstage, in the middle of a party. Am I correct?"

We nodded. I looked at Harry and asked if we could speak to them alone. The detective and Sanchez signaled to a few of their men, and we moved into the area we used as a dressing room.

"Sergeant Sanchez, you might want to check with the Zanifran consulate. I happen to know Sonja was working undercover guarding the prince's Afghan Hound. I also know that she went missing this afternoon. If Bill isn't here, he's probably with the dog at the consulate."

"Does this have anything to do with the attack on you?" Sanchez asked as he entered my information into his small black notebook.

"I don't know." I found myself reaching for Harry's hand again, needing his strength. "If there is a connection, I don't yet know what it is."

Sanchez scanned the room and sighed. "I'm going to have you and Harry give your information to the officer here and then you can leave. We'll need to talk to you again first thing in the morning."

"Sergeant, I know you have your work to do here, but I have a rehearsal scheduled in the middle of your crime scene for tomorrow morning at ten and a sold-out fashion show scheduled for tomorrow night. I have contact information for the models, but there are between three and four hundred people with tickets whom we can't contact."

"I take it from that poster, this is your event," Sanchez remarked pointing to the subtly lit poster behind me. "We'll do what we can to get this cleared out. I'll keep you posted. I've got your number. " He handed us off to a policeman at the table by the door.

I saw Lucy was now with Cora and Alice. Relieved that I was no longer needed, I sat and gave full attention to my statement. As soon as Harry was finished, we walked in silence to the elevator and went back to our room. My mind spun with images of joy and horror and I told Harry that sleep would be impossible. Harry suggested we get out of the hotel and take a walk, so we changed our clothes, leashed the dogs and headed out. What we needed was some peace and sanity.

CHAPTER FOURTEEN

It felt good to be outside in the crisp, cold air. Turning right, we started our walk around the block, moving in silence, lost in our own thoughts. I'd been trying unsuccessfully to clear my brain, but the harder I tried, the more my mind filled with unwanted images—one of them struck me as curious.

"I don't know what it means, but the thing that was sticking out of Sonja's neck…" I took a breath, shivered and continued, "That piece of metal looked very much like a knitting needle. It's not the kind I use, but I recognized it as a needle for knitting lace." We walked a little further. "Harry, do you think whoever killed her wanted to implicate me?"

"If you mean the fact she was killed with a knitting needle on the runway for your show that's based on knitting? Then I rather suspect it is a possibility."

Harry reached for my hand and finished his thought. "It might mean someone is trying to involve you, or it might mean something entirely different. We don't even have the right questions to ask yet, to say nothing of the answers. You're not the easiest person to be engaged to, Miss Killoy."

I looked up at him. "Okay my mathematical super stud, if you look at the facts carefully, this whole thing—the attacks on me and Agnes and now murder—it's all got one common denominator; Zanifra."

"Super stud?" he asked, grinning.

"I thought that would get your attention. If we were to sit down later and start associating people with links to the reference point of Zanifra, we might have a better chance at figuring out not only the likeliest suspects, but a possible course of action to catch them."

"In other words, I should view it mathematically and work to bring logic to the problem. You are a woman after my own heart." He hooked our arms together, "I take back what I said about our engagement. You are the best person to be engaged to, Miss Killoy."

We continued walking, but the silence had lost its earlier tension and a warm, understated companionship had taken its place. I watched the dogs trot before us, enjoying the cold, what my dad had called *Samoyed weather.* I began thinking aloud again. "Agnes seemed very interested in my relationship with you and not too happy about it."

"I understand that, because of the circumstances, she'd not be thrilled."

"That's what's strange. Why did she get me so gussied up if she didn't want me to find someone?"

"Gussied up?"

"You know what I mean. If she wanted to keep men away from me she should have left me as I was."

"Speaking for myself and all mankind, I'm glad she didn't." He grinned and gave me a quick hug.

"Well, I trust you and Maeve does as well."

"Padraig isn't so sure."

"That's because he's always treated me like a daughter since I look so much like Maeve did at my age. Believe me, he trusts you, or you wouldn't be standing here." We continued to walk and I pulled my collar tight as the damp cold began to seep in. "That ring around the moon means snow is coming soon. I hope it holds off until after the fashion show—if there is a fashion show. There, ladies and gentlemen, is still another unanswered question."

Harry pulled me close kissing me lightly on the forehead, and I found myself leaning into him. In companionable silence we listened to the muted sounds of the city; the occasional horn or siren, the trucks making late-night deliveries, the traffic still rushing by and the people, though not a lot of them, hurrying to get wherever they needed to be at that hour.

We had just turned the third corner of the block around the hotel and had barely walked twenty feet when suddenly Dillon spun around and growled.

"What the hey?" I looked around and didn't see anyone. As I bent over the dog to see what was wrong, I felt the wind shift as something brushed by my cheek and pinged off the wall.

"Kate, down." Harry grabbed me and threw me hard to the ground, shoving me under a parked car. He pushed his phone into my hand. "Call 911."

I forced my fingers to move on the buttons as several more pings hit the wall above our heads. The next one hit the fender of the car. I gave our location and the fact that someone was shooting at us to the 911 operator while at the same time dragging both dogs underneath with us. While the operator told me to stay on the line, I saw someone's feet hit the street from some vehicle. Scuffed boots strode steadily in our direction. The next series of pings went into the sidewalk a yard from where we lay, and I heard Harry cry out and begin to swear. I wasn't ready for what happened next. As the man in the boots bent, bringing his gun down to our level, a deafening bang went off in my ear. Boots man dropped to his knees. With the damn fender in the way, I couldn't see his face. He dragged himself back to whatever vehicle he'd been in as the sound of cars with sirens blaring came 'round the corner. I tilted my head and saw the shooter's van, a windowless, muddy, tan panel van, do a one-eighty and speed the wrong way down the street making a two-wheeled turn at the corner.

I let out my breath and moved my hand. Something warm and wet was under my hand. The metallic smell of blood filled my nostrils and seemed to surround me. My hands did a quick check. Both dogs were fine. Dillon whined and licked Harry's head. He didn't move. I couldn't reach past them, but I saw his head butting against Harry's and not getting a response. I pulled Dillon back so I could see past him. Harry's eyes were closed and he had his head lying on the ground; he was bleeding. I felt a scream rip from me and, with my next breath I yelled for help.

Gentle hands reached to ease my head and shoulders from under the car while working not to touch Harry. Someone was yelling for an EMT. Both dogs scrambled out after me, but Dillon turned back and pulled hard on the lead, whining as he tried to rouse Harry. I heard someone crying as rough hands dragged me away, breaking the hold I didn't realize I had on Harry. Someone screamed something about trying to stop the bleeding. After a few seconds, I realized that someone was me.

"Just let the paramedics do their job, Miss. Let us take care of him. Can you get the dog out of the way so we can bring him out?"

I called Dillon, who reluctantly crawled from under the car and came to sit by me, but didn't take his eyes off Harry. The policewoman at my elbow had to repeat her request. "Tell me your names and what happened."

I shook my head to stop the ringing that still echoed in my ear. Without taking my eyes from the spot where they were easing Harry from under the car and onto a gurney, I gave the officer the information. Harry was lying much too still. What of his face that wasn't bathed with blood was dead white. He wasn't moving and I couldn't even tell if he was breathing. I must have made a sound because Dillon shoved his head into my arms and laying it on my shoulder with plaintive *roaw, roaw* sounds. I looked down and saw blood on his coat. The cop must have understood my panic, because she checked and said it was transfer from Harry. Ajax leaned so hard against my other side that, without Dillon holding me down, I'd have been pushed over. Suddenly I heard running feet and then Sergeant Sanchez was in front of me. "Kate, what happened?"

I closed my eyes and took a ragged breath. Opening them, I told him, "Harry and I were walking the dogs when Dillon suddenly barked. I bent over to see what was wrong and felt something whiz by my head and ping off the building. Harry grabbed me, gave me his phone to call for help and we dove beneath the cars with those pinging noises sounding all around us. Then a man wearing scuffed boots and jeans—I didn't see his face—got out of the car and the pinging began bouncing off the sidewalk so close to us I could feel the concrete bounce. Suddenly a huge bang went off by my ear and the guy dropped to his knees, bleeding. Yelling, he scrambled back to his car just as the cavalry arrived. He escaped, going the wrong way and turning at the corner. Sanchez, Harry's hurt." Sanchez rushed to the side of the gurney as the paramedics rolled it into the street and I became aware that Detective Williams had moved next to me, petting Ajax's head.

Harry moved his hand to grab Sanchez. I was in motion before my brain could form the thought. I flew to his side and knelt, my eyes staring into his which seemed to radiate pain. I wanted to gather him up and hold him, but was afraid to touch him, afraid I'd hurt him.

"Harry, it's Kate. You've got to be okay. You've got be here with me. You can't leave me. Please, please be okay. I need you. I love...." The EMT pushed between us and clamped an oxygen mask over Harry's face. His eyes stayed on mine as they lowered the gurney to roll it into the ambulance. Harry's hand grabbed mine and squeezed. The ambulance doors swung open and Harry was lifted with the gurney and loaded into the back. I moved to get in with him, but Sanchez stopped me.

"They won't let you bring the dogs. Just get into our car; we'll be right behind them." He loaded me and the dogs into the back of the cruiser. Taking the wheel, he switched on the lights and siren as Detective Williams slid in on the passenger side. The ambulance sped away with Sanchez right behind.

We reached the hospital right still behind the ambulance, and I jumped out as soon as Sanchez opened the door. I focused on the gurney being wheeling in through the doors and broke into a trot. He and Williams were right beside me. Hospital personnel stopped us from following as Harry was rushed into surgery and I stood helpless twisting the dog leads and staring at the doors that kept me out.

"I realize you have other things on your mind right now, but we've got to talk," Detective Williams said. "I need to know, Kate, why someone is trying to kill you."

CHAPTER FIFTEEN

I stood watching the doors through which the gurney had disappeared. Someone bellowed, "You can't bring dogs in here."

Ignoring them, I moved forward until I rammed into a massive white chest that befit a halfback but belonged instead to stubborn nurse. "And you can't go in there either. They're taking him to surgery. You're going to have to wait and we've got rules against animals in the hospital, so you must wait somewhere else. I suggest you leave immediately."

I tore my attention from Harry to rest on the giant before me. What he was saying finally registered. I reached into my bag and pulled out a pair of laminated ID badges, as Detective Williams stepped up beside me. He grabbed them from my hand, glanced at them for a second, then pulled his own ID and badge and told the nurse, "Police dogs. They stay."

My attention had already slipped back to what was happening behind the doors. I felt him stuff the badges into my bag and steer me toward a garish orange couch with metal arms that epitomized ugly combined with discomfort. I winced as I gently lowered myself onto this bed of nails, realizing now that I hurt everywhere. My gaze shifted to my hands and the leather leads wrapped so tightly around them my fingers were white. I relaxed my grip and reached to bury my fingers in Dillon's ruff. His head leaned against my left side while Ajax leaned in on the right.

Williams had just sat next to me and reached for Ajax's ears to scratch. "I had a Shepherd when I was a kid," he mentioned, looking down. He saw blood dripping from the rips in my jeans and jumped up. "You're bleeding."

My first thought was annoyance. I liked these jeans, but I could see they were toast. I shifted the leads to my other hand, only to find that the leads were sticky with blood and my hands stung as though they'd been attacked by hornets. Williams ran for the nurse and suggested I needed to be treated as well. He reached down and eased me to my feet.

I had gotten a lot less steady. Moving forward, I was stopped when the burly nurse pushed me into a wheel chair that had appeared from nowhere and rolled me into a cubicle. A nurse, female this time but definitely the tougher of the pair, breezed into the room. Taking one look, she ordered me to change into a gown and get on the examination table.

"Somebody get rid of these hounds," she yelled.

"No." My voice also brooked no argument. "They're police dogs. They stay."

I dropped the leads, thinking they'd need to be cleaned with leather cleaner, and gave a quick hand signal. Both dogs dropped to the floor, their bodies alert for any sign of trouble. Keeping one eye on the ever-alert dogs, the nurse helped me stand and get out of my boots, jeans, jacket and shirt. With surprising gentleness, she eased my arms into the cotton gown and helped me stretch out on the examination table. A minute later, a doctor who could easily pass for one of my sixteen-year-old twin brothers' pals walked into the room. "Well, what have we gotten ourselves into tonight?"

I glared at him. "I don't know what you've gotten into, but my fiancé and I have spent the evening finding a dead body and being shot at, so I suspect your evening is better than mine. If I were you, I'd ditch the fake cheerfulness or I'll tell the dogs it's time for lunch."

He pulled up short, took in the dogs, and said, "Absolutely." After the fastest examination on record, he explained, "You seem to have surface lacerations. I'll just clean them up and bandage the worst of them. You'll be fine."

I reached to grab his hand. "I need to know how Harry is doing. He's in surgery."

"I'll get someone to check." He stepped to the curtain, mumbled something and returned. He worked quickly, and soon I was bandaged and inching my way back into my clothes. When the nurse pulled back the cubicle curtain, Sanchez and Williams were waiting. They wheeled me back into the waiting room.

We'd only been there a few minutes when the huge male nurse came in and asked, "Are you Kate?" I nodded and he reached for the back of the chair. "Your fiancé is out of surgery and asking for you. I'm afraid the dogs aren't allowed in the recovery room, so they'll have to stay here." Williams took the leads from my hand. "I'll watch them," he reassured me. "You go check on your young man." He patted my shoulder. I nodded and gave the dogs a down command.

Harry was stretched out in a bed, not moving under the white blankets when we got to the surgical recovery area. His eyes were closed and his color was still dead white. He was hooked up to monitors and IV bags. I gripped the bars at the side of the bed and listened, wanting to hear him breathe, but the only sounds were the squeaks coming from the machines. I'd been wheeled to the side of the bed and left there alone. The small room seemed to vibrate with my panic and I forced myself to slow my breathing. Pulling myself closer, I reached for his hand and saw his eyelids flutter before they closed again. I sat watching his chest rise and fall.

After a while, a doctor, looking as drained as I felt, pushed past me, grabbed the chart and, checking the monitors, made some notes. Finally he leaned against the head of the bed, looked down at me and smiled. "Your fiancé is a very lucky man. Most of the bleeding came from a cut on his head. Head wounds are notorious for being bloody. He also took a piece of shrapnel that, luckily, missed all his vital organs. The bullet in his shoulder was a through-and-through that didn't damage anything vital. He should keep the full use of that arm. From the scaring I saw, I take it that it's not his first time he's been in this situation?" He raised his eyebrows to punctuate his question.

"Former FBI." I mumbled, still looking at Harry.

"He's going to be sore as hell, but you can take him home once he's awake, provided he comes back tomorrow to get his dressings changed. He'll be a little woozy for a while because of the anesthesia, but I'll prescribe something for his pain. He'll recover. Damien will be here in a few minutes to wheel you out to the desk so you can complete the paperwork. Knowing how long the new forms take to fill out, Mr. Foyle should be ready to leave when you're done."

After he left, I felt Harry's hand grip mine hard. I grabbed the safety bars at the side of the bed and pulled myself up to stand. His eyes flickered open. He tried to say something but I couldn't hear him. I moved closer and bent over him, bringing my face nearer to hear what he wanted. A second later I found out as I felt his undamaged arm wrap around me and pull my mouth to his. The kiss didn't last long, but the power behind it left me limp and convinced me that, even suffering from a gunshot, he was incredible. When he broke the kiss, my breathing was ragged and my heart pounded hard enough to be heard.

From the doorway came a laugh followed by, "Oh, my." The nurse had arrived. I felt warmth rising up to heat and color my face but Damien, the Super Nurse, just grinned down at me. He continued to chuckle as we headed for the checkout desk.

An hour passed before we were finally finished and Sanchez and Williams took us back to the hotel. When we arrived, Sanchez got Harry to our room while Detective Williams helped me take care of the dogs' needs. They left once I returned to the room, but said they had a lot of questions for us tomorrow.

Harry hadn't said anything since we left the hospital, and I wondered if he was in shock from the injury to his head or the bullet that went through his shoulder. He sat on the edge of the bed and stared at me, his eyes tracking my every move. I gave each dog a biscuit and told them to go to their kennels. I wished Harry were as easy to settle for the night. My body was letting me in on the news that I'd been trampled by elephants. There wasn't an inch of me that didn't hurt. Leaving Harry sitting, I grabbed my PJs and headed for the bathroom. In record time I'd changed out of the bloody clothes. I didn't bother with a shower because it would just get all my dressings wet, but I did a quick clean up and pulled my night clothes gently over my bandages.

Opening the door I saw Harry hadn't stirred. His eyes again locked on mine but he didn't speak. "Harry, you need rest," I began, but got nothing, no response, no acknowledgement. He just stared. I reached out to touch his good shoulder. "Harry?" Nothing. I put my hand on his forehead. No fever. It was as if he were here, but at the same time, not here.

Sighing, I reminded myself that, after growing up with four brothers, I wasn't without experience in bedding down males who were somewhat out of it. The boys had all been known to overindulge from time to time and need help to keep the extent of their bender from our parents. I unbuttoned his shirt and eased it off. The bandages were clean and no new blood showed. I tossed the shirt on the chair and squatted down to pull off his boots. These I tossed in the closet and shut the door, not trusting Ajax since he was still a puppy at heart. Next I reached for his pants and undid his zipper. I pulled back the blankets, reached under his arms and managed to hoist him up, shoving down his pants at the same time, and then lowering him with his head on the pillow. I finished pulling off the pants, hoisted his legs onto the bed and reached to pull up the covers.

Harry's hand gripped my wrist. His eyes hadn't left my face this whole time. "Kate, please," he finally whispered.

I looked at him and, realizing what he wanted, I nodded. Turning off the light, I pulled aside the covers and gently lay next to him, trying to avoid his injuries.

A minute later, Harry pulled my back tight against his chest and locked his arm tightly around me. I lay still, listening, until I felt him relax. After a few minutes, I heard his breathing slow. His body released its tension; eventually I allowed myself to relax as well. Thousands of questions chased their tails in my head, but I had no answers. Harry's even breathing warmed the back of my neck, and I felt my body snuggle close to his as I too slowly relaxed. I placed my hand over his, the day's exhaustion taking over, and with him warm against me, I gave in to sleep.

CHAPTER SIXTEEN

I was so relaxed and warm and comfortable, opening my eyes just seemed too much like work. I felt wonderful. I snuggled further under the covers and froze. Slowly, I opened my eyes to see the familiar green ones I found so fascinating staring back only inches away. My mind snapped full awake. I was lying draped over Harry's body, my head resting on his uninjured shoulder and one of my legs straddling his waist.

"Good morning." He smiled into my eyes. Where I was and what I was doing hit my brain like a tsunami.

"Oh, my God!" I scrambled off him, fighting the covers and landing hard on my backside on the floor. "I am so sorry. I don't know what I was doing lying on you like that. I could have injured you more. I am so, so sorry. I don't know what came over me."

"Kate stop. Please stop talking." Harry leveraged himself up to sit on the edge of the bed. Reaching down, he took my hand and pulled me up to sit beside him. Guilt shot through me and I was just beginning another round of apologies when he placed his hand over my mouth.

"Kate, last night I was in a bad way. It might have been a little PTSD from being shot again, but mostly it was the shock of almost losing you. I zombied out on you. All I know was that I needed to hold you, to know I hadn't failed, that I hadn't lost you. Your climbing into my bed and letting me hold onto you and your strength got me through the night without the screaming terrors. As for waking up to find you lying across me with your sweet head cradled on my shoulder, that was just a bonus." He grinned. "You didn't do anything wrong. You showed me more kindness than I've ever known, and I thank you."

"But your shoulder, your arm... Are you all right?"

"I'm going to be fine. As bullet wounds go, this was nothing. I'll have to go get the dressing changed sometime today, but other than that, it's not a big problem. So tell me.... After the best start to a day I've had…ever, my darlin' fiancée...what's on your agenda for today?"

The shock of waking in Harry's bed had completely pushed my other problems out of my head. "Oh no! The show! I don't know if we'll be able to rehearse or do the show if it's a crime scene. Am I a horrible person for thinking of my fashion show when someone's been murdered? Though I didn't particularly like Sonja Kunar, nobody deserves to be stabbed to death. Harry, she was stabbed with a knitting needle. The police might think it's mine, though it was obviously a lace needle, probably a triple zero steel, and I never do lace and wouldn't have that kind of needle, but they might think that I do because of the knitting connection...." Harry had placed his hand over my mouth again, then lifted it away. "But the police...." I stopped when he raised his eyebrow. I really needed to learn how he did that.

"We are going to get dressed, take the dogs downstairs, and get some breakfast. Then we'll call Sergeant Sanchez and find out if the rehearsal can go ahead. Once we know that, we can schedule the rest of the day. Just let me use the bathroom then you can shower and get dressed." I nodded and stood, letting the dogs out of their crates. With a last glance over my shoulder to be sure he was okay, I went to find my clothes.

All the talk in the green room was about the murder. While I let the dogs finish up, Alice noticed Harry's arm was in a sling and stopped by to ask what had happened.

Harry glanced at me and answered, "Mugging last night. They took off after they realized what they'd done. The sling's just a precaution."

We made a quick escape to the elevator. "Mugging?" I said, eyeing his sling.

"Would you have preferred that I explain how you were shot at because some master criminal thinks you're your cousin?"

"Good point. Oh, how much do we tell Sanchez? He's already told me he wants to know why this guy was trying to kill me. We've been assuming the connection with Agnes is the reason, but we don't know that and we have no proof. We should probably talk this over with Agnes first."

When we reached the room, I unfastened the leads and both dogs dashed into their crates and to sit waiting for their chow. Meals done, I latched the crates, grabbed my schedules and attached the Do Not Disturb sign to the doorknob.

As we headed for the elevator, I fished out my phone to call Agnes. It went right to voicemail so I called Maeve. Niall answered. I asked him to check to see if Agnes was still there while I grabbed the menu and gave it a quick scan.

"Order me blueberry pancakes, sausage, a small orange juice and a large pot of tea, please. Oh, Niall, is she there? Well, then I'm going to have to talk to Maeve. Could you have her call me as soon as possible? You're a darling. Thank Sally for that delicious lunch yesterday. I'll see you again before the weekend's over and we'll find some time to chat."

Harry clicked off his phone. "Sanchez wants us up in the ballroom at nine, so eat up." We finished quickly. Afterward I realized I had been starving and had polished off everything—including my second cup of tea.

"I have no idea why I was so hungry."

"Well," Harry leaned over to whisper to me, "I've been told that when people sleep together, their appetites...." I felt my face burn and scrambled to my feet.

Harry grabbed my hand. "Let's go."

As we headed into the lobby, it was a struggle to get through the crowd. Arrivals had moved into overdrive. We grabbed the dogs from our room and hurried to the green room before the day got too involved. I noticed that even there, the flow of handlers, groomers, and gossip in and out seemed to be escalating. However, the fact that there had been a murder of one of their own less than twelve hours ago didn't change the fact that today was business as usual. *How would people have reacted if I'd been killed last night?*

Harry must have read my mind because he wrapped his good arm around me and kissed the top of my head. "Kate, I think they'd be acting differently if they had known her. But she wasn't part of their crowd and in the short period of time she was among these people, she did nothing to make friends." He was right. I might not have cared so much if I weren't so involved.

Sanchez was waiting to let us into the ballroom and had us sit at the table where we'd given our statements last night. "How are you two doing?"

"We're fine, though it would be nice to go a whole day without one of us getting hurt," Harry told him settling more comfortably in his seat. I looked at the envelope in front of Sanchez as he got down to business.

"First," he began as he reached into the manila envelope and pulled out a plastic bag, "what can you tell me about this?"

I felt Harry's hand on mine and I took a breath. Then I looked at the needle in the bag, trying to ignore the blood on it. "It looks like a lace knitting needle, steel, about twelve inches long, probably size triple zero. They usually come in sets of four or five. They're available in some yarn shops but more commonly at online knitting shops and even the big-box chains."

"Is it yours?"

"No, I don't use that kind of needle." Sanchez waited without talking for me to continue, which I figured must have gotten a lot of guilty parties to reveal information over the years. I knew I had to explain. "The kind of knitting with which I'm involved is called intarsia or picture knitting." I pointed to my sweater; it depicted a Samoyed standing in the snow on a hill looking down at a sled team. "The patterns I design are written for straight needles in sizes between US 4 to 8. I design for worsted weight yarn. Now that doesn't mean someone couldn't use another weight of yarn and reproduce the chart, but they'd have to make sure the gauge was proportional and wouldn't cause distortion to the design." I stopped to see if he was still with me. "When I create the samples for the show, since so many have to be made quickly and to the correct gauge, I use a mid-gauge knit weaving machine, a scaled-down version of those machines that produce commercial sweaters. I'll be using this smaller machine to produce the sweaters in my ready-to-wear line. My machines are set to match the gauge of my hand-knit patterns so they produce a match for the designs I sell to knitters. Before you ask, I don't have the patience to do lace knitting and I don't own lace knitting needles. I run a design business with a manager and four sample knitters who work part time, leaving me to handle most of the administrative and design duties. I also run a breeding and boarding kennel with a full-time training program for dogs in conformation, obedience, agility, tracking, search and rescue and, recently, police-dog work. I don't have time to sit and knit scarves and doilies on tiny needles for fun."

"What about in your booth at the show?"

I reached into my briefcase and pulled out my master notebook for the booth. "As you can see, the stock I sell, other than patterns, includes yarn in the gauge to work my designs and needles in the sizes I mentioned. If you want to check, there's a list of what we sell inside carton number one, which is already in place, waiting to be unpacked in the booth. I carry needles in bamboo, carbon fiber, metal and wood in the sizes I indicated, both in the straight, single pointed style, which come in sets of two, and the circular style which has a point on either end and is sold singly. The people managing my booth, Jennifer Santos and Heather Miller, will be happy to show you anything. They work at The Tail of the Dog which is owned by Jennifer's mother, Cathy Santos. I know nothing whatsoever about how or why that needle came to be used to kill Sonja Kunar." I looked down to see my hands had been gripping Harry's tightly enough to turn them white. I let go and looked at him to apologize.

"Okay, we'll check into it and we'll want to talk to you again. But now you are going to tell me what the hell was going on last night."

Harry leaned forward. "After leaving the party, Kate and I decided to get some air. We changed clothes and took the dogs for a walk. We were circling the block when Dillon spun around and barked, making me aware of a van coming up beside us with its door sliding open. It was an unmarked panel van without side windows. I didn't get the plate number. Kate bent to see what was bothering Dillon and I heard a bullet whiz by just missing her head. We dove beneath the cars, flat on the ground, calling 911. Bullets sprayed the area, fired from an automatic with a silencer. When the guy jumped out of the car to get a better angle on us, he got off a couple of shots, one of which hit me before I shot him in the knee. He dragged himself back to the vehicle when he heard your troops coming. The van did a one-eighty, sped the wrong way down the street and ran the light turning onto Sixth Avenue."

"Do you have any idea why a shooter would target you two taking a quiet walk?"

"They didn't stick around long enough for me to ask. I just figured it was New York street crime."

"Thugs rarely use high-priced automatics with silencers to go after random victims. There's something you two aren't saying and I hope you know what you're doing. I don't want to find one of you dead on my next call." Harry and Sanchez stared at each other for a moment.

Harry pointed out as he stared across the table, "We don't know why this is happening, but that doesn't mean we aren't trying to find out. I promise to contact you as soon as we have any real information to share."

"I guess that'll have to do. But two attempts in twenty-four hours tells me that whoever's doing this is serious. Watch your backs." Sanchez tucked the murder weapon back into the envelope and sighed.

"Sergeant," I turned my head as noise came from the other side of the door. "I can hear my people gathering outside the door. Do we have permission to have our rehearsal and fashion show, or does the crime scene have to be preserved?"

"Our people finished with this area last night. You can go ahead with your show. However, an officer will be stationed inside the door to keep an eye on things. Oh, and by the way, I've got a full day ahead of me, so if you two could stay out of trouble, I'd appreciate it."

CHAPTER SEVENTEEN

As though someone had just pulled the cork out of a bottle, people, dogs, electricians and others in Ulysses' crew all poured in, anxious to get started. However, once inside, they had to be checked off by the cop, who had a copy of my master personnel list. Everyone surrounded me asking questions at once.

The cop called me over when Bill arrived surrounded by the three guards who were now familiar to me. I gave the okay for them to stay to guard the dog and pushed my way toward the runway, people stopping me practically every two with questions.

An ear-piercing whistle brought everything to a stop. Harry reached into the crowd, grabbed me around the waist with his good arm and swung me up onto the runway Winking he waved for me to begin.

"Thanks, everyone, for coming. Sorry you had to wait, but on the plus side, we've been cleared to go ahead with the show. Ulysses' people will have everything ready for a rehearsal in"— I looked over in his direction, and he flashed his fingers, "twenty minutes. Great. That's the perfect timing for our walk through. Ah, Denise, there you are." I reached down to help Denise up onto the runway. "Everyone, this is Denise Simpson, one of my former professors and a good friend, who also happens to be *the best* fashion-show narrator in the business. Her voice will make every eye focus on you, so if she makes a suggestion, take it as cast in stone. She will go over pronunciations with you to be sure your name is perfect. Park all your things over behind that curtained area, where there are chairs. That will be your dressing area tonight. Ahh, and I see that the coffee, tea and goodies have now arrived."

I hopped down from the runway, instantly regretting the move as pain from last night's injuries reminded me of what had happened. I turned to hug Denise who joined me.

"Kate, look at you, all grown up and having your own show. I always knew you'd be a success; I just didn't know exactly how your niche would work out. However, listening to your fans in the hallway, I would say you were right on the money when you told me you knew what dog lovers want."

"That's high praise indeed, coming from you, Denise. Here's the narration book. The only change," I grabbed a pen from my bag, "is to change Jimmy's name and replace it with Harry Foyle and Ajax. Oh, Denise, this is Harry."

"How do you do, Ms Simpson," Harry said, shaking her hand. "It's good to meet so many people in Kate's life since we've become engaged."

I was startled when Denise hugged me. "I'm so happy for you, Kate! She's a wonderful woman, Mr. Foyle, as well as a talented designer, so I hope you know what a gem you've gotten, sir."

Harry moved to stand behind me, laying his good hand on my shoulder. "Believe me, I know how exactly how wonderful she is."

I squirmed under all this praise. "Um, let's get to work. Okay, everyone, finish up your snack and as you hear your name called, get into line. This will be your order for the show, so be sure you know who's in front of you and who's behind. If Kathy is trying to lead her Newf, Tenney off the runway, Barbara, don't go rushing out with Toto or we may have a Cairn pancake. It will be Denise's job to keep everything flowing smoothly, so stay focused and riveted on what she says. Ulysses' people will take care of all the special effects so the pictures match the live action. The rehearsals will help you to know where you should be every step of the way as your position must match the commentary. The reason for the walk through is to let you get the motor memory of where you are at each step. The lighting effects will be disconcerting. I want you confident first so nobody is disoriented and falling off the runway."

I paused for a moment for breath then continued. "You should have your dog sit in heel position to relax him when you reach the spot on the runway behind the curtain. Scratch his ears and do your pre-ring focusing. If you do this before stepping out onto the runway, you'll send your dog a message to focus totally on your commands and not be thrown off by all the sights and sounds around him. If you have a focus word, use it as you make that first step out onto the runway. I can't stress enough that there will be an incredible number of distractions for the dogs. It will be ten times harder than any show competition. So keeping their focus on you is vital. And if, for some reason, you get off your pacing or something causes you to get behind, don't worry about it. You're working with professionals. They'll spot the bobble and make it look as though it was planned as part of the show. So just keep going. Okay Denise?"

Denise went over what she would be doing and the signals she'd use to get them up the runway and back smoothly. "Those of you wearing capes, skirts or scarves, be sure the audience can see them to full advantage. That means that you will do a slower turn when you get to the end of the runway than the other models, holding the garment out to give full view to the design. I'll count out the turn for you with the first run through. If I say your name or that of your dog wrong, tell me and I'll correct it. Also, as you return up the runway, prior to exiting, watch for a signal from me to see if you need to add another 360 turn before exiting. I will make sure that you're right on beat. I see that Ulysses is ready for the first walk through. Kate, why don't you stand right behind the entrance curtain since you're more familiar with entrance cues? Oh, and lastly, when you are going up and down the steps, use the railings whether you feel you need them or not. There will be flashing strobe lights and in some cases, pitch darkness. We don't want anyone injured."

"Ready, Denise?" came the call from the back of the room.

I lined up everyone in order, dogs on the left. Climbing the steps, I took my place at the edge of the curtain that blocked the entrance from the view of the audience.

Denise pressed the buzzer that cued Ulysses and, with a voice like silk, began to create a fantastic world populated with dogs and those who loved them. She spoke lovingly about each breed and pointed out what each did that made it unique. She described the pictures knitted into the sweaters, shawls, and dresses as each pair went down the runway. Ulysses was in the front, telling them how to walk, showing them when and where to turn. I was in the back, getting each model ready to hit his mark. By a piece of good fortune, it only took two run-throughs before they were ready for the full dress rehearsal with all the bells and whistles.

I realized I was holding my breath when the room grew suddenly dark. Underneath the melody, a continuous thumping beat provided a pace for each of the models. Denise's voice came out of the darkness as she presented her introduction, and then the music changed. A ten-foot-high projection of Richard, laughing as he held Spike high above his head, the dog staring down at the Chihuahua design on his sweater, flashed across the backdrop curtain. Simultaneously Richard and Spike stepped forward onto the runway. The beat helped control Richard control his steps and turns as he moved forward and back his projection vanished as he exited down the stairs, and a projection of Alice holding the training wing as Lucky pointed filled the entrance. As each pair finished the trip down the runway and back in front of their projected portrait, a ten-foot, hard copy banner of the projection was unrolled and spotlighted on a side wall of the ballroom.

One after another, they went. Susan and Angus were heeling in style when, as they turned, the Corgi began barking and trying to herd the sheep that had been suddenly projected as a hologram before him on the runway. Someone had found a small red wooden wagon for Hugo to pull as Cora and the Bernese displayed his breed's historical occupation. The aloof disdain Ralph and his Borzoi, Wolfgang, projected led to cheers as he paused to give a royal wave. Chance the Poodle was high stepping beside Lucy the length of the runway. As she bowed low to spread out the cape at the turn, he leapt over her back and whirled in circles beside her down the far side of the runway on their return. I was relieved that Lucy didn't seem too rattled by last night's horror.

The flow continued when Byron, who had added a Churchill-like cigar to his performance, worked the runway quietly chatting with Winston, his Bulldog, and waving his arms to lend animation to the discussion. Maria showing her Cavalier, Bitsy, took advantage of the full skirt as they whirled and danced a parody of the jitterbug all their way down and back. Bringing a change of pace, Tenney, the Newfoundland, pulled a large rescue buoy while Kathy, showing off her sweater depicting a rescue, carried the ropes and blankets. Barbara went with tradition, it seemed, just heeling with her Cairn 'til they got to the end of the runway where she lifted the sides of her cape to show the Cairn design worked into it then turned to show herself beneath, dressed as Dorothy in the *Wizard of Oz* complete with ruby slippers. One after another they performed, and the music slowly built, as Mary and her Sheltie, Wizard, finished.

Bill was second to last and stepped forward to music that now featured an overtone of the Middle East flowing through the melody.

Harry and Ajax came last. Harry handed me his sling as they got ready. I held my breath as they glided to the end of the runway in perfect step. Ajax stacked in a perfect show position. Harry stepped forward and did his turn, showing the sweater with the design that matched the dog. Then as Harry passed him, Ajax slid into heel position man and dog moving in perfect symmetry. Harry looked at me and winked as he turned and headed down the steps. I let out my breath. Suddenly the music changed and became frenetic. The strobe lights blazed, lighting the side banners like Fourth of July fireworks. The noise and flashing lights built, whirling, crashing then suddenly…*silence.* The room went black.

Like everyone, I was holding my breath. One after another, the vague shapes of people and dogs moved past me into place. Out of the silence came a fanfare and the lights surrounding the runway blazed, showing the entire line of owners and dogs, who stepped forward and back to bow one at a time. Then all joined hands and bowed together in perfect timing to the final note.

A cheer filled the room. I didn't realize I was crying until Dillon began whining beside me. I squatted down and gave him a hug, then strode forward to tell everyone how great they were. Ulysses agreed they had been perfect. I explained they should relax and plan to be back at seven tonight. I answered a few questions for Ulysses, then hugged Andy and thanked him, unable to express how blown away I was by what he had created with the projections. Denise had a few questions and I thanked and hugged her, telling her I would see her later.

Finally turning to Harry, I said, "If I don't get

out of here immediately, I'm going to start bawling like a baby."

"We can't have that, so let's get moving," he said heading for the elevator. "I thought you were happy about the rehearsal?"

"I am. It's a girl thing; these are tears of joy."

CHAPTER EIGHTEEN

We headed down to take care of the dogs' needs and for Harry to change out of the Shepherd sweater. I checked my watch. "It's almost noon. I have two tapings this afternoon. Why don't I see if they can do them now since they don't seem to be taping anyone at the moment? You can grab us some lunch. The dogs can stay with me. Then we can take a few minutes to talk before we have to head to the hospital to get your dressings changed."

"Sounds like a plan," Harry said as I dashed over to talk to the director. At my thumbs-up signal, he took off for the deli up the street while I ended up doing three interviews, two spots to run during this afternoon and tonight and one to be run as a voiceover for clips of the fashion show they had decided to put into the Monday-night broadcast of the dog show as color. I thanked them profusely and was just getting up to leave when Harry arrived with bags of food.

"I don't know about you, but I'm starving," he opened the first bag and sniffed. I got you a tuna and cheese sub toasted, and me a meatball grinder."

We quickly headed up to the room. Harry pulled the food from the bags, handing me a bottle of water and opening a can of root beer for himself. The dogs settled down with their treats as we began polishing off our picnic.

"Okay, which do we cover first; the problem or what we know?' I said. "I'm afraid it's all jumbled together in my brain at the moment."

"This is where math can be your friend," he instructed with a grin. "Let's first list what facts we know. Later tonight, I can work on giving items on the list values and weights in helping to determine the solution."

Now it was my turn to grin. "You sound so sexy when you talk math."

He gazed at me for a moment, and then with a shake of his head went on. "Right. The element that seems to be consistent through this whole thing is Zanifra. First the information Agnes was passing to the State Department concerned Zanifra. Also, Bill is handling the prince's dog because some political something is keeping his daughter and granddaughter from leaving Zanifra. We need more information from Bill. Zanifra and Naro are scheduled to begin peace talks at the United Nations the middle of next week. Maybe Sadie can dig up more information on what's at stake in that peace treaty. Why is our State Department so interested in what's happening between a small principality and an equally small democratic republic? So far as I know neither sits in control of any of the world's natural resources."

I began ticking off items on my fingers. "Then, getting into stickier subjects, why was Sonja Kunar, a supposed dog groomer who was, in reality a body guard for a dog, murdered? And why was she murdered on the runway of my fashion show? Does the killer have a problem with me? We're assuming the killer knows Agnes disguised herself as me and has a problem with Agnes. But then there were the attempts on my life. I want to know how the killer knew I'd be leaving that Chinese restaurant just when I did, since I didn't know I'd be eating there until twenty minutes before I arrived. And the big one.... How did the killer know we'd be taking a walk with the dogs after the party? Is there any way the killer could be tracking me—or my phone?"

I stopped talking and dug into the carrot cake Harry had brought me. Murder never trumps carrot cake. I looked up to see him staring at me, his pen not writing.

"What?"

"I think you're in the wrong line of work. If you ever need a job…."

"I just tend to be curious about things I don't understand. Those are our questions. Do we have any answers or possibilities?"

"I'm afraid the answers will have to wait or I'll be late for my appointment to have my dressings changed, and we'll end up sitting in the ER all afternoon."

Both Harry and I checked the street as we crossed to the taxi stand and hailed a cab. We also made sure we weren't drawing attention when we arrived at the hospital. We didn't see anything. However, my nerves kept me on edge. It was a classic case of *if you are a hammer, everything looks like a nail.* I was sure a man with a gun was lurking around every corner.

Harry kept me close as we headed inside. Because of the dogs, we were stopped again at the entrance, but the big burly nurse, Damien, who'd been on last night, waved us through. He told me I'd have to stay in the waiting room with the dogs, though, while Harry got his dressings changed. He steered me toward a room painted hospital green with clashing orange plastic chairs. It was a relief to see the room's other inhabitants were female and seemingly oblivious. I led the dogs to the farthest side of the room, where no one else was sitting, and sank into one of the chairs. In barely a minute, I concluded that whoever had designed the chairs did it purposely to drum up business for the hospital. They were making me feel every bruise and scrape from last night. I slid my parka off my shoulders and down onto the seat to give some padding to my bruised tush. With a hand on each dog's head, I settled in to wait.

The hammer-and-nail analogy flashed in my head when a man entered the room. He was, I guess, about Harry's age, though with his heavy jacket, his baseball cap pulled down blocking his face and his slouch, it was hard to tell. His eyes searched then zeroed in on me and he headed my way. I counted twenty empty chairs, which he ignored in his stroll across the room. When he sat next to me, he graduated from ten-penny nail to massive railroad spike. The atmosphere in the room shifted. Thinking to flee rather than fight, I was about to move when something hard was shoved into my side. Glancing down, all I could see was his hand in his pocket.

Under my hands, the dogs had gone from relaxed to attack alert in a nanosecond as they read my fear.

Spike Man leaned in, forcing me to reel back from the smell of cigarette smoke, and spoke in a whisper. "You're gonna stand up and walk out of here without them pooches. If you try to call for help, you're dead."

I turned toward him, but he hissed, "Keep your eyes front. Just stand and walk."

"Are you kidding me?" I asked in a voice that wasn't at all quiet. The panic that had been building as he walked toward me instantly gave way to temper and exasperation. "You have *got* to be nuts! First someone tries to push me into traffic, next someone commits murder on the site of my show, and then they shoot at me and wound my fiancé. Now you have the gall to walk into a public hospital, point a gun at me, and think I'm going to be stupid enough to walk out of here with you? You've got to be crazy." My voice had been rising as I delivered my diatribe, and now everyone was watching, and the dogs were standing, hackles up, staring at Spike Man. I glanced at them, ready to give the attack command.

"Enough talking, just shut your yap, get up and walk. Leave those ugly mutts behind."

Ugly mutts? That did it. There was no way I was going anywhere with this homicidal maniac who obviously knew nothing about dogs. My temper took over.

"No," I shouted loudly, not moving.

"I said get up and walk," he growled, shoving what did feel like the muzzle of a gun against me, "unless you want to be dead."

Who did this guy think he was? James Cagney? My eyes scanned the room then looked down at the dogs. They were ready. Only their training held them in check.

"You can forget getting me to go anywhere with you," I said deliberately, still looking straight ahead. "However," I added as my voice took on the commanding force that for years had gotten people and dogs to follow my directions, "I suggest *you* might want to walk, without any sudden movements, out that door. You see, if you shoot me, I might end up dead, but I guarantee so will you. If you look about, you'll see a lady across the way in a brown cable -knit sweater. You'll see that she's taken notice of you because her knitting needles are no longer in her hands, and I'd say her finger is now on the trigger of whatever weapon is in her knitting bag. The guard at the desk has stopped flirting with the cute blonde nurse and has flipped off the strap holding his gun in its holster. His hand is resting on his weapon. My friend Damien to his right is a nurse, but at three-hundred fifty pounds of solid muscle, I think he could take a couple of bullets and still bring you down. And then there are these pooches. If you were to check their ID cards, you would find that these pooches are trained police dogs. Of the two, the cute white, fluffy one that's smiling and watching your eyes is the more dangerous. You'll also notice they're in full alert with their hackles up. 'Hackles up' is dog speak for locked and loaded. They are on hold, focused, waiting for any sign, no matter how tiny, to tear you apart. Now I have no intention of moving from this spot. If you shoot me, I'll have a hole in me and may die, though I should point out we *are* in a hospital, so the chances are better than even that I might also live. However, if you shoot me, the pooches will definitely take that as a signal and the coroner will require a search to find your body parts, which will be scattered around this room. The dogs are faster than you, and there are two of them. Your choice, but if I were you I'd leave. Now!"

When Harry entered the waiting room a minute later, he found me, flanked by the dogs and bent over, throwing up into a wastebasket held by an old lady in a brown sweater while Nurse Damien placed a cold pack on the back of my neck. Damien looked at Harry and said, “This lady has guts. No brains, but guts.”

CHAPTER NINETEEN

Sergeant Sanchez responded to Harry's call and managed to get videos that covered the waiting room from two different angles with sound. The hospital had recently upgraded their surveillance in an effort to keep their insurance company from jacking up their rates. Sanchez and Harry watched the videos while the doctor who had just changed Harry's dressings checked me out. His comments were almost as annoying as they were accurate. I just sat there trying to figure out what had possessed me to do verbal battle with a killer. I'd definitely lost my mind. I suspected my family would call it a toss-up between my Irish temper and my stubbornness.

"Call me Manny," was the way Emmanuel Sanchez began our discussion of what happened. I wasn't sure if he wanted to be friendly because we've seen so much of him lately or if he was just humoring the crazy lady. They'd gotten good facial recognition off the video and this time the guy was in the system. Manny put an APB out on him but figured his boss would just use someone else next time. I wanted to argue with the sergeant's guarantee there would be a next time, but I couldn't. We went over the whole thing twice, even though it was there in glorious black and white, and it was two-thirty by the time we were finished. He sent us back to the hotel in a cruiser.

As soon as we got to the room, I got out the notebook so Harry could add the details of today's misadventure to our collection.

Harry sat looking at me for a few minutes without saying anything which was beginning to annoy me. I was about to tell him to get with the program when my brain froze. I felt Harry move me to the far bed and sit me down. He took off my shoes and made me lie down. I vaguely knew he was there but I couldn't focus on him or on anything. I began to shake, so I curled up in a ball with my knees up to my chin. I heard the closet door shut and felt the bed dip as he lay down beside me, covering us both with another blanket. When his hand touched my side, I stiffened. I hated my body tensing up but I couldn't help it. He was trying to be nice and my body lay rigid against him. I felt his large hand gently stroke up and down my arm. He didn't talk, his hand moving up and down, up and down.

I felt my muscles ease, one at a time, and I found that letting go meant letting go. Sobs poured from me. Harry tightened his grip. I heard him on the phone asking Sadie whether she'd found anything. He was quiet for a moment, listening to her response. Anguish filled me as if all the grief of my life had come here to this spot right now. It swam through my head. The deaths of Dad and Gramps of, friendships past, of beloved dogs, fears of not being good enough.... It went on and on, and there was no way I could stop it. Then, as if I'd been drained of every tear and left empty, the misery, heartbreak, sorrow, despair, mourning—all of it—faded to a whimper. The world of warm hands stroking my back faded. I slept.

Sometime later, I felt him slip away. The loss, sharp for a minute, faded as I slid back into sleep. I don't know how long I'd slept when I heard Harry on his phone. "Sadie, what else have you found?" He was quiet for a few moments. "Right. This is escalating and there may be a possible link within the Bureau. I need it yesterday. You've got it. Thanks, Luv."

Harry answered a knock and let Sanchez in. I didn't have the energy to open my eyes, but could hear the sergeant speaking softly, filling Harry in on the guy with the gun. They were checking on a few leads they had on his known associates. Harry, in turn, filled him in on what he'd gotten from Sadie and some other sources he wouldn't name. They went over security for tonight. Sanchez said his boss had that covered. They especially didn't want trouble since it seemed the commissioner's wife was going to be taking donations for the charity. "She thinks your girlfriend is wonderful and has a bunch of her sweaters," he said.

After Sanchez left, I heard Harry walk over to stand by me, but I didn't want to move. A minute later, I heard the sound of Dillon's front paws on top of his crate, and I knew exactly what he was after. I relaxed and drifted off again. When I finally woke, I rolled over and smiled. Dillon was almost purring and next to Harry was a large pile of hair.

"You realize since you've done that once, he'll expect it all the time. Dillon loves to be groomed," I said stretching and standing up.

"I think my arm is going to fall off. How do you do this all the time? My muscles are screaming."

"I've got fourteen of these guys at home counting all the old retired dogs, and the puppies. Everyone gets brushed out at least every other day, so I've built up the muscles. Remember, I've been doing this since I was a little kid. Gramps used to say I was grooming dogs before I could walk." I stood looking at Harry for a minute. "Thanks for…" I nodded toward the bed.

He grinned, "Believe me, it was my pleasure."

I felt a blush heat my face but this time I smiled.

Once I'd washed the remaining sleep from my face, changed my clothes and run a comb through my hair, we took care of the dogs then headed down for an early supper. I spotted several of my models who had the same idea and waved as Harry and I found a quiet table in the back. We'd been holding hands when we came in. My friends were kind enough to give us some privacy.

Harry reached across the table after we'd placed our order. "What you did at the hospital today still terrifies me. I can't believe you just talked to that killer and convinced him to leave quietly."

"I've never understood why, in books and movies, the stupid girl always thinks she'd be better off going with the killer. If he wants to kill you, he'll kill you. The question was his place or mine. Of course, his choice was made easier after I explained what was behind door number two," I added with a shrug. "As Sanchez said, speak softly and carry a big dog or in this case, two."

"You are a remarkable woman, Kate Killoy. You're beautiful, smart and have the guts of a Marine."

"I'm not sure many people would say I was smart today. I was just lucky it worked." A chill of fear shook me for a minute.

Harry was about to continue when our food arrived. After losing my breakfast into a wastebasket and not having eaten lunch, I dug in with enthusiasm, even polishing off a piece of chocolate pie for dessert along with two cups of tea.

While we ate, Harry told me what Sadie had found. "There were rumors some group was trying to stop the peace agreement. The word that Sadie heard is that if the talks between Zanifra and Naro work, the agreement would change things and certain deals with multinational corporations would be rendered null and void. Billions of dollars are at stake, Kate. And with those numbers, the lives of a few Americans are a small price to pay. Sadie doesn't have the plan or the schedule of what's going down, but she figures that it has to be during some televised event. The only event scheduled to be shown both here and in Zanifra is the dog show because of Ashraf, so we've got the time, but we don't have the plan."

"Did either Agnes or Maeve call when I was out of it?"

"No. Tomorrow I think we should visit the family again."

"You just want another of Sally's meals."

"Guilty as charged. But we've got to find out what the plan is. And only Agnes knows."

"I still can't understand why Agnes doesn't call or text. She didn't even call to wish me good luck." The hurt I felt must have been obvious. A big hand enfolded mine and Harry's thumb began its familiar stroking of my palm. Feelings of pleasure flowed from that palm and caused my breath to catch. I looked up, losing myself in his eyes. I had to admit I liked being Harry Foyle's fiancée. We stood to go back upstairs and Harry kept hold of my hand. I found myself leaning into him.

It was rather a shock when we walked out of the restaurant to find Agent Donner waiting for us along with another agent I recognized but couldn't quite name.

"Foyle, Miss Forester, you need to come with us. The director wants to talk to you."

"Donner, don't be an ass. You know perfectly well this isn't Agnes Forester. Bill, what's going on?"

"Well, Donner says he has proof that this lady is Miss Forester; so until we see the two of them together, we'll have to assume you're wrong, Harry," the man he called Bill answered.

I turned to Harry and asked, "Who is this man?"

"Kate, this is Bill Hendrix, the agent I told you I was visiting in the city. Bill, I'd like you to meet my fiancée, Kate Killoy."

Surprise and dismay played quickly across the man's face but were just as quickly replaced by a fake smile. "When did you get engaged? You didn't say anything when we were at lunch."

"We've been seeing each other for a while, and I proposed on Thursday evening," he explained then smiled at me. "And, much to my delight, she said yes."

"Foyle, you must be in on this charade as well." Donner seemed determined to chew this bone until all flavor was gone.

I finally had had enough. I had a fashion show to run and didn't have time for this. "Agent Donner. You insist that I am my cousin, based on no proof. And you, Agent Hendrix, say you need to see us together. Well, I claim that you have seen us together and are for some reason not informing Agent Donner of that fact. You saw us together at Reilly's restaurant last November. You were sitting at a table nearby and spent most of the meal staring at both Agnes and me. Harry can testify to that fact because he was there with you. In fact, it was right after that evening that he got someone to introduce us and we began seeing each other. So if you agents want to continue wasting tax dollars, do it somewhere else. As for your claim that the AIC wants to meet with us, I doubt it. Carter Billings will be accompanying his wife to my fashion show this evening; she's vice chair of the charity that sponsors the event. Now you may have time to waste, but we don't. Good evening, gentlemen." Squeezing Harry's hand, I pushed past them and headed for an open elevator. We entered and the door closed on the angry faces of the two agents.

The whole ride up Harry just stared at me. At the door to our room, he stopped, turned me around, and said, "You are an exceptional woman." I looked up to say something, only to find his mouth on mine with a kiss that was not in the least tentative. Somehow my arms found their way around his neck and when we finally pulled apart, I had to hold on just to stay standing. Harry smiled and my heart did a flip that brought a grin to my face.

Once in the room, I grabbed my slacks, silk blouse, sweater and a pair of pretty leather two-inch high heeled boots and disappeared into the bathroom. Again wearing his Shepherd sweater, Harry looked up when I emerged. "Ten minutes flat, dressed and ready to go. You continue to prove you are a very rare member of your species, my sweet Kate, in every way."

"My life is too busy for silly primping. We should get upstairs and double check that there aren't any problems." I knew I needed time to process what had happened outside the door. Suddenly a thought popped into my head, and, stopping I burst out laughing. "I just realized that Sal was right. After my day, both bad and...very good, a mere fashion show for the movers and shakers of New York, is going to be a piece o'cake."

Grinning, Harry reached out and kissed me fast. "Let's go."

I felt a surge of joy pulse through me. I threw my purse over my shoulder, and Harry helped me do the same with my briefcase. As I took the dogs, and we headed out, I reached over and grabbed his good hand. On the way to the elevator, I asked, "How is it the FBI always knows were I am, every minute of the day?"

Harry didn't answer, just looked at me curiously and frowned.

CHAPTER TWENTY

The first person we spotted as we stepped from the elevator was Detective Williams.

"Kate, Harry, how are you doing? I heard you had an interesting time around noon at the hospital. In light of the fact people seem to be interested in killing you, Kate, and since we had a dead body turn up on the runway of your show, I'd like a few minutes of your time tomorrow to discuss what happened to Miss Kunar."

"I'm not sure how much I can help, but if you want to talk, I'll be happy to meet with you tomorrow. However, right now I have a fashion show to run, so please excuse me."

I walked into the room, giving Harry a quick eye roll. It was fairly quiet inside. Ulysses wandered over, shook Harry's hand, and gave me a quick hug. His people had finished setting out the chairs in neat rows, with sections of the front row designated as reserved seating. A flash went off and I glanced up to see Andy's grinning face behind the lens. He waved then turned to stake out the best spot for getting shots, both of the show and the audience.

Denise came through the door, which I noticed was being monitored by two policemen, and headed for the podium to stash her bag. She took Ulysses' arm on the way to walk with her, waving papers with her other hand. I glanced at my watch and walked to the area behind a curtain where chairs were set up for the models.

Harry took a chair and placed it to the right of the runway entrance out of the way, but close to me. The sound of voices filled the room. I stepped forward as the models pushed the curtain aside and surged into the small space. En masse, they pushed closer to get my attention. Luckily, knowing the models would need reassurance, Agnes had arranged for her agency's crew of makeup artists to be there. Before long, they had everyone in chairs, holding mirrors while they worked their magic. Grinning at Harry as he submitted to some primping, I moved around the room, ensuring the models had everything they needed from safety pins to aspirin.

I heard raised voices at the door and looked out to see Bill along with Huey, Dewey, and Louie, having an argument at the entrance. The new cop on duty had stopped the group because only Bill's name was on the list.

I hurried over and let them know the trio would be providing protection to the prince's dog, and should be allowed in. I stopped Bill and made him introduce me to each of the men. They obviously bristled at the thought of a woman in charge, but shook my hand when offered. I let them know how relieved I was they were there to provide protection to Ashraf and Bill so our police could focus their attention elsewhere. I gave them my condolences on the death of Sonja Kunar. This seemed to make peace, and as we moved toward the curtain, Bill patted my shoulder. We ducked out of sight as I noticed the first of the attendees beginning to arrive.

The makeup artists had finished working their magic—combining powder and lip color with a hearty dash of confidence building. The models, now relaxed and ready, sat and chatted quietly.

About ten minutes later, Ulysses stepped into the midst of the group and everyone went silent. He waved those standing to their seats and, in a quiet voice reviewed exactly what the models could expect on the runway. He told them not to be nervous about the crowd.

Cora laughed, "We deal with crowds all the time and so do the dogs. At least tonight isn't a competition."

Everyone was smiling, even Ulysses, which was a sight I had rarely seen before any show. He leaned over and whispered to me, "I had my doubts about these dog people, but I'll tell you Kate, they're some of the most professional models I've ever worked with." I smiled and hugged him.

After that he went back to his setup in the rear of the room. Denise and I reviewed pacing, calling up two of the models to go over details of some minor adjustments. I demonstrated what I wanted then, patting the dogs and nodding to Denise, went to sit on the steps and snuggle my dog. Dillon had been napping on the edge of the runway, not the least bit impressed with all the hoopla. Bill wandered over and sat, relaxed, in the chair Harry had just vacated to go chat with Manny Sanchez.

"Kate," Bill said in a hushed voice, "I can't thank you and Agnes enough. You have given me back my family, my life."

"Have you heard something?"

"My daughter called. They are, at this hour, changing planes in Germany and will be arriving at Kennedy tomorrow morning. The State Department was able to get them out, thanks to the information you got to them."

"Well, I was just a small part of it last November."

"Yes, but that was the final piece of information they needed to work a deal and gain their freedom. Without you and your long braid, I would have been observed passing the information. Nobody suspects a child."

I chuckled. "I've grown up a bit since then."

"Beautifully, I might add. Your Harry is a lucky fellow. If I can ever do anything for you, just ask."

Denise tapped me on the shoulder to tell me it was time. Bill kissed my cheek and went back to his guards and Ashraf. Harry and Ajax returned to their spot and everyone sat up straight, patting their dogs, ready to begin.

I mounted the steps and, through a break in the curtain, looked out at the crowd. Dad and Gramps would have loved to have seen this. I had to believe that they were looking down on me now. I missed them incredibly at this minute.

I felt a thumb wipe the tears from my cheeks as Harry squeezed onto the platform beside me. "They'd be so proud, Kate."

Startled, I looked into the eyes of this man I'd known such a short time. He understood me so well. Could it really be only two days ago that he bumped me and my world had changed? Agnes had told me at lunch yesterday that I didn't know what being in love was. But I knew this man, this wonderful, brave, amazing geek, who though he look at the world though numbers, really understood me. If what I felt for him wasn't love, then love didn't exist.

Harry pulled me into a hug, which ended with a kiss until Denise leaned over and whispered, "Sorry to interrupt, but its show time."

I felt myself blush and was grateful for the darkening of the room. I moved into position at the runway entrance with Dillon at my side, and peeked through the curtain again.

The place was packed. I spotted the mayor, and many people from the kennel club. Scanning the front row I gasped in surprise. There, sat Maeve and Padraig alongside Agnes with Sean Connelly, Sal, and my whole family. I was about to say something to Harry when the music began. Instead, I stepped back, checking to ensure everyone was ready.

The room went totally black and the beat changed. Denise began her welcome and introduction, and we were off.

The collective gasp from the audience told me the banner of Richard and Spike had been projected, and I tapped my old friend's shoulder and patted Spike as Denise introduced them. Counting the beats in her head and in her heart, I aligned each model pair. The flow went forward to cheers and applause. I felt my whole being swell as I heard the handclapping, laughter and shouts.

As each of my friends moved forward, tears of gratitude filled my eyes. They were doing this for me. They were bringing the dream of a twelve-year-old girl to life, and I would be forever grateful. Finally, Bill walked out with Ashraf and Harry stepped up beside me.

He slipped off his sling and handed it to me then hooked his thumb into his pocket to steady the arm. I felt him squeeze my hand just before he stepped forward with Ajax, looking as though they'd trained together for years. My eyes followed them down the runway and I saw the sheepish half smile he gave me when he returned up the runway. I knew he had spotted the family.

Denise went into her commentary, directing the audience to look around and enjoy the distinction of being the first to see the premiere Kate Killoy Fancier Fashions Collection.

The room exploded into a light show with throbbing music and flashing lights making the banners lining the walls on both sides of the room seem to come to life. Andy's photos were so good I expected the dogs to bark. The whole production built to a breathtaking crescendo of light and sound. Then the room went black and silent.

The audience held its breath, as a solo flute played a haunting melody which twisted and turned in the darkness, rising slowly until it swooped up into a high, unbearably sweet note. So wrapped in the sound, I barely felt the quiet swish of movement as each dog slid past with his owner in the darkness to stand onstage. Then Denise pushed the button to signal Ulysses.

A beat came in underneath and with a blast, the full orchestration hit as the lights flashed and flooded the runway displaying all the dogs and their owners wearing my designs. The crowd went nuts. Denise's voice broke through the applause as she announced my name and Harry stepped over to escort me the length of the runway. Dillon moved proudly at my side as I smiled, reaching out to touch the hands of each of my friends. I turned and applauded them as they did me.

As the cheers died down, Denise announced that refreshments were available and buyers could pick up packets from Jennifer and Heather located at the table to the left of the entrance. I glanced at Agnes, who nodded, gave me a thumbs-up and turned to a woman behind her pointing toward the table. Then came the hugs and cheers from my models as they surrounded me, all happy for themselves and their dogs, but more so for me. They gave me three cheers before moving from the stage to find their friends and refreshments. I felt a warm hand grasp mine as Harry and I went to greet the family.

CHAPTER TWENTY-ONE

Harry strode beside me down the runway stairs. "Kate, you were right to wonder how they knew where we'd be last night. Deciding to take a walk after the party wouldn't have been a normal thing to do. We've got to talk to Manny."

We'd reached the crowd. I leaned into him to whisper as we stepped forward, "Brace yourself, sweetheart. You're about to meet the family."

Suddenly, I was swung up into air and tossed from one set of hands to another. Finally hands reached up and snatched me to safety as Maeve burst into the crowd, slapping the young men involved in a spirited game of 'Toss the Kate.'

Harry held me to his chest as he turned on the group and quietly warned, "If you lay one hand on my fiancée again without my permission, it'll be your last move."

Shock stopped them for a second and Maeve took advantage of it. "Okay you unruly Killoys, listen up. You are in a civilized place, and you will mind your manners. Since I am the one who brought these two together, I get the honor of introducing you to Kate's fiancé, Harry Foyle. If you want to know specifics about him—without pestering your sister, who will be busy enough tonight—talk to Sal, who knows Harry well. I will tell you that he and Kate have been seeing each other since I introduced them last fall. I want you all to know Padraig and I, and Agnes and Sal, think this engagement is wonderful. So, young Killoys, you'll behave, or you'll answer to me."

Harry and I watched as the revelation passed across the faces of the Killoy clan. He bent down and whispered in my ear, "Have they every really taken a good look at you?"

I, introduced him to my mother and grandmother then labeled each of my brothers. None of the boys looked happy, but Harry immediately found a friend in Grandma Grace. She slipped an arm through his and I watched them slowly traverse the room. I wondered what they were talking about.

Agnes appeared at my side, accompanied by Sean Connelly. I'd known Sean most of my life. His father was Padraig's best friend and they lived two towns over from me in Connecticut. Sean was rising in the ranks as a Connecticut State Trooper and enjoying it thoroughly, according to his father.

What was curious was to see him with Agnes. Under possible escorts for my cousin, traditionally, Sean would rank last. He and Agnes had been at war, constant squabbling, since they were ages twelve and ten respectively. I'm sure neither remembered what the original fight had been about, but it didn't matter. They needed no excuse to snipe at each other non-stop, so to see them together had me greeting him with wonder. "Sean, it's so great to see you. Glad you could come."

"Your cousin brought me, and I'm glad she did. I must say Katie, you've certainly changed since I last saw you. Did I hear someone say that guy with your grandmother is your fiancé? He's to be congratulated. What does he do? Where is he from?"

"Harry has his own security company. He used to be with the FBI, but chose to go independent. He lives in Boston."

"Sounds like someone I should get to know." He smiled and glanced at Agnes then headed over to talk to Harry.

I looked after him and asked Agnes, "Is there something here that I should know?"

"The number of things you should know is limitless, cousin. But right now, Andy looks like he'll have a coronary if we don't let him take his pictures."

The next fifteen minutes was taken up with lots of smiles and flashes as Andy set up photos of me with the commissioner's wife, of me and Agnes with the mayor, of us with the show chairman, then with the committee...and so it went.

I smiled at Andy and said, "It's great that you were here tonight, not only to get the runway shots but also these publicity ones."

"It has less to do with me being nice and more to do with a phone call I got from your Mr. Foyle. He indicated people mixing up you and Agnes was becoming a problem. So he thought some shots of both of you together might solve the problem. He gave me a phone number, and I made one phone call. Suddenly, I've got eight papers and two magazines calling and offering big bucks for coverage with all the high muckity-mucks. Harry was the one who set the dominoes falling. I owe him."

I realized Harry must have figured that showing the two of us together would prove to the world I wasn't Agnes. I hoped his plan could work, and he would personally send a copy to Agent Donner which gave me the idea of having one more shot of Agnes and me with the FBI's AIC and his wife. She was delighted and told Andy she'd love to have a copy. Sean came up and said he hated to break this up, but he and Agnes had quite a drive ahead of them and should be leaving. They each hugged me and then, hand in hand strolled toward the exit.

A comment from earlier this evening popped into my head and I called after Agnes to wait. Quickly I asked her questions about the thumb drive. She answered me and I stepped back to watch them go.

Donovan stepped up beside me and looped his arm through mine. He chuckled, "Now I believe in miracles. Those two have been fighting since dinosaurs roamed the earth. You'd think that they were engaged."

I didn't answer, but I knew I had more questions for my cousin.

Harry returned and wrapped his good arm around my waist. Heading off my siblings' cross examination, he told Tim his sister was starving.

Not to be upstaged by his twin, Seamus made a quick foray to the desserts table for treats which he had the staff pack in take-out containers. He told Harry, "She always gets hungry for desserts after a big win, and there is no kitchen here to raid." I realized Seamus knew me well and ate with enthusiasm, slapping Harry's hand as he stole treats from my plate.

Sal brought my mother over. He introduced her to Harry and assured her he was a good man and good for me. My mother stepped forward without a smile. She'd finished visiting with all her old friends and now found herself in a position where she must talk to her daughter. I could see her disappointment was palpable but couldn't tell if it was with the show or the engagement.

"Well Kathleen, at least you seem to have found a way to make some success from all the time you spent at that little design school. This career, if you can call it that, is better than spending all your time running around with those silly dogs. I'm afraid your father and grandfather spoiled you. How they could allow you to waste what little mathematical ability you have in this way I'll never understand. But what is this about you becoming engaged? Why didn't you tell me? Didn't you think that I'd be interested in the fact that my own daughter was seeing someone?" She looked around at her family, who seemed to be waiting to see what was going to happen next.

I felt as though I'd been kicked and, without thinking, struck back. "No, Mother, I didn't think you'd be the least bit interested in this or any other part of my life."

"Well, I am," she answered, not the least bit stung by my comment. "Who is this man and why should I even consider him as someone I'd choose for my daughter?"

Harry began to speak but my temper could not be held. "Mother," I began sarcastically, "with midterm exams coming up I wouldn't dream of distracting you with anything as trivial as my engagement. So being aware of what your requirements would be for someone to marry into your family, I weighed the variables and chose according to your strict standards. I happen to know you'd approve of Harry because he's as much, if not more, skilled in mathematics than you are. However, the deciding factor was that Dad and Gramps would have happily welcomed him because they'd have realized, he makes me happy."

Seeming to know I had blown out my anger, Harry stepped forward offering my mother his hand and introducing himself. Sure that he would survive, I walked over to talk to my grandmother, though I kept the pair in sight.

"If this were not your evening to shine, Kathleen, I'd take a paddle to you. You father would be washing your mouth out with soap, party or no party. That was an unfair fight and you know it. You mother understands numbers the way you understand words. What you said may have had a grain of truth, but to say it in public is not the way we do things in the Killoy family. I expect your behavior for the rest of the evening to be up to Killoy standards and I expect you to apologize to your mother."

I stood there feeling about two inches tall. Grandma Grace could always do that to me. I turned, most of the shine taken off the evening, and walked back toward Harry, only to hear my mother ask him a question.

"Harry Foyle? Wait. Are you the Foyle who published a paper two years ago on the integrating factors of inhomogeneous linear ordinary differential equations in AMS?"

Harry blinked, saying he had. Kate grinned as her mother launched into a discussion of Duhamel's Principle. Seamus stepped up to them and managed to steer his mother to talk with Alice Simmons, who was an old family friend as well as one of the models. My older brother Tom joined us.

"Congratulations, Foyle, you have just crossed the Rubicon, my man. My mother would love to marry all her sons off to girls who write for AMS. You, my lad, just waltzed in carrying a *Get Out of Jail Free* card that, I guarantee you has bought her unwavering loyalty for life."

Sal joined them and asked, "What the hell is going on? Harry, you're wearing a sling and Kate is nowhere near as excited as I would expect for someone who just pulled this off."

"I'll give you the details later, but the bottom line is that someone has access to everywhere Kate and Agnes might be and seems to have a team of assailants who can attack at any time. Who can you think of that has that kind of accessibility?

"Off the top of my head, a bunch of high-tech criminals or—" he stopped and stared at Harry.

"Yeah, we'll talk later. You might want to check some of your sources, but on the q.t." Harry smiled at Sal then strolled with me over to where my friends were saying goodbye to everyone. I hugged and thanked both Andy and Denise.

Jennifer and Heather came over with the paperwork they'd gathered. "Kate, I hope you're braced to be a success. The buyers were placing solid orders, and two of the buyers also represent boutiques out West that they hadn't told about the show. They'll be contacting Ellen with their orders on Monday. They were all excited about the graphics. The styles that were in greatest demand were the square neck sweater, the tuck-scarf and the short cape. If you want," Heather suggested as she sealed the oversized envelopes, "we'll have the hotel overnight this paperwork to Ellen, so she'll be ready for the calls next week. You're going to be busy enough with the dog show." I thanked them both, hugged them and waved them off.

Harry and I checked to be sure Ulysses had everything in hand, and I gave him a hug, thanking him for making the show so special.

"Kate, at school I thought you were a little off the beam with this dog obsession of yours, but working with these people the last few days was great. Anytime you want to do this again, give me a call."

The last to leave were the family and Sal. Harry and Seamus slipped over to the refreshment table and put together a doggy bag for us to take back to the room. Finally we said goodnight to everyone and promised to see them soon. Herded by Sal, the Killoy contingent headed out. I leaned my back against Harry as I waved my family off.

"I like your family. Your brothers are great. Tom is a little protective, but his threats to destroy my livelihood through numbers manipulation and encryption tampering if I hurt you would have carried more force, if I hadn't realized that Fortune 500 companies hire me to provide protection against that kind of thing every day.

Gathering our dogs and doggie bags, we headed toward the elevators, only to have Detective Williams join us. "I know you've had a big evening, you two, but we've got to talk."

"How about tomorrow at…" Harry grabbed his phone and pulled up my schedule, which he'd apparently downloaded. "Eleven o'clock. Kate has interviews before that and at one o'clock she needs to be at the 42nd Street branch of the New York Public Library."

Detective Williams frowned but agreed and stepped into the almost-full elevator just as the door was closing.

We waited for the next one. I put leads on the dogs and when I turned I noticed a serious expression on Harry's face. "What?" I asked.

"I was wondering when you had stopped being a job and become something so much more?" I looked up at him as we entered the empty elevator and headed down. I had been on such an emotional roller coaster all day that I didn't think I had any sensation left in me but from somewhere, perhaps deep in my heart, joy filled me and I couldn't keep it from showing on my face. Apparently that was the only answer he needed as he drew me tight against his chest and bent to give me a bone melting kiss.

CHAPTER TWENTY-TWO

We had our snacks in the room before taking the dogs down for one last visit to the green room. I had been sure I wouldn't sleep a wink but in the end, with the comfort of having Harry nearby, I don't even remember my head hitting the pillow.

It being Sunday, we were up early to take care of the dogs before heading across the street to early Mass. The old Church of St. Francis of Assisi had been a place Gramps, Dad and I would attend whenever we were in the city on a Sunday. The animal-loving saint is honored in this beautiful, more than one-hundred-year-old Greek-revival church. The place always gave me a sense of peace. Kneeling, I bowed my head, losing myself in prayers of thanks to the Lord and all the saints who watch over fools and dog lovers. I spent time before Mass going over the many good things that had happened during the week since my last Mass. I also asked forgiveness for being harsh on my mother and I asked guidance in dealing with her. Grandma Grace's rebuke weighed heavily on my mind. I realized Dad had always told me that I should make an effort to understand Mom, but it seemed so hard. The boys would just brush off the thoughtless things she said that cut me, saying it was just her way and forget it. Maybe I was too sensitive. Maybe I just felt like an outsider in my own family because I wasn't focused on math.

If it hadn't been for the dogs…,I looked over at Harry, who sat relaxed at my side. The lack of hesitation in his responses to the priest told me, without my asking him directly, that he was a practicing Catholic. I knew that question would come up within the first five minutes of my return home on Wednesday.

"Let's eat." Harry said as we left the church after Mass and made our way across the street. "I'm always twice as hungry after all that praying. Oh, and I want to get the papers." We detoured to the newsstand and lugged the heavy Sunday editions into the restaurant with us. The *Times* had us above the fold on the first page of the Society section whereas the *Post* and *Daily News* had us right on the front page with a tie in to the dog show.

Andy had been as good as his word and Harry said he hoped this would show those who were trying to kill me that I wasn't Agnes. Hopefully, the drive-by shootings would stop. He said he felt sick whenever he thought about what could have happened yesterday. "That's a great shot of you and Agnes hugging as well as the one showing both of you with the Mayor and his wife."

"I hope Agnes wasn't too uncomfortable in that bulletproof vest. I think Sean was delighted to be her escort for the evening. I've never seen him smile that much. He's a nice guy and they'd make a great couple."

"How did you know she was wearing a vest?"

"I hugged her. Plus it would have been stupid not to, considering she's obviously a target. She was headed back to Connecticut with Sean after the show and either spent the night at his place or with Sal. She'll come back to the city in disguise tomorrow. Since it was her idea in the first place, I'm glad she got to be at the show after all her hard work. It wouldn't have been the same without her."

"And I got to meet the family." Harry said, looking me in the eye.

"I'm so sorry about that. I had no idea they were coming. I hope you weren't too uncomfortable."

"Not at all. I was surprised when I went down the runway with Ajax and saw a lineup of males that all looked so much like you. You're right about the Killoy family having a resemblance. I really love your Grandma Grace, and your brother, Seamus, reminds me of myself many years ago."

"Seamus and I are close because he understands me more than the others do. I tend to be the odd one out as you may have guessed. Since my math skills, other than what I use in design, comprise mostly parlor tricks, I'm not really Killoy material. If I didn't have the dog thing going with Dad and Gramps, they would have given me away."

Harry turned me around and stared at me, frowning. "I think that you and I have more in common than I first thought." I wasn't quite sure what he meant, but I knew that sharing any bond with him could only be good.

"We shouldn't dawdle," I mentioned as we went to get the dogs. "I've got a television interview at nine fifteen in the lower lobby followed by a taped radio interview over near Twenty-Sixth and Twelfth. We've got to talk to Detective Williams at eleven then get to the New York Public Library so some city youngsters can read to the dogs. After all that, we get to the best part. We've been invited to head uptown for dinner at Maeve's."

"Ah, one of Sally's meals. That can make the whole day worthwhile."

We fetched the dogs and took care of their needs before I sat down in the interview area that had been set up to one side of the green room. They were just finishing up a segment featuring a huge male Great Dane and a tiny teacup Chihuahua.

I smiled when they turned to me, and I eased into the interview, speaking with excitement about the fashion show last night. I even managed, within the allotted time, to pitch my patterns promising they would be available in my booth at the dog show at the pier. I also stressed that many of the designs from last night's show would be for sale soon as ready-to-wear items.

I introduced Dillon and mentioned that he'd won the National the year before last and did my classic thirty second speech describing the breed's ancient lineage. I finished up saying I hoped people would come out and see us at the dog show. The director signaled we were out and I took a deep breath. That was one down and one to go. I signed the waiver and made sure that they would send me the clip.

When Harry and I got up to the lobby, I pulled out my phone I called Jennifer to see if the booth needed me. She told me everything was under control, and the paperwork from last night had been faxed to my studio. They'd seen the live broadcast that had just finished and said they thought it was terrific. The director told me that the spot would be run three more times between now and Tuesday, which was fantastic.

Since we had our coats with us, we just headed out to find a cab to get us across town. Twenty-Sixth is one way in the wrong direction for us, which meant the cab needed to go around the block. Traffic was jammed. Not wanting to be late, I took the dogs and hopped out of the cab when we were still down the block. Harry followed close behind and we dashed between the trucks that were blocking traffic.

Dillon and I, then Ajax and Harry, squeezed through the revolving door, and I checked in at the desk, letting them know Harry was with me. Looking at the time, we hurried up the steps, through the turnstile, and into the elevator which took us to the ninth floor, and finally through the glass doors of the reception area. Harry and the dogs waited in the lobby with its massive windows looking out over the city and the Hudson River. During the radio show which was broadcast over satellite radio, my host and I discussed our shared love of dogs. We chatted about her Chows and Frenchies and my Samoyeds, about the fashion show and about the upcoming dog show. I was amazed we were able to fit so much into that short time.

Once again on the street, we began watching for cabs so we could get to the precinct. As we headed east, I told Harry my reasoning that it would be easier to catch a cab on the avenues rather than the cross streets. We hadn't gone more than a dozen steps when I spotted a familiar tan van slowly maneuvering around an unloading truck. I grabbed Harry's arm and started to run, looking for cover. We heard a siren and the van sped up turning the corner, as a cruiser pulled to the curb right by us. "Get in," Sergeant Sanchez called and we thankfully accepted the ride. "I've got the description, but the plate number was covered with mud, making it unreadable."

I quickly reeled off the plate number. "They may have covered their back plate, but the mud they splashed on the front has worn off and the numbers were clearly visible. I caught it when they came around the big furniture truck, just before they took off."

Harry looked at me. "Is that one of your so-called parlor tricks?"

"I can remember strings of numbers. It's just something I do."

"That's a handy talent. I wish I had it." Sanchez called in the information on the truck and added the plate number.

"How did you happen to be Johnny-on-the-spot here this morning?"

"You told us your schedule last night. I just guessed you'd be finished with your interview about now."

Harry grinned. "Good timing."

Our hope that the photos being splashed around would draw the killers away was fading, and I didn't relax until we were in the precinct building and on our way up to talk to Detective Williams. He took us to an interview room. Williams began the interview by asking me where I had been between two and six o'clock on Friday.

"Let's see, by two o'clock we'd finished up the photo shoot and grabbed a snack on the way up to Central Park. Dillon and I and a group of the models were part of a demonstration of precision obedience set to music, which was filmed for television. When we finished that, we went to my Aunt Maeve's for a late lunch and to get Harry's tux. Then we went back to the hotel to get ready for the party." I turned a guileless gaze on the detective, daring him to accuse me of anything.

"You say 'we.' Do you mean you and Mr. Foyle?"

"Yes."

"I'm told you know most of the people involved with this show."

"All but a few technicians."

"Can you tell me who had a problem with the victim?"

I thought for a minute. "I can tell you I—and I suspect the other exhibitors who were involved with the show—had never met Sonja prior to Thursday. She arrived as Bill Trumbull's groomer, but I later found out that was just a cover. Her real role was to act as bodyguard to the prince's dog, the Afghan Hound, Ashraf, that Bill was handling. Her abrasive nature, I think, had more to do with her responsibilities than with any real dislike of the people who'd be in the fashion show. She felt the dog would be exposed to more danger if he was involved. However, the prince wanted him in, so she had to bite the bullet. Excuse me, poor metaphor. She normally accompanied the dog everywhere. However, Bill told me, she came to him Friday afternoon with the dog and told him that he must guard Ashraf with his life. When he asked where she was going, she didn't tell him but just left. We saw him waiting for the troop of bodyguards to arrive from the consulate when we returned to the hotel, and he told us about Sonja's unusual defection. When Huey, Dewey and Louie arrived, they left."

"Huey, Dewey and Louie?"

"Sorry, it's my name for the troop of royal body-guards who are guarding Ashraf now. I just learned their real names when they arrived at the fashion show last night."

"So I take it that you don't think that any of these people you worked with disliked her enough to kill her."

"I don't think they knew her at all. Many of them are old friends I've known since childhood, and that would include Bill Trumbull. Others were top breeders I'd met over the last few years. I think only a crazy person would become so pissed at someone for usurping their dog-bathing time that they'd take it to the point of murder."

"And then there's the knitting needle. Do you have any insight on that?"

"Well, now that you mention it, I do. While we were sitting around last night waiting for the show to begin, I asked several breeders if they'd ever seen a knitting needle used for grooming dogs. It turns out many of them use one for untangling matted coats. I checked with Bill and it seemed that Sonja had one that she carried for that purpose. So I'm afraid the needle used had less to do with knitting and more to do with its availability. Since she carried it in her pocket, the killer could have just grabbed it and used it because it was there. I'm assuming you didn't find one in her pocket. I don't know when she was actually killed, but the ballroom was filled with workers until three-thirty and then again starting at five."

"That's what Mr. Jones said."

I started gathering my things together, thinking we might be done, but both Harry and Manny shook their heads.

Detective Williams set the files that had been in front of him to one side and reached for another stack. I glanced at the time foreseeing any possibility of lunch before the library event disappearing.

He cleared his throat and settled his glasses. "Now as to the matter of the man shooting at you Friday night and the threat you received yesterday.... Oh, and Sergeant Sanchez added your being shoved into traffic on Thursday to my pile this morning. New York isn't a crime-free city, but you must admit that your being here only three days and getting three attempts on your life is not improving the city's statistics. Could you tell us why someone wants you dead?"

I glanced at Harry and said, "No, I can't. As you say, I've been in the city for three days almost all of it involved in getting ready for and putting on a fashion show. I haven't had time to give anyone a reason to kill me."

There was a tap on the door. Sergeant Sanchez opened it and whispered something to Williams. "Bring him in."

The door opened to allow Agent Hendrix to enter the room. Harry sat up and looked quizzical.

Williams said, "Agent Hendrix, I think you've already met Kate Killoy and Harry Foyle."

"I already know Foyle from the Bureau. It's Miss Killoy I need to talk to here. I have learned that Agnes Forester is your cousin. Is that true?"

"Yes."

"When did you last see your cousin?"

"I saw her last night at the fashion show. If you saw the *Times, The Post,* or *The Daily News* this morning, you might have seen photos of us with the mayor, the show chairman and, if I remember correctly, the AIC of the FBI."

"Where is your cousin now?"

"I have no idea. Agnes is a big girl and we both lead our own lives. I was just happy she could attend my fashion show since she was vital in getting it set up. She's a real sweetie. She left with a guy so I imagine that she had plans. In fact my entire family was at the event. Though I could lay a guess where my mother, grandmother, great aunt and uncle are about now, the location of my four brothers would also be a mystery."

"Foyle, why didn't you say something to me on Thursday? I told you that I was following Agnes Forester?"

"I probably didn't tell you because Kate and I have been focused on each other not other people. My mind was on proposing this weekend, not trying to figure out why my fiancée's cousin, whom I met for the first time last night, was of interest to the Bureau. I don't think anyone mentioned at lunch on Thursday why they were interested in her. I freely admit, Hendrix, my attention was elsewhere."

Harry grabbed my hand under the table and smiled at me. "You should congratulate me, Hendrix. This beautiful, smart, funny dog nut is the best thing that ever happened to me. By the way, what has Agnes Forester done that she's being tracked by the Bureau?"

"I can't discuss that."

"Excuse me, gentlemen. I'm afraid we have to leave." I stood as did all the men. Dillon and Ajax moved from under the table where they'd been resting. "We're scheduled to have children read to these dogs at the Public Library in forty minutes and I don't want to be late," I said. "Let me know if I can be of any more help, Detective."

When we reached the sidewalk, Harry turned to look at me. "You aren't intimidated by detectives or FBI agents at all, are you?"

"Hey, there's a photo of the Mayor hugging me in the *Times* this morning. The police commissioner's wife wore one of my sweater designs to the show last night." I laughed. "These guys don't scare me."

CHAPTER TWENTY-THREE

Keeping an eye out for tan vans, we worked our way up to Forty-Second Street. From a cart on the way, we grabbed a lunch of huge pretzels, which we dipped in mustard. We made it to the library in plenty of time. Dillon and Ajax were delighted when they saw the huge stone lions that guard the entrance. I patted these giants for luck, which had been my ritual since I was a child. We made our way to the children's room where Cora met us at the door.

Inside, it was a small but merry collection of children and dogs. A troupe of other dog owners had been drafted to be part of this event cosponsored by the Westerland Kennel Club and a local Literacy Volunteers group. Several board members were on hand to enjoy the fun as well. The noise built as more people tried to cram themselves, their children and the dogs all into the same room. As we waited, I introduced Harry to some friends he hadn't yet met. The TV camera was finally moved into position to tape the event for later broadcast and everything was ready.

Local schools had sent kids who'd been identified as having reading problems to participate in the program. Allison Silver, the head of the Children's Department, explained that each child could pick a book and choose a dog as a reading buddy. Then child and dog would find a comfortable spot on the rug. The owners and parents would sit outside the reading circle. The librarian invited each child by name to select his book, take the dog's leash, and go to the spot he chose. This went quickly, and soon the room was filled with the voices of children reading. Harry whispered that he was astounded that these two dogs, who might have torn my assailant to pieces yesterday, behaved today like sweethearts with the kids. I reminded him that *this* was their normal behavior.

Harry sat with his arms around me, squashed into a spot beside the picture books. We watched the children, who had begun reading hesitantly, grow more confident as the dogs snuggled closer to listen. I whispered to Harry that my dog club at home did this once a month at the public library and Dillon loved it.

I pulled out my phone and was able to get several wonderful shots of a young boy, his hair a mass of cornrows, who had finally ended up using Dillon as a pillow while he read *Arthur's New Puppy* by Marc Brown. A tiny girl had chosen Ajax. Their heads were level as they found their spot. She was wearing a beautiful blue sari over her leggings and snow boots. When they finally settled, both sitting, she was so small that she ended up between Ajax's front legs as she read *A Dog Called Kitty* by Bill Wallace. As she finished each page, she'd hold up the book so that he could see the pictures. I took several shots of that and sent one off to Sarah and one to her husband Pete in Afghanistan. After all, this was why our troops were fighting.

When the reading was done and the dogs had gotten their hugs and kisses from their new friends, we moved toward the exit with the other owners. Cora leaned in toward me and told me a friend of hers would record the broadcast later today. She would send me a copy.

When we got outside, I stopped beside one of the lions to rearrange what I was carrying. I heard my name and looked up just in time to see Harry snap my picture. Pulling out my phone, I snapped some of him beside the lions and then with each dog. I laughed when he made a face, and he took another then stepped up and tucked his arm behind me, his face against mine, to get a shot of us together.

As Harry looked around, his smile faded. He noticed a number of people watching us. I didn't want to lose the joy of the moment, but when he pointed out a guy with a scarf around his face and his hat pulled down giving us the once over, we slipped into caution mode and quickly hailed a cab for our trip uptown.

As our cab fought traffic, I remembered I hadn't told Harry about the discussion I'd had with Bill right before the show. "I talked with Bill. He was in seventh heaven. His daughter had just called from Germany. The State Department was finally able to get her and his granddaughter out of Zanifra safely and they are probably landing at Kennedy Airport right now."

"That's great. How did they do it without the last piece of information that was passed to Agnes?"

"Well, that's the curious thing. When I asked, he said the final piece of information was the chip he buried in my braid the morning of my makeover. He swears he never passed any other information after that."

"But what about the information Agnes got from him?"

"I asked her before she left last night. She said it was passed to her by a man she'd seen with Bill a minute before. She said she assumed Bill had used the man to steer suspicion away from himself."

"She was set up?"

"It seems so. She didn't have time to decode the whole message, but thought the beginning looked like some kind of plot." We both sat in silence for a minute. "If the FBI caught her in possession of that information, they could probably arrest her for espionage. Maybe someone was trying to get her in trouble. What I want to know is who gave her the information and who sicced the agency on her? It wasn't Bill Trumbull, and it certainly wasn't the State Department."

The cab pulled to a halt, and we stepped out onto the sidewalk, our minds still wrapped up in the problem. The door at the top of the stairs opened, and Niall welcomed us, telling us Agnes should arrive soon. I was glad we were having dinner with Maeve. There were too many unanswered questions. This was a puzzle that needed all the brain power we could gather.

After hugs all around, Harry and I settled into the wonderful feast that had been prepared to celebrate the success of the fashion show. Maeve and Padraig insisted that we eat before we discuss our problem with them.

The party was in full swing when the call came. Niall walked into the room holding the phone, looking more disconcerted than I had ever seen him. "It is Mr. Connelly, sir; it appears the Connecticut State Police phoned to tell him… It seems there was an explosion and fire at young Sean's house. Mr. Connelly is leaving to see what he can find. He'd appreciate it, sir, if you'd go with him." The monotone of Niall's words screamed louder than a shout.

"Tell him I'll be ready." Padraig stood, looking as if in that moment, he'd aged ten years. He kissed Maeve then stared at me for a minute. Putting a hand on Harry's shoulder they traded unspoken words, and he left.

We sat in silence. I felt numb, unable to move or even look around. Nodding to Maeve, Harry went around the table to pull my chair back and help me up. Niall came up beside him and listened to Harry's instructions. Then he went to Maeve, and drawing back her chair, he allowed Harry to take her an arm and lead both of us to the library. I walked because his arm propelled me forward.

Niall soon wheeled in a tea cart, which also contained brandy and scotch. He poured Maeve a brandy while Harry pulled an afghan off the back of the sofa to wrap around her legs.

I was frozen. I couldn't move. I sat because he'd put me on the sofa. I was vaguely aware that Harry had poured me a cup of cocoa. I blinked at seeing the generous dose of brandy he'd added. He served himself a scotch, and joined me on the sofa. Wrapping an afghan around me, he held the cocoa out to me. I knew I should be doing something with it. I could only sit. He set the chocolate down on the table along with his drink and then shoved in next to me. On some level I must have known he was there, but my brain wasn't open for business.

Harry coaxed me onto his lap, and held the cup of cocoa for me to drink. At first I couldn't respond, but eventually the words he was saying, his tone gentle as he stroked me, reached into that place where I was hiding, slowly guiding me out.

I turned to look into his eyes, and he smiled. "Welcome back."

I couldn't manage a smile in return, but I finished my cocoa and then, as if I'd been doing it for years, put my head on his shoulder snuggling into his arms.

Time passed, and he spoke quietly with Maeve, who was more alert and focused than I on Harry's discussion of his strange childhood. He spoke of going to Caltech from elementary school, being away from his family for years, but, at the same time having those who surrounded him look upon him as normal. He told about how his father was uncomfortable with having a son who wasn't like other boys.

Maeve told him that being a Killoy meant that she was surrounded with math geeks from birth. I let the stories of her growing up with Gramps and Sybil in Ireland descend on me like a warm blanket. She said something about understanding Kate that I knew I should pay attention to, but I could not keep my eyes open and just drifted off.

Niall came in. Yanked from sleep, I watched as he went to the extension phone and brought the receiver to Maeve. He spoke to her softly and pressed the button which transferred the call.

"Sybil." She listened. I saw Harry watch her face, trying to fathom the news. After a minute she sank back on the couch and closed her eyes. "Thank God. Yes, call whenever you hear anything more."

Niall took the phone and closed her hand around a fresh brandy.

Staring into the glass, she said, "They got the fire out and have been through the house. No bodies were found. Apparently, Sean's SUV was found near the Fairfield train station. They might be in the city or anywhere, but for now, it seems, they're alive."

Niall interrupted, clearing his throat. "I have talked to Himself on his cell phone. They are going to check out the house and then spend the night at Mrs. Sybil's who is in a bad way. They'll be back sometime in the morning. He suggested that Miss Kate and Mr. Harry spend the night here, so I've made up their rooms."

Harry looked at me. I still hadn't moved. It hadn't completely registered what I'd heard.

"What do you need to show Ajax in the morning?"

My brain felt the fog lift. I turned to stare around the room, not knowing how I'd gotten there. I felt renewed warmth in my hand and was surprised to find a new cup of cocoa there. Realizing where the warmth that wrapped around me was coming from, I looked at Harry. Running a hand through my curls, he repeated the question.

"Oh, right. I've got to show Ajax tomorrow." The habits of a lifetime pulled me back and substituted for actual thinking. I drank the rest of the cocoa and slid off Harry's lap, sitting up straight. "I can borrow what equipment I need from Maeve. I should text Sarah to bring his show benching crate and grooming table." I pulled out my phone, but stopped and stared at it, wondering how it worked.

Harry took it and keyed in a message. It buzzed almost immediately with an irate message from Sarah wondering where I was. He texted back that we were staying at Maeve's for the night. but would see her at the pier in the morning. He suggested she take the shuttle bus over. Slipping the phone into my pocket, he watched me as reality shot through my body.

I turned to Maeve. "I know Agnes will find a way to stay safe. She's with Sean and even though they fight like cats and dogs, he'll make sure she's safe and not taking any chances."

"They used to fight every time they got together, and even last night they were bickering on the way to the show." She looked at me, smiled, and raised her eyebrows. "But the bickering was different, and now they're on the run together. Interesting."

I met Maeve's eyes and slowly returned her smile.

CHAPTER TWENTY-FOUR

We all stood after a few minutes. Maeve walked over and hugged Harry and me.

"You two need to sleep. Tomorrow will be a busy day."

Then she left, looking slightly closer to her actual age than she had at the beginning of the evening. I reached for Harry's hand and headed down the stairs to see about the dogs. We were met by Niall coming up.

"Dillon and Ajax have been fed and exercised and they are bedded down, asleep. Breakfast will be ready at six. Mr. Harry is in your father's room so you can show him the way. I'll see you in the morning, Miss Kate."

I reached out and hugged the old man, who after a moment of surprise, unbent and hugged me back. "Off with you now."

When we reached the top of the stairs, I stopped at the second door on the left.

"You're in here." I opened the door, pausing to take a breath and straighten my shoulders before stepping inside. It was a gentleman's room, filled with heavy oak furniture that hadn't been altered since the house was built. For a moment I just stood there, breathing in all the years of memories.

"I haven't been in this room since…." After a moment, I pointed. "I'll be next door," I pushed open the connecting door, then stopped. "Harry, I want to thank you for being with me today. It was good to have someone sharing my world again. I haven't been able to do that…in a while. And thanks especially, for staying with Maeve and me tonight." I stopped, then stepped forward and gave him a quick kiss, turned and closed the door.

I found that Sally had laid out an outfit for me to wear tomorrow from show outfits I'd stored here over the years. She had added a royal blue military jacket that must have been Maeve's which fit perfectly. I smiled. Like a good luck charm the jacket acted as a touchstone to my past and she knew it would give me some of Maeve's strength to face the day.

I'd checked my schedule, plugged my phone into the charger on the nightstand and now lay flat on my back, wide awake. My brain did hamster imitations, running in circles going nowhere, as it moved from Harry to Agnes to Sonja to Bill to the faceless killer and then to back to Harry, definitely to Harry. In three days I'd be home, sleeping in my own bed, in my tiny house. I'd be safe. Harry would be back in Boston, job done. I would no longer be the focus of his day. Life would go back to normal. So why did normal make me feel so miserable? I rolled over once, then twice, and again. I punched my pillow and tried to think about anything else. Then I heard the door click.

"I heard you tossing and turning and wondered if you were all right." Harry stepped into the room, wearing a loose plaid-flannel robe over pajama bottoms that stopped about three inches above his ankles and were cinched way in at the waist. They'd been Dad's.

I sat up in bed, not the least tired. "In the old days, I'd be worrying about tomorrow and showing, but to tell the truth, I have too many other things on my mind."

"Agnes? The murder?"

"Both. I can't turn off my brain. I've been reviewing the evening. Agnes coming out of hiding must have been what placed Sean and her in danger. Putting our photo on the front page of the papers might have pulled the killers off me for a while, but at what cost? What I'm really having trouble with is how they got onto Sean so fast. Someone at the event must have fed the information about Agnes' connection to Sean, on to someone else. They not only IDed him, but were able to locate his home and arrange to bomb it. Am I wrong, or does that take serious skills?

"Incredible skills. Very much like the skills of finding you hurrying from a restaurant, us walking the dogs late at night or you sitting unguarded in a hospital waiting room. In fact, few organizations have the tools to carry it off at all." Harry frowned as he settled himself at the foot of the bed, leaning against the footboard of the four poster.

"That's what you and Sal were whispering about?"

"Yeah, I'd find it harder to accept if I didn't have my own history with them. Something seriously wrong going on in the Bureau, but I don't have any proof...not even a clue. All I have are questions."

"If you remember in the letter Agnes sent, she did say not to trust the FBI." We sat for a minute in silence, each of us buried in our own thoughts.

Harry frowned. "There was one thing I didn't ask you about at the time since we never really got a chance to discuss Agnes' letter. What was all that stuff about Nana? Who's Nana and why is she so important?"

I looked up and stared at him taken aback. "I am such an idiot." I threw off the blankets and ran from the room, down the stairs, and into the library, with Harry right behind. I dashed straight the back of the room and the shelves at that held older books. I slid my finger over the titles, carefully checking each one. On the fourth shelf I found my prize, *Nana*. Hugging the book, I threw myself onto the sofa, tucked in my cold feet and, leaving room for Harry, opened the book.

"Nana is the name Agnes and I gave this special illustrated copy of James M. Barrie's play, *Peter Pan*. Nana was the character modeled after Barrie's own Landseer Newfoundland dog. Since this is an illustrated copy, it contains a section which Agnes and I loved as children, that shows a photo of the dog. The book is large, and we would hide notes inside. That way we could whisper to one another in passing, saying, 'Visit Nana,' and the boys wouldn't get it."

I looked at the open book. It looked perfectly normal, but when I began checking between the pages, sheets of copy paper—some with writing and some with rough diagrams—appeared. The text looked normal until you tried to read it. I could feel anticipation build in Harry as I passed him the first page.

"Kate, this will take time. I can tell you it doesn't fit any of the simple substitution patterns. A key is needed. This must have something to do with Zanifra. They're Muslims, right? Maybe they used the Quran."

"No, they're Coptic Christians. Try *The Bible - King James Version,* I'm pretty sure that's what they use. One of my part-time knitters is Coptic. There should be a copy on the third shelf next to the *Jerusalem Bible*."

He stood, found it and headed toward the desk. Within seconds, he was lost in deciphering the message. As he reached the end of each page, writing the decoded part of the message out on a legal pad, I'd hand him another.

We worked together until it was done. Then we gathered all the papers and returned to my room where we could talk.

By now as the temperature of the house had dropped considerably, and I was freezing, so I slipped on a cardigan, pulled up the covers and took the notes from Harry. He grabbed the extra quilt from the bottom of the bed, sat next to me, and threw it over his legs.

"Now we've got to try to figure it out. This is obviously a plan that was secret. And my first question is why were they giving it to Agnes?" I looked at the information before me.

"Perhaps the person who wrote the plan was someone who might be searched if they tried to leave the consulate. Or who didn't want to be seen meeting with the one who would be getting the plans. Planting the drive on Agnes, who was above suspicion, meant it could be taken from the building easily." Harry postulated aloud.

"Okay, they've planted it on Agnes, who is walking around with the plans for whatever secret plot they've made. What would they do next?

"First they tried unsuccessfully to run her down that night. Then on the following day, after she leaves, her apartment is searched, trashed and the drive with the plans is taken."

"So why, if they have the plans, are they still trying to kill Agnes? Or kill me, thinking I'm Agnes? Why would they suspect she could possibly read what was on the drive? It was in code and nobody would think she could read code. The fact that she can is a Killoy secret."

"Maybe someone who knows that particular Killoy secret has decided not to take any chances."

"The only possible people other than family who might know are FBI agents who might have read the classified reports she's worked on."

"If that's the case, they probably want to eliminate the possibility that she'd be able to pass on any information she might read. They know she hasn't so far, because they would also know if an operation was being prepared to stop the plan. All they have to do is eliminate Agnes and, of course you—in case you really are Agnes in disguise—and then they'll be able to complete their plan without discovery."

I stared at him. "Harry, you told me your business was to take each assignment, assess it, evaluate the risks, weigh the options, appraise the consequences, project results and formulate plans. I know you do this mathematically and use algorithms to develop these plans. However, since we don't have much time and this case is unique, that is to say involving both my life and Agnes', could we go from assessing the problem straight to formulating the plan without the middle steps?"

"Fine. From these notes, it looks like there's a kidnapping planned. The question is why here and why now? Taking the last part first, I'd say it has to do with the peace talks scheduled to begin on Thursday."

"Having the plan the kidnapper intended to use can't hurt, providing this is what they still have in mind to do." We curled up side by side on the bed and spread the papers out, placing the text in one pile and the two graphics next to it.

"Okay, the graphics are numbered in the order they were found in the book. According to the text, team one will shadow the subject to the place. They just refer to it as Zone A, followed by seven-thirty, which might be a time."

I picked up the graphic depicting cross hatchings with a spot labeled, 'A.' There were no labels on the cross hatchings, but it looked familiar. I held it up, turned it upside down and, smiling, began to sing, "'New York, New York, a helluva town.'

"Don't you see? I won't do the whole musical, On *the Town* but as the song says, "the Bronx is up and the Battery's down."

"What?"

"It's Manhattan!"

"You're right. This must be the Battery, and this is Times Square, and this empty section must be…"

"Central Park."

"Okay, if we know it's a map of Manhattan, what's on the spot they marked?"

"The Garden. This has got to be connected with the dog show." I grabbed the other graphic and studied it a minute. "This building is the Garden. The central section is the show rings, and there's the grooming area, and this is the main entrance."

"The section of the plan here is where they assign units to different tasks—distractions, disarm, acquire, extract. The next section is withdrawal, then contact and completion. Each of these has a page of cryptic details. However, I've read the whole thing twice and nowhere is a time given except maybe seven thirty." Harry's frustration at working outside his system of numbers was beginning to show, but he struggled on. "Well, whatever is going to be done must happen either on Monday night or Tuesday night, because that would leave Wednesday to send out the demands. Tomorrow would be the first logical time."

"What do we know that connects Zanifra, the Garden and tomorrow? Only the fact that Bill is showing the prince's Afghan Hound and, considering the quality of the dog, he's probably going to win the breed. He will most likely be showing at the Garden in the evening competing in the group. That means that it could happen then. The other possibility, though it would be a longer shot, would be if he were to win the group. Then it could happen on Tuesday when he competed for Best in Show."

"But that assumes the dog will win the breed."

"Right, but I pretty much know what's showing out there now. This dog is definitely the best. I'm pretty sure that, unless some dog I don't know about is entered, he'll win. Bill is too good a handler not to show him at his best, and that's really good."

"So if this is going to be a kidnapping attempt, who will they want to kidnap?"

"Have you seen any publicity about the prince making public appearances? Do we even know if he is in the country? Does anyone know what he looks like?"

"Not that I am aware of."

"According to Bill, the prince loves this dog, which he bred and trained himself. I suspect the kidnappers are counting on his pride in his dog to make him come out of seclusion. I think their target is the prince."

"This is where we've got to turn this information over to the powers that be to organize a way to stop them. It's going to take man power. I'll notify the Bureau and…"

"No. You can't notify the Bureau. I know you worked there for five years, but you, more than anyone else, must know there are people within that organization who can't be trusted. I know you and Sal suspect that someone in the Bureau is behind the attacks on Agnes and me. They've been tracking us using our cell phones. Someone who knew Agnes was helping to get Bill's family out of Zanifra took advantage of that information and used her to get the plans out of the embassy. However, we do have someone we can trust who has the manpower. We need to meet with Manny tomorrow."

"Good idea. We can share what we know with him, let him know we suspect there's a mole in the Bureau and give him what we've found so they can come up with a plan to stop the kidnappers."

"Without getting me killed."

"Oh believe me, that most of all," Harry said. He leaned in and kissed me.

My mind stopped thinking about plots and dog shows. My mind stopped thinking period. I just felt and what I felt was new and wonderful and I never wanted it to stop. I turned toward him, reaching up and sliding my hand up his chest and around his neck. My whole being cried out for more, and, at the same time I felt clumsy and awkward and stupid for not knowing what my body wanted.

Harry lifted his head and stared into my eyes. "You have no idea how much I want you right this minute, but we're in Maeve's home, and she trusts me to be a gentleman. Do you trust me?"

"Yes, of course."

"Then trust me when I tell you that stopping now is the hardest thing I've ever had to do. You need your sleep because you have to show a dog tomorrow. I'm going to try to get some sleep as well. Tomorrow we'll talk to Manny about what to do with this information. I promise I won't do anything without you. But for now, as much as it kills me to say it, you sleep and dream of me." He kissed me gently, tucked the covers around me and retreated into the other room.

CHAPTER TWENTY-FIVE

I grunted, rolled over, and opened one eye, my mind taking a few minutes to realize where I was. I barely focused on the fact that someone was moving in the room and the light was on. Then the aroma of chocolate caused the other eye to snap open as my brain finally registered the presence of Sally holding a steaming mug of cocoa.

"Ah, you're a saint, Sally. What time is it? Is Harry awake yet?" I sat up, piling up the pillows behind me and lay back, wallowing in the pleasure of drinking the cocoa in bed. I felt like a princess as I let the comforting chocolate work its magic.

Sally's gray braids still held a hint of the flaming red that had always been her crowing glory. In her late sixties, she was still strong and active, though age had added to her girth slightly. She was still what Grandpa would have called a fine figure of a woman. She and Niall had been with my aunt since Maeve had moved from Ireland to England to work in MI-5 following university.

When Maeve and Padraig decided to marry, there was no question but that Niall and Sally would join them in their new home in America. As far as Killoys were concerned, they were just additional members of the family. Sally opened the hamper, plucked out my clothes from yesterday to wash, and pulled my snow boots from the closet. Shoving the closet door shut with her hip, she crossed to the bed, and flipped back the covers.

"Mr. Harry is up and dressed. He's out back with the dogs. It's five thirty, so you can't be lollygagging in bed, Miss Kate. Get along with you now. I put Mr. John's backup show bag on the table by the back door, so you'll have what you need to work on young Ajax at the show. Niall and I will take care of Dillon and see that that he gets bathed. I don't know what you've been doing with that boy, but he looks as though he's been rolling in the streets. I even found car grease on him. Oh, you should know; we've had a bit of snow overnight." She headed for the door, inspecting the room to see that everything was done.

"How much?"

"Twelve inches, according to the weatherman on the television set. Niall will use the Land Rover to deliver you to the dog show."

I slid my legs over the edge of the bed as soon as she left, grateful for the warm wool carpet beneath my feet. I really did need to get a rug for my bedroom at home.

Grabbing my old green flannel robe from the foot of the bed, I threw it over my shoulders and went to peek out the window. It was still dark, but city dark—which meant I could see the snow which was still coming down at a good clip, and the cars parked beneath the street light across the way just looked like white lumps. Closing the curtain, I glanced at the clock and dashed into the bathroom to take a shower.

Standing under the hot water, I tried to focus my mind on the discovery we'd made last evening only to find my body's focus drifting to the discovery I'd made later. I tried to shake it off as I hopped out and grabbed a towel, drying my hair and attempting to shake some sense into my brain. I wrapped the towel around me, enjoying the luxury of the thick bath mat and the heated towel racks Maeve had in every bath. Some European traditions were absolutely wonderful.

Once I was dry, I ran a quick brush through my hair then fluffed up my short curls with my fingers. I don't know how many times I'd blessed the day Agnes convinced me to cut my hair. I went back in my room and dressed while mentally going over my list for the day. I had just pulled on Maeve's jacket and was checking the look in the cheval mirror that stood beside the bureau.

"You decent?" A call came from beyond the connecting door.

"Always. I'm even dressed and ready," I quipped, feeling suddenly cheerful at the effect of the jacket on my outfit.

Harry entered, smiling and red cheeked. Though there was still snow on top of his head, he looked warm bundled in a heavy Irish-knit sweater. "This is going to be fun. They haven't plowed yet, all the airports are closed, and the trains are on a limited schedule. A perfect Monday rush hour."

I picked up the boots from beside the padded chest at the end of the bed and pulled them on.

He walked over and sat next to me on the bed. I suddenly wanted to close the space between us, but felt clumsy and awkward. He looked back with his sparkling eyes and smiled. It was clear I was not controlling what was happening here.

I looked away and said, "We can show a dog and then build a snowman."

"Sounds like a plan," he grinned, leaning back as though he'd read my mind. "Where did you get the outfit? You look nice."

I stood, raised my hands and waved, indicating the room. "You're sitting in my home away from home. For seventeen years, I've been staying in this room during Show Week. It's got a lot of my things like clothes and some of my trophies. Padraig and Maeve would often let me stay with them when the sibling testosterone got to be too much. We'd go to Radio City, skate in Rockefeller Center, or visit a museum. Dad would take me and whichever dog was mine at the moment and drop us off here. He could tell when dealing with my brothers, kennel work, or the pressures of school and show competition was getting to me. He'd just wake me up early with a hot chocolate, declare it New York Days, and tell me he'd already cleared it with my teachers."

I found myself moving around the room, my fingers seeking connections; first the desk, then the rocker, and, finally, the bureau. A framed photo rested on top. I reached out and picked it up. It was taken at a show and showed three people. I was grinning, holding a beautiful rosette, my hand resting on Dillon beside me. Behind me stood Dad and Gramps, each with a hand on my shoulder and both of them smiling.

"Kate, they'd be proud of you now."

I set the photo down and turned. With sudden tears running down my cheeks, I stepped into his hug. "How come you always know the best thing to say?"

"It's a rare talent that comes from kissing the Blarney Stone at the age of seventeen," he murmured, running his fingers gently through my curls. "Anyway, I just call it as I see it." He pushed me gently back and tipped my chin up. "Unfortunately, being cursed with honesty, I must mention you'd better wash those tears off your face. Right now, the dogs won't know you and you'll terrify the judge. That's not the look of a winner."

I dashed into the bathroom and groaned, but emerged only a minute later, back to normal. I grabbed my empty cup and my scarf from the closet and tucked my ring shoes into a tote bag.

Harry and I ran downstairs. Passing by the main floor, we tore down to the kitchen. I put the cocoa cup in the sink and hugged Sally, who now smelled of the yeasty bread she had rising on the back of the stove. Harry stopped in the kitchen, but I threw Niall's ancient mackintosh over me and headed out into the yard to check on the dogs. As I romped with Dillon and Ajax and threw snowballs, which they chased but couldn't quite catch, I spotted Harry watching from the window. I needed to talk to someone about what I was feeling after last night, but I couldn't think of whom since Agnes wasn't here. I cleaned up after both dogs and stomped back into the kitchen, covered in snow. "It's really coming down out there. I hope they made sure all the judges stayed in town last night. They're going to need a few Hummers to get them to the show site. I wonder how many dogs will miss showing. Ahh, breakfast."

"Don't you go bringing that wet snow into my kitchen, young Kathleen," Sally admonished. "You can sit right there so as not to track that wet mess all over my clean floors. You'll be leaving by the back anyway."

Harry was already settled at the table, devouring oatmeal, eggs, bacon, sausage, potatoes, fried mushrooms, and tomatoes. A heavy, white, ceramic pot of tea sat in the middle of the table, and scones, still hot, filled a basket. I fell into the chair next to Harry and began making inroads on my full plate. As Harry watched my food disappearing, He grabbed a mug, which he filled with tea, adding the right amount of milk and sugar before sliding it in my direction. I looked from the cup to him in surprise.

He said sheepishly. "Sorry I told you I notice things."

Sally finally stopped fussing at the stove and took a seat across from us, pouring her tea.

"Agnes?" I asked.

"Himself called this morning. Mrs. Sybil is taking it hard. To have criminals chasing her granddaughter has got to be worrying her something awful. But they apparently got a message, what they call a text, from Maine by way of a burner kind of phone, saying they were okay. According to Mister Connelly, Sean must have contacted a friend who bought this phone, sent the message, and then somehow disposed of it. Thank God she's with young Master Sean."

"Do you think they can keep the peace between them as they try to stay hidden?"

"Those two may have been fighting like wet cats since Master Sean was still in short pants, but they know this is important."

I laughed, knowing, that if Agnes had a choice, she would want to be with anyone else...though, maybe not. Sean had turned from an awkward teenager into a surprisingly handsome man. Plus I remembered her saying she was helping him plan a party. Hmm.

Sally pushed a picnic basket across the table. I peeked inside and saw cheese, scones and apples packed inside along with two Thermoses. I grinned and hugged her. "You are a saint, Sally."

Niall came in the door, leaving the shovel outside and reaching for the mug of tea Sally handed him. I leaned back, absorbing the warmth of this big room, its sunny-yellow walls and bright blue curtains framing windows hung with sun catchers made to look like illustrated letters from the *Book of Kells*. They had fascinated me as a child. The long oak table where we sat shone with both the wear and care it had received over the years. In the corner sat Sally's rocking chair and the table holding the lamp and stacks of fabric. On the other side, the tall wooden sewing box holding all her threads and tools for the many quilts she made. We all treasured the ones she'd made us over the years.

Niall cleared his throat. "We're good to go now. Everything is in the Rover and since it will take some extra time, we should get young Ajax and head out. I'll drop you at the pier, and you can call if you need picking up."

Harry clipped on Ajax's lead, grabbed the basket and followed me out. I'd abandoned Niall's coat for my stylishly feminine white parka, which made me feel like the Snow Queen. Harry loaded Ajax into the crate in the back then hopped into the front seat. He handed me the basket, which I held close, inhaling the aroma of fresh-baked scones.

CHAPTER TWENTY-SIX

"How long will we have to stay after the judging?" Harry turned in his seat to ask.

"We should be able to take off right afterward."

"So what's the game plan?"

"Sarah should be meeting us there. Since she's bringing the crate and grooming table from the hotel, I hope she takes the shuttle bus. It'll be safer and definitely faster than a taxi today. Carolyn, Ajax's breeder, is staying with her after the judging because they want to talk about lining up stud services for Ajax. He's just old enough and is only one point from finishing his championship. He still has more tests to do, but the early tests were good, so they don't expect any problems. Sarah will stay 'til the benching ends then Carolyn will help her get the stuff back to the hotel. Now do you think that you can play nice with your sister for a couple of hours?"

"I'm willing, but I don't know if she'll behave."

"It may not be fun, but we'll get through it. I'm counting on you not to bait her. I don't need her throwing a hissy fit in the middle of the benching area. She doesn't need that kind of reputation. Besides, I need you watching my back in case some of Agnes' fans decide that I'm really she after all."

"Not a problem."

We made good time, all things considered and joined the line of cars, vans and taxis disgorging passengers and dogs. The huge buildings had been the place where for years ocean liners had taken on passengers and cargo; now they'd been converted into something that was perfect for showing dogs. The entrance to the T-shaped building was located where the two strokes intersected. The police kept the line moving quickly, and when we pulled up to the curb, Harry and I both jumped out, Harry gripped Ajax's lead and signaled him to leave the crate as I grabbed my grooming bag, purse, and tote. Passing him the basket, I pulled out my entry papers and his ticket. With thanks to Niall, we were entering the building in just over a minute's time.

Just as in the old TV show, *Cheers*, everybody knows your name when you've shown here for seventeen years. I checked in and was immediately surrounded by people talking about the fashion show. As Harry and I edged our way forward, I answered questions and took their teasing about the strange-looking Samoyed I was showing.

Instead of heading left into the benching, I called, "No, this way," as I turned us to the right and the vendor area. Jen and Heather were just putting the last of the photos on display. The poster of Agnes as me with my old dogs held pride of place above the booth. It was surrounded by smaller photos Andy had taken of the models. In between the sample sweaters were racks of bright-colored yarns and bins of needles and other knitting tools. Candid shots from the fashion show and the reception also hung there, thanks to Andy, including the one of Agnes and me with the mayor. Arranged across the front of the countertop were books of sample patterns, and, a line of my faithful customers was already checking out the new designs. I greeted them and signaled Harry I'd be a few minutes. He and Ajax wandered off to explore the different booths while Jen, Heather and I went over all the last-minute details.

Once all the business details were covered, I allowed myself the luxury of a couple of minutes to chat with people about the show. The crowd around the booth was really beginning to build when Harry came up beside me, saying Ajax was getting antsy.

"This is great, guys." I called to Jen and Heather as Ajax tugged me out of the booth.

We walked back through the restaurant near the entrance and moved with other exhibitors down the closest aisle between the rows of plywood platforms. A sign hanging in the rafters above our heads identified each row, giving the row numbers and the breeds to be benched there. The noise—not of barking, but of hundreds of human voices—made it hard to hear anything. Harry's height had come in handy; he tapped my shoulder and pointed when he spotted our row. Then the challenge was to weave, carrying all our gear and with Ajax on lead, between the groups setting up wire dog crates and grooming tables. The crates allowed the dogs to be seen while at the same time, protecting them.

We finally located our spot and had Ajax jump up onto the bench while I tucked most of our equipment underneath. The wooden dividers designated a set amount of space for each dog, depending on the breed's approximate size. We'd no sooner gotten settled when people began coming up to tell me how much they missed Dad and Gramps and how much John and Tom had meant to the world of dogs.

I looked at Harry, and he saw how these well-meaning friends' stories had me fighting to keep it together.

He broke in and, with a smile, introduced himself as my fiancé and the brother of Ajax's owner. That took conversations in an entirely different direction and enabled me to pull myself together. Finally, Harry reminded everyone we needed to get Ajax settled and relaxed. Being breeders, they agreed this was vital for him at his first benched show. As soon as they left, Harry gathered me in for a quick hug.

"Oh, Harry," I said, hugging him back. "I knew this would be hard, but knowing it and living it are two different things," I said with a shuddering breath. Harry held my face for a minute and, looking very serious, kissed me on the end of my nose. I giggled. Now at head level, Ajax pushed forward, now being at head level, contributing a wet sloppy kiss of his own. Harry chuckled and shoved Ajax over, giving me some room to sit. He poured us some tea from one of the Thermoses Sally had put it in the basket and split a scone for us to share.

"You'd better not be feeding my dog any of that sugary stuff." Sarah's voice slashed through the moment. "It's a good thing this collapsible crate and grooming table thing you had me get has wheels, or I'd be wiped. The staff doesn't provide anyone to help."

"This is a dog show, Sarah, not the Hilton," I reminded her, reaching for the equipment. "Let's just get the crate set up and Ajax settled." I looked around until I saw a spot clear of people for a foot or so in each direction and rolled the crate there.

Harry moved forward, took the crate from me, and began setting it up. "I see that he's still around," Sarah sneered, pointing at her brother.

I planted myself in front of her just a few inches from her face. In a low voice, I said, "Yes, Sarah, your brother is still engaged to me and is, therefore, still around. I would appreciate it if you would attempt to be civil at this show. Not only does *your* reputation in the dog world depend on it, but your dog's reputation hinges on it as well. No one will breed to a dog whose owner makes snide comments about other people at shows. You may think what you want, but keep it to yourself in public. Do I make myself clear?" I finished with an emphasis on each word. The effect was the same as if I had shouted at both Sarah and Harry—stunned silence. This was right up there with things I didn't need right now. I turned on my heel, picked up Ajax's lead and handed it to Sarah.

Shouldering her to one side in the crowded aisle and making sure I had some room, I reached for the crate and flipped it open, startling Harry. He took it from me, lifted it with the door facing out, and inserted it into our assigned cubicle on the bench.

Still pissed, I grabbed the legs of the grooming table and swung them open. Harry stood it up and jumped aside to see what else was needed. I had suddenly morphed into the wicked witch scaring the children, which was fine with me. I hadn't put all this work into the dog for their antics to blow it.

I began to formulate another lecture in my mind when I thought I felt a cuff on the back of my head. Turning, I found no one there. I closed my eyes for a moment, took a breath and climbed down off my high horse. I realized it was my conscience, reminding me with one of my father's mental slaps, that telling people off might feel good, but nobody elected me God. I looked at both of them and asked, "Pax?"

They looked from me to each other and shrugged, nodding. Since the crowded aisle was filling up, I figured

I'd better claim my work space while I could. I patted the top of the table, and Ajax jumped up, placing his front feet on it. Then, with a swoop of my arm under his stomach, I hoisted him onto the table. I flipped open Dad's grooming kit, which resembled an old-fashioned doctor's bag, and placed it on top of the crate. Spreading a towel next to it I laid out the combs, brushes, dry shampoo, spray bottle of water and scissors. Taking off my blue jacket, I put on the lab coat I always wore to stay clean at shows.

"Everyone on the bus over,"— Sarah ducked, lowered herself onto the bench in the empty cubicle next to ours, and spoke in a cautious manner, not wanting to get told off again—"was talking about a woman who was murdered. They said she was found on the runway of your fashion show."

My mind turned to Sonja—first, her desperate need to stay with the dog, and then hours later, her walking away from him without so much as an explanation. Could she have found out something about the kidnap plot? Had she been involved in the plot herself? Could she have known something and been so over confident that she would try to stop it herself?

I heard Harry say, "Yes, that's true. She was found there during the party the evening before the show. Her name was Sonja Kunar, and she worked as a groomer for one of the handlers."

"Why was she on the runway? I thought only owners were modeling for you."

"They were. The police have no idea why she was there."

"According to the talk on the bus, she left the dog with her boss and just took off then turned up later, dead."

I nodded soberly. "I wish we could find out what happened to her or why she was found in that exact place. She had nothing to do with the fashion show."

Harry leaned in to hand me a spray bottle of water and a towel to clean the effects of the snow and mud off Ajax's legs. As he did, he whispered, "You've thought of something; I can see it in your face. We'll talk later. Better not to say anything here where you could be overheard."

"Well, there you are, Ajax...and aren't you looking just fine?"

Tall, broad shouldered and looking as though she had stepped from the pages of an *L.L. Bean* catalog, Carolyn Schultz swept in along with two other women. "Ladies, this is the male I was telling you about. He's by Niklas out of Tova. He is turning out exactly as I had hoped. We will see soon how he works in the ring," she paused to run her hands over Ajax's body, checking him out from shoulder to hock, "but what I see and feel here leaves me sure he'll work very well in next year's breeding schedule. Hi, Kate. I know I wrote you at the time, but let me say again how much John and Tom are missed. I am so glad that you're here and showing my boy. Sarah, you've done a good job with him. He is everything you said he was in your last email." Turning to look at Harry, she asked, "And who's this?"

"Harry Foyle, Kate's fiancé." Harry said before either Sarah or I could respond.

"Kate, you're engaged? Well, good for you. I see you've put him to work, and that's a good sign. You be good to this girl, young man. I've know her all her life, and you won't find better." Checking her watch, she took command. "Sarah, we've got thirty minutes until our ring time so why don't you go get Kate's armband? It's ring eight, and you want number thirty-three. Kate, give me Ajax's lead and Carrie, Hope, and I will make sure he relieves himself before he goes into the ring. You and your young man just take a break and relax for a few minutes." Clipping on Ajax's lead, she was gone in a whirlwind.

"Wow, is she always like that? Harry asked in amazement. She could easily lead an army, run a country, or at least be CEO of a major corporation."

"Her husband has that job, but I know for a fact that he pays attention to everything she suggests and tells people she's the reason for his success."

"I can believe it. I got the feeling that she was talking to us, but was also aware of everyone else around."

"Exactly. You can be sure that she's summed up

Ajax's competition just walking down the aisle. Nothing escapes her notice. I'll bet she'll be back in the handler area, schmoozing and checking out the dogs back there. The class competition is small, but the best-of-breed competition will be tough.

"I wonder if Jimmy ever made his flight. He's the one you replaced in the fashion show. I haven't seen him, but the bitch he's handling is the number one Shepherd, and if he makes it, she'll be the one to beat. This snow was probably what he was dealing with in the Midwest on Saturday. We'll have to wait and see who actually makes it into the ring."

We were interrupted by a commotion as a white-haired man raced down the aisle, out of breath and yelling, "Kate, I need your table now!" He threw down his bag and swung his Shepherd bitch up onto the table. Throwing his coat and blazer onto the bench, he yelled, "Towel, water, brushes…"

CHAPTER TWENTY-SEVEN

"I've got it covered, Jimmy. Just take a deep breath. You relax while I get her ready." I let the bitch sniff me all over and slipped her a dog treat before getting to work. "How did you get here? I heard the airports were closed."

"I drove. My van is probably being towed as we speak, but I knew I had to try to make it."

"Harry, pour him some tea and give him a scone." I directed, keeping my voice calm. "Jimmy, when you taste these scones, you'll think you've died and gone to heaven. They were made this morning by the best cook in the city."

Jimmy perched on the edge of the benching and ate with obvious enjoyment. He raised an eyebrow in Harry's direction. "They're fabulous. And you are?"

"Harry Foyle, Kate's fiancé," Harry answered and shook Jimmy's hand. "Kate drafted me to take your place in her fashion show."

"Congratulations. I'm Jimmy Burke. You've got the best girl ever. Kate, do you think your dad and grandpa would have liked him?"

"They'd have loved him. He's a mathematician."

Jimmy laughed. "You're right about that. Math is the family vocation if you're a Killoy. But if you were in Kate's show, what dog did you use?" Jimmy asked.

"His sister co-owns Ajax, one of Carolyn's young males, whom you'll see in the ring with me today. I think you'll like him. He's very much your type," Kate responded.

"If he's Carolyn's, I probably will. I've wanted to talk to Carolyn about Alexa. If she takes the breed and group today, I plan on pulling her to be bred. Is Carolyn here?"

"She'll be back in a minute with Ajax."

"Kate, what are you doing grooming someone else's dog?" I looked up and saw Sarah standing with her hands on her hips and a sour expression on her face.

"Sarah," I frowned at her. "This lovely *bitch* is Alexa, who will be handled by my friend Jimmy Burke here. Jimmy, this is Sarah Mondigliani, who co-owns Ajax with Carolyn. Isn't Alexa gorgeous Sarah? She's the number one Shepherd in the country." I kept my gaze firmly on Sarah as I went back to brushing down the bitch.

Sarah looked none too happy but shut up.

I said casually, "Jimmy's planning on breeding Alexa and wants to take a look at Ajax." I turned when I heard Carolyn's voice calling my name.

"He's all set and raring to go, Kate," she called from the end of the aisle as she and her friends wove their way toward me. Glancing at the benching, she yelled, "Jimmy, you made it. Oh, thank God Alexa is here." She turned to look at the bitch after giving Jimmy a hug. "She really is lovely, and from the way she handles all this adulation, I'm sure she knows it." Carolyn reached over and stroked the bitch's neck. "Don't you, princess?"

Jimmy slipped a show collar over Alexa's head and attached a lead. He gently lifted her down, much to Ajax's delight. I pulled off my lab coat and slipped my arms into the blue jacket Harry held for me. Carolyn attached my armband, and Sarah pulled a bag of bait from her tote. Carolyn took it and dumped it onto a paper towel; then, taking a knife from the grooming bag, she cut the chunks into tiny pieces and slid some into my pocket. "You want the bait to be so small the judge doesn't have to watch the dog chew it," she explained for Sarah and Harry's benefit. "Kate won't need much, if any, with her style of handling."

We all moved toward the ring. Harry slipped in next to me and took my hand. "You really love this," he whispered in my ear.

I glanced up at him and grinned. I could feel I was getting back into the groove of showing. "Absolutely." I stepped forward, feeling the old excitement return. I hoped Harry saw a different person from the slightly insecure girl he'd seen all week. Moving through the crowds in the grooming area, we took on the speed of a salmon in an upstream battle, but we finally made it.

Jimmy and I passed through the check point on the exhibitor side of the rings while Carolyn led everyone else to the other side to find seats or standing room amid the crowd. I noticed that one of Carolyn's friends spotted her and waved her over to sit in the front row. From her hand gestures, she was asking her young companions to give up their seats so that Carolyn and the obviously pregnant Sarah could sit.

While waiting for the judging to begin, I saw Harry watching his sister begin to enjoy herself and relax. I'd noticed how surprised he'd been when Sarah didn't say anything nasty when she saw me grooming Jimmy's bitch. I wondered if he realized how, with just a few words, the situation was under control. Maybe they could learn to talk to one another instead of always assuming there would be a problem? I watched as he turned his head to look behind me and, following his line of sight, I caught Sergeant Sanchez striding toward me. I was about to wave to get his attention when I heard the ring steward say, "German Shepherd open dogs into the ring, please." This kidnapping business would have to wait. I had a dog to show.

I gave Ajax a pat and entered the ring. Having watched what the judge had done setting up his earlier classes, I knew exactly where to stand. I walked into place, and Ajax, needing no extra urging, went right into his stack with his rear legs positioned with one under his hips and the other extended so the hock stood straight up. I glanced to see if the judge was ready, but he had taken a break between classes for a cup of coffee and hadn't finished yet. After a quick scan of the competition, allowed myself a second to look at the crowd. Like radar, my eyes met Harry's wink, which put a big smile on my face.

I focused my attention on the job at hand as I turned to face the judge. The judge took his first look at the entry. I stepped in front of Ajax, allowing a good twelve inches of space for the lead to drape in a loose curve, showing the dog's control and natural beauty. The dog behind us was nervous and fidgeted while the third entry's handler had to hold it in position. I thanked God for all the hours of obedience training Ajax had gone through. It was paying off with his ability to focus totally on me. Catching the judge's signal, I slipped into place beside Ajax, gave him a flick of the lead, and we were off, trotting in a line around the ring. When the judge had seen us all move, he stopped us and began his individual examinations.

I had shown numerous times under Judge Hyram Phillips. He was a big man, tall as well as broad, with a deliberate grace that came from his years as a handler. I knew he favored movement over beauty, but if you could bring both to the party, it gave you a real shot. I was ready to show him both when he asked to see the bite. I pulled back Ajax's lips so that he had a good view of the teeth. Then shifting to stand in front of Ajax, I held bait so his head was at the proper angle to show off his excellent neck and shoulder layback. I watched Phillips' eyebrows rise slightly as he slid his patient, sensitive hands over Ajax. I knew his style of structural examination was gentle, quick, and thorough.

Once finished, he stepped back, admiring the dog's solid patience. After one more overall look, then he asked me to move him in a triangle. I turned Ajax to align his start, slipping in a quick "Good boy" With a quick snap of the lead, we moved. I started slowly, making sure we had the judge's full attention; then we sped up 'til we hit the perfect speed to show off his rear in motion. I wanted all parts working perfectly together. We swung into a neat left turn, our gaits now matching. I moved Ajax across the ring showing off his side gait in the classic German Shepherd's flying trot. Finally, reaching the corner of the ring, we turned for the home stretch. I glanced to make sure we were heading in a straight line then we moved diagonally from the far corner across toward the judge to show his front-end movement. Just before we reached the judge, I gave a slight flick of the lead that was a clue to Ajax to come to a halt, shifting smoothly into a perfect stack, frozen in place, watching me.

Phillips approached, stepped in next to me and, putting his hand to his mouth, made a noise. Ajax instantly switched his focus to the judge who smiled and told me to take him around to the end of the line. I circled him around to the back of the line enjoying the applause of the crowd from ringside. Once there, I told Ajax how good he was and gave him a treat. I also allowed myself the treat of a glance into the stands receiving a smile and thumbs-up from Harry, a nod from Carolyn, and a frown from Sarah. *Oh well, you can't win them all.*

I watched as each entrant was put through the same paces as we had been. Neither dog had Ajax's calm assurance or smooth movement, what my dad use to call ownership, in the ring. Dad would stand at ringside and point out the dogs who approached showing with an attitude that said, "I'm here, so the rest of you can just go home." He drilled into me that this wasn't something that could be taught, though if the puppy showed any sign of it, it should be encouraged. Time and again he would point to a dog, and I would see that it stood out from the rest. Call it ring presence, charisma, self-assurance or what Gramps would call *savoir-faire*, but when it was there, it would draw everyone's eye and more often than not, would be the judge's choice.

The judge finished with the third dog and then walked down the line, comparing each dog to the standard of perfection he had memorized. He then signaled us to move our dogs around the ring. As we completed the circuit, he pointed at Ajax for first place, the third dog, for second and the other for third. Since this was the only class for males, this automatically meant Ajax qualified for the point being awarded today. That was all he needed to complete his championship, so I knew Sarah and Carolyn would be happy.

I stepped out of the way for the handlers bringing the bitches into the ring. Placing the ribbons on a nearby table so I could get them when I was done, I settled to watch the bitches go through the same routine. I also took the time to look up into the bleachers at Harry. Standing instead of sitting, he was and looking behind me and to my left. I turned, but the wall of humanity blocked me. I looked back at Harry and saw him relax and sit. Then he turned to me and smiled. I looked back at the ring, where several nice bitches were showing, but none was anywhere near the quality of Jimmy's Alexa.

Then the bitch judging was done, and the specials pushed past me into the ring. These are the champions who, along with Ajax who had been chosen winner's dog and the female who'd just been chosen winner's bitch, would compete for Best of Breed. The judge finished checking the armband numbers on the dogs' handlers.

Then the fun began. At a show like this that gets international attention, owners of champions travel great distances to compete. The prestige is huge and worth the effort, but it makes for a crowd. Once we had circled the ring twice, the judge divided the class and parked half of them outside the ring so he'd have room to move the remaining dogs.

The routine followed the same pattern as the classes. Once the first group was done they got parked and the rest came in along with the winner's dog and bitch and the pattern repeated. Finally, the judge brought in the first group and double checked his assessments against the whole group.

Ajax occasionally looked at me to see if we were going to do something, but his training had prepared him for long periods of inactivity, so he didn't fuss. The judge went down the line and brought to the center eight champions, plus the winner's dog and winner's bitch. The remaining handlers were thanked for showing and dismissed.

We then spread out. Jimmy was at the beginning of the line. Judge Phillips began moving dogs in pairs across the ring and back. He signaled for Ajax to cross the ring three times with different male specials. He repeated the action when pairing Alexa and the winners bitch. After one last walk down the line making his noise to alert each dog, he crossed to the steward's table, marked his choices in the judging book with the steward doing the same, and signed it. He returned to the center of the ring, carrying the collection of ribbons for Best of Breed, Best Opposite Sex, Best of Winners, Select Dog and Select Bitch, plus Awards of Merit. He then pointed to Alexa for the Best of Breed, walked the length of the ring, and pointed to Ajax as the Best of Opposite Sex and the Best of Winners, pointed to two others as Select Dog and Bitch and a final two won Awards of Merit. I was thrilled for Carolyn and Sarah.

Everyone in the ring congratulated Jimmy and me. The handler of the Winner's Bitch asked about Ajax, and I referred him to Carolyn for any discussion of breeding.

I finally got through the crowd to give Jimmy a hug and congratulate him. "It was worth the drive, I take it?" I joked.

He grinned, shifting Alexa into position to have her photo taken with the judge. I grabbed the rest of Ajax's ribbons off the table and placed him properly for his photo. Judge Phillips asked who the breeder was and was pleased when I told him. He also teased me about my new look. Knowing this was an important photo, I was glad I'd worn the blue jacket since it would look really good behind Ajax. Then Jimmy and I moved out to the lobby where everyone was waiting.

Sarah was ecstatic, and Carolyn, taking hold of Ajax with tears in her eyes, grabbed my hand in thanks. But the best reward was when Harry scooped me up, whirled me around and kissed me.

He finally set me on my feet. "That was fantastic. I see why you love it."

I grinned, knowing he needed to know a lot more to really understand why I love it, but he was getting a peek into my world and his enthusiasm made me hope there might be something for us in the future.

I was still grinning when I headed back to the grooming area, only to find Sergeant Sanchez blocking my way. "Kate, we've got to talk."

CHAPTER TWENTY-EIGHT

Sarah's face had lost its usual pinched expression and now embodied the definition of "wreathed in smiles". This Sarah, grabbed me in a warm hug and did the same to her brother–who, after a split second of shock, hugged her back, blurting out his congratulations.

His smile looked a little wobbly, but genuine. My hand sought his, and when he looked my way, I nodded and grinned. Harry's surprise at her complete happiness was obvious. Carolyn and Sarah continued accepting congratulations from those around them. When Harry's phone buzzed, I looked over his shoulder and saw a text from Sal telling him to congratulate Kate and Sarah, and that he had seen the judging live on his computer.

Harry leaned in and showed the text to Sarah then introduced Manny Sanchez to everyone, mentioning he was an old friend of Sal's.

Sarah was immediately friendly when he congratulated her on Ajax's win. He told her he'd spent time with Harry and me during the week and had really been impressed with her Shepherd.

Our group was causing congestion by the ring, so we worked our way slowly down the center row through the masses of people and dogs, heading toward our aisle. Jimmy was waiting when we arrived, and, before I even got Ajax into his crate, he and Carolyn had pedigrees spread across the grooming table and were instructing Sarah in the qualities each dog listed could contribute to possible puppies.

As soon as my hands were free, Harry placed a cup of tea into them; I exclaimed with a sigh, "Ah, tea," I exclaimed with a sigh, "the staff of life. Just what I needed!"

The crowd of shepherd admirers still surrounded Sarah and several were asking to take photos and get copies of his pedigree. One man pulled Sarah aside. I heard him ask about using Ajax at stud.

I interrupted and told him he'd have to go through Carolyn as she supervised Ajax's limited service to select bitches. As the man moved away, I smiled and whispered my advice that Sarah use that line on anyone who approached. "Until you know the pedigree for every bitch suggested to you, six generations deep, you can't take a chance of breeding Ajax to just any bitch. The resulting puppies, might sully his reputation."

She looked over my shoulder at Jimmy and Carolyn talking and nodded, "You're right. I'm just so happy everyone likes him."

Harry handed his sister an apple and gave one to me. Smiling at Sarah, he said, "This will take the edge your off your appetite until you have time to eat. You want to take care of that baby. Mom is thrilled at the prospect of a grandchild."

Sarah was the startled one this time, but, continuing the spirit of détente, she smiled at her brother. "Thanks."

Carolyn sent her friends off to buy them lunch then she and Sarah sat on an empty bench. I glanced at Harry and Manny, who nodded. Harry got my coat and reached for my grooming case. Hugging Carolyn and Sarah again, I made our excuses saying I needed to get back to Dillon, and Carolyn shooed me off, saying she had everything under control.

Again, we moved slowly through the crowd like salmon fighting our way upstream. As we neared the exit, I stopped. Opening the show catalog Harry had bought, I checked the judging schedule. "We're just in time," I said, heading back toward the rings. In the fifth ring down, the Afghan Hound Best of Breed judging was just about to begin. Flanked by the three bodyguards, Bill stood, relaxed at the ring entrance with Ashraf.

I leaned in and whispered to Manny. "Be patient with me on this; it relates to your case." I studied the crowd, easily spotting the delegation from Zanifra. With my arm through Harry's, I nodded toward the delegation. "Can you spot which one is the prince? All their robes are magnificent."

Harry looked at the group of men and boys, who looked as if they'd stepped right out of *Arabian Nights*. "Judging from the keffiyeh on their heads and the thawb and bisht, which are the robes, I'd guess the tall man, third from the left. The rest are all members of the royal household." Looking around, he pointed out several agents standing nearby on the right. Manny identified a group of New York's finest in plainclothes standing casually nearby, to the left. Looking to the ring Manny leaned in close. "Which one will win?"

"The silver should," I told him. "He's better than any of the other champions in today's competition."

The judge pulled out several champions for final consideration then pointed to the silver male as Best of Breed. The group from Zanifra began celebrating.

"Let's go." I took Harry's hand, and we hurried to the area where the shuttle busses were loading. We climbed aboard one to return to the hotel. Luckily, the back seat was empty so we could all sit together.

"You realize what that result in the ring means," I whispered as I moved my bag and tote to my lap, focusing on Harry. "Both the Afghan and the prince will be at the Garden tonight for group competition. I heard the number one and two hounds missed showing because of the snow, so he's got a good shot at winning the group. Tonight could be when the kidnapping is planned."

Manny stiffened, "What kidnapping?"

Harry leaned in, speaking softly. "We need somewhere private and secure where we can fill you in on what we've found concerning our attacks and possibly your murder."

Manny inclined his head then pulled out his phone to tell the precinct he needed the conference room. Two men who got on the bus after us had taken an interest in our conversation, but with the loud chatter between a Saluki breeder and the woman with a pair of Wirehaired Dachshunds in the seats between us, our position was as good as a cone of silence. I wasn't surprised to see them right behind us when we exited the bus a few blocks short of the hotel. We began walking toward the station when I stopped at a deli we were passing to get some bagels. I purposely dawdled, and when I stepped out of the deli, noticed our shadows duck into a doorway of a shop displaying rolls of fabric.

"If we don't want people to know that we're talking to the police, someone's going to have to do something about the two guys tailing us." I pulled the hood of my parka tighter around my face as the bone-cutting February wind tossed last night's snow back up at us.

"Got it covered, Kate." Manny nodded at a pair of supposed tourists walking toward us, their map flapping in the wind. I glanced at a shop window's reflection and saw them stop the men, getting in their way to ask directions. Manny shoved us through the next shop entrance. We ran, out the back and down an alley then repeated the process a block over, which brought us out across the street from the entrance to the Fourteenth Precinct. In less than a minute, we were across the threshold, upstairs, and pushing in the door of the conference room. The table in the center of the room could have seated a dozen but from the dings on its surface, I suspected it had seen its share of regulation shoes resting on its surface. A big screen on one wall and various electronics on a cart nearby brought the room into the new century. Manny and Harry got themselves coffee while I poured the last of the tea from Sally's Thermos. I laid out the bagels and cream cheese while Harry pulled his notes and the decoded message from his pocket. The note from Agnes was back in the hotel room, but I could recite it from memory. A raisin bagel covered with cream cheese kept my gut from gnawing through my backbone. I finished my tea, as Detective Williams walked in and took a seat.

Harry nodded for me to start. I began with last November, my trip into the city and the information sleight of hand concerning Zanifra. I spoke of my makeover, which guaranteed nobody would know I was the kid in the park. Details I gave about Bill's family explained why Agnes and I had gotten involved, and I told Williams about learning Bill's daughter and granddaughter had returned safely to the States two days ago and, how, after two months of quiet, Agnes again was contacted.

"The only difference from the earlier contacts was that this time, she got an email from Bill, instead of a face to face meeting. During a fundraiser for orphans at the Zanifra Consulate, a thumb drive ended up in her purse. She spotted it when she checked her makeup. Since her apartment was only four blocks from the consulate, a friend offered to walk her home. As they started to cross the street in front of her building, a car tried to run them down. It chased them onto the curb, hitting another car and a parking meter. Once safe in her building they called the police and reported it, but said the license plate was covered with mud, obscuring the numbers. Her friend left, making sure Agnes double locked the door. This wasn't an accident but an attempt to kill her." I paused, searching Williams' face for understanding before I continued.

"Now, in spite of the whole supermodel thing, Agnes is smart. She can add two and two and come up with a thumb drive. In the past, the passing of information had always happened within the hour if not set up differently. After three hours, she knew something was wrong, so she plugged the drive into her spare laptop. Only two small files came up, one text and one graphic. The text file was in code. Since she didn't have a key, she knew it would take time to decode. To be on the safe side, she printed it out then had her doorman ship both the printout and the laptop, along with some clothing, to safety." I paused again to see if Williams had any questions. He didn't say anything, so I plunged on.

"She put the drive in her jewelry box. The next morning at seven-thirty, a stranger knocked at her door, claiming he had come for the package. He wouldn't give his name, and he offered no password, so Agnes played dumb. He then began to get nasty. Sean Connelly, who's a Connecticut State Police trooper and a friend, showed up then and made the guy leave. Later that day, someone tried to push Agnes off a subway platform. A woman grabbed her just before the train came in. While this was happening, someone broke into her apartment and stole the drive. Since then two additional attempts have been made on her life. She decided to go into hiding and chose to disguise herself as me. Unfortunately, they were able to track her even in that disguise. So she went into serious hiding." I'd cleaned up the bagel detritus from the table as I spoke. The detective kept glancing at Manny with a raised eyebrow. It must be a Y chromosome thing. "I hope I'm not boring you gentlemen?"

"How does this tie in to our murder?" Williams' focus was totally on his own case.

"That's coming." I stood and took the bag to the trash, tossing the proverbial ball into Harry's court.

Harry sat up and restacked the papers. "The people tracking Agnes were now hunting the girl in the poster, so Kate became their next target. Getting her name from the poster, they tracked her phone, which was why they were able to locate her outside the restaurant when we walked after the ball and in the hospital waiting room. I thought that by getting Agnes out of hiding at the fashion show, and, by showing Kate and Agnes were two different people, we could get them off Kate's back."

Manny interrupted, picking up a file. "That doesn't seem to have put them off. We picked up the guy who pushed you into traffic. He was stalking you at the show this morning while you were standing outside the ring." I looked at Harry, realizing that's what he'd seen behind me. "He was carrying a hypodermic." Manny flipped some more pages. "We haven't analyzed it yet, but I suspect you would not have finished showing that Shepherd."

"Thank you." I felt someone tap dance on my grave and turned to Harry. "That's what you were looking at when you stood in the bleachers. And, in the meantime, there has been another attempt on Agnes' life. This time it took place in Connecticut. Sean's Connelly was guarding her, and, last night, his home was blown up. They escaped, but now they're both hiding, even from us."

"How does this tie in with the murder?" Detective Williams was not long on patience.

"I talked with Bill Trumbull. During rehearsals, I had found out Sonja was a trained bodyguard. It seems that her family has been guarding the royal family for generations. She was young and eager to prove herself ready to join them, so she felt as though it was a slap in the face when they assigned her to guard a dog. That accounted for her temper. When I threatened to pull the dog if she didn't behave, she panicked and begged me not to. When I told her the prince was trusting her with his most precious possession, she looked guilty."

Studying their faces, I said, "You men may think my woman's intuition is nuts, but I think she may have been involved with someone who wanted to kidnap the dog. When I pointed out Ashraf was something the prince treasured, she may have realized he could be used as bait to draw the reclusive prince out. She was smart and, in the long run, loyal. I think she may have tried to stop the kidnapping plot—and that's what got her killed." I understood her frustration all too well. "Since she'd been in the room earlier in the day, she probably felt safe when she met her attacker."

Harry picked up the papers "Agnes sent Kate a cyphered note, which told her where the coded kidnapping information was hidden. Last night, we found it, and I decoded it with Kate's help." I smiled at the credit. "What we'd found was a kidnapping plot, which will be set in motion at the Garden either tonight or tomorrow. It's all detailed here." Harry shoved the papers across the table into eager hands. "Agnes and Kate, and now Sal and I, are beginning to suspect that there's at least one FBI agent involved. This is why we didn't take the information to the Bureau. If the mole discovers the information is out, he'll still do the kidnapping, but change his game plan. Right now, they don't know we know their scheme."

Manny took the papers and scanned them, passing them to Williams. "The question is, "Will it be tonight or tomorrow?"

"Can you set up covert units for both nights? Kate, can give you the logistics on where the dog would be at any time."

I leaned forward. "I wouldn't recommend using Bill Trumbull since he might give the game away without realizing it." I reached for a copy of the building layout. "The prince's delegation will probably be seated here. It's usually reserved for dignitaries so that the cameras can find them while their dog is showing. The Afghan Hound would be benched in this section." I drew a red circle around the hound benching. "Guards should be placed here, here and here, in case the prince comes to see his dog before or after the judging."

Manny gave me a worried look. "You don't understand. That's not how these operations work. Protocols are involved. If this involves a possible international incident, the NYPD could get fried if I don't report it and get the FBI involved."

Harry took my hand. "Kate, you're going by what was in Agnes' note about not trusting the Bureau. Look, I worked with these guys for five years. I agree with Manny, we've got to bring them in."

I gasped, feeling as though I'd been slapped. I pulled my hand back and shot to my feet. "Fine. You shits can do whatever you want. Just count me out." I tugged on my coat, grabbed my bags, and headed for the door. "Go ahead and guard your butts. You can feel sanctimonious as hell while you're investigating my murder." I stormed out, slamming the door, and tromped down the stairs to the street without looking back.

CHAPTER TWENTY-NINE

I jumped, my heart in my throat, when a hand grabbed my shoulder. I spun, braced to fight. Harry's face looked like thunder.

"Where the hell do you think you're going?" His yelling caused people around us to step away. I moved closer to the building and out of traffic. "I'm finding a taxi, heading back to Maeve's and getting my dog, who at least gives a shit about whether I live or die. Then we're going to get ready for tomorrow's dog show. You can go back to your friends and plan World War Three. But, please, don't endanger my family or my dog." I shot out a hand, bringing a cab to a stop, and before Harry could open his mouth, I jumped in and told the driver to go.

After taking a breath, I gave the driver Maeve's address, leaned back, and tried to shut off the voices in my brain. My bruises and aches from the last few days throbbed, guiltily reminding me that Harry had saved my life. Harry wanted to protect me and the cops thought I was hysterical.

Meanwhile, the bad guys wanted me dead because I might have dangerous information. *Well guys, now I do.* Fat lot of good it did, since the cops were going to blow the whole deal. The bad guys would kidnap the prince and kill me and the peace talks would never happen. Then everybody else would live happily ever after...or not.

I pulled my notepad from my tote and wrote furiously. As the cab pulled up in front of Maeve's building, I saw Niall waiting on the porch. I stomped up the steps, ready to bite the next person who spoke.

"Congratulations."

"Huh?" Oh, the show. So much had happened since then, it had slipped my mind. "Oh, thanks. What are you doing freezing out here on the porch?"

"Mr. Harry called and said you were on your way. He said that you had a headache and needed some peace and quiet. Sally's made you some tea, and I'll send Mr. Dillon up to you. You've been doing too much and need a rest. I'll call you for supper." That is how I found myself coatless and heading up the stairs before I could confirm the lie.

I stopped, reached into my pocket, and took out the paper that held what I'd just written. "Niall, could you please give this to Maeve?" He took it, and I continued up the stairs, the headache having finally arrived.

Dillon was at my side by the time I reached my room. I closed the door, dropped my stuff and slid down beside the bed, my face buried in his heavy white coat. Then I let tears of frustration and anguish flow.

Dillon hates crying, but, this time, he just leaned into me, making small whooing sounds. Tired, stiff, and finally all cried out, I lifted my head as Dillon's rough tongue sandpapered the top three layers of skin from my face. Pushing him aside, I shed my clothes and climbed into a pair of worn sweats. My phone rang. I saw it was Harry and let it go to voice mail. With no strength left, I slid under the covers, ready to sleep for a week. Dillon jumped up next to me.

"Dogs are not allowed on beds." We both ignored the command as I wrapped my arms around him, blotting out all the arguing voices in my head and letting sleep pull me under.

***

My eyes opened in a dark room. I was alone in the bed. I listened for the screams in my head to continue, but there was only silence. Anger and fear were now gone, leaving only acceptance. The bed squeaked as I turned over and saw the time. Not wanting Sally's fussing, I slid my feet to the floor and made my way into the bathroom. The overly hot water seared my skin, soothed my aches and seemed to ease my soul as well. I looked in the mirror and saw no sign of the great flood. The room's temperature had me dressing quickly and I was halfway down the stairs when Niall met me with news. Guests had arrived for dinner.

"Mr. Harry has brought three gentlemen, Mr. Sanchez, Mr. Williams and Mr. Hendrix. They are in the drawing room with Herself. Sally sent me to bring you for a snack before you have to entertain them as dinner won't be until seven and she knows you don't like cocktails."

Walking quietly at his side, I made it to the kitchen and the smell of scones and marmalade. Sally pushed a mug of tea at me and ran a quick hand across my brow, checking for fever.

I smiled. The gesture took me back to my childhood, where any slowdown on my part must mean I was sick. "I'm fine, Sally. I just needed sleep."

I'd just started on my second scone when Dillon shot down the stairs, Harry following a minute later. He pulled out the chair opposite me and took the tea Sally handed him before she and Niall left the room. I had just finished putting jam on my scone when he cleared his throat.

"Remember when I first bumped into you and I said I was an idiot? Well, that's true, especially where you're concerned." I looked up at him. His face was all planes and angles hewn from granite yet able to show a sweetness that called me. He stared into my eyes. "Kate, you are a riddle wrapped up in a mystery inside an enigma, to quote Churchill, and you scared the shit out of me today when you took off. Your feelings were obviously hurt, though I'm too confused at the moment to know why. The amount I don't understand about you could fill oceans. And when I flounder around, trying to impress, I seem to have an incredible ability to hurt you."

"The cops don't need to be impressed," I said, pouting. "They pretty much think you walk on water." I stood, took both of our empty teacups to the sink, and washed them.

"The cops weren't the ones I was trying to impress." He swept the crumbs from the table and handed me the plates to wash. "You're right that we need to stop the kidnapping. But, above everything else in the world, I need to keep you from harm. You hold something of mine that would be destroyed if anything happened to you." He reached for my hand and I felt that now-familiar pull as his thumb stroked my fingers. My whole being focused on that magic thumb and my body leaned in. Then I remembered the guests upstairs which poured ice water on the moment.

I pulled my hand away. "You brought company." My protective walls slid into place as he leaned back and adjusted his glasses.

"Yes. The NYPD needed to involve the Bureau and I brought Hendrix here with Manny and Williams, so that you could tell them your plan. I've known Hendrix since I started at the Bureau. You can trust him to handle this right."

Thrown off by the statement about Hendrix, it took me a moment to realize what he was saying. I stared, wide eyed, mouth open, shaking my head. "What plan?"

"The plan you'll come up with in the next thirty minutes that will save the prince, involve both the NYPD and the Bureau and keep you from getting killed." Harry straightened his jacket and tie, then flicked some invisible lint from his sleeve and grinned. "That plan."

My incredulous stare transformed into a scowl. I folded my arms, stepped back, and stiffened.

Harry reached for my hand again. "After you left, we talked and agreed. Your life is on the line, so it's your safety first. But by using Hendrix, we can get the word back to the Bureau without alerting the people possibly involved in the kidnapping. Also, this way the department doesn't get slammed, nor the plans get changed. I told them you know this world like the back of your hand and you might be the best one to come up with a plan of action."

I snorted and stood tall, shoving my hands in my pockets. "You assume these men are going to listen to any plan that I suggest?"

"Kate, this is your world; you know the building, the people, everything involved. How much time do you need to come up with a plan?"

"I have no idea."

"Take all the time you need, provided it's no more than two and a half minutes."

He walked over and stood eye to eye with me for what felt like an excessively long minute. Then his mouth covered mine and his arms drew me in so I could feel his racing heart. I wanted to go with the moment, but I couldn't. I lifted my head. "We'd better go; your guests will be waiting."

He tried to pull me back, but I nodded toward the stairs. "This was your idea." I turned to trot up the stairs.

Maeve was holding court in her chair before the fire, and Padraig, back from Connecticut and looking normal, sat on the arm, his hand resting on her shoulder. The proverbial long arm of the law was spread along the sofa and Connolly, looking five years older, relaxed in the chair opposite Maeve. I hoped this drama wasn't going to flop.

"Sorry not to be here when you arrived, gentlemen, but I'm afraid that after the fashion show and all the activities, today's showing wore me out. I needed a nap so I'd be in shape to show Dillon tomorrow." My hand dug into the hairy white head by my knee. His hackles were up, which made me scan faces.

Harry pulled a chair forward for me and stood behind it with his hands resting on my shoulders.

I smiled. "Sally tells me we're having a celebratory dinner for our engagement." I looked over my shoulder at Harry. "I know that Sal would have loved to have been here, too, but I needed him to hold down the fort back in Connecticut. I hope you don't mind, but I asked Sally to time the meal so we can watch the group judging tonight. I wanted to see how my friend Jimmy does in the herding group. His bitch Alexa will probably be bred to Ajax this year and those puppies will be special. A group win wouldn't hurt their value. I know your sister would be delighted." I looked up at Harry again.

He smiled back. "She's already over the moon with you finishing him by going Best Opposite today. Your friend Bill will be in the hound group with the Afghan and I saw online that both Richard and Lucy took their breeds."

Manny laughed. "Carsley's Chihuahua, Spike is a shot and a half. For such a tiny dog, he knows how to grab attention."

"That's the thing. Spike doesn't believe he's small," Maeve pointed out. "Richard has always had dynamic Chihuahuas. Spike's grandfather was the same way."

Williams looked at Maeve and the trophies on the shelves at the side of the fireplace. "These dog people all seem to know each other. Yet there are hundreds of them."

"Thousands." Maeve sat forward warming up to a favorite topic. "Each weekend, they come together and compete against one another. Still, with a few exceptions, they remain friends. It's a 'build a better mouse trap' mindset of trying to breed the best dog within your breed possible. The way they can have their opinion of their dog's quality verified is to compete. Of course, it's still the appraisal of one person on one day, which is why you need to get the valuations of a variety of judges over the dog's career. Winning group and best in a show means three different judges agreed your dog was best in one day. It's what everyone wants, but to do it at this show—that's our super bowl."

"Well, Kate and Maeve can give us a blow-by-blow account after dinner, if you gentlemen aren't in a hurry. I never knew anything about this dog-show stuff 'til last week, but I must say it's fascinating." Manny got nods from the men on the sofa as Niall appeared in the doorway, announcing dinner.

The roast lamb in mint sauce, baby new potatoes, asparagus with a light hollandaise sauce, and individual loves of spinach bread had everyone enjoying the pleasure of perfectly cook food. My favorite dessert chocolate cake with cherry filling followed the main course. Coffee, tea, and brandy made the rounds to wrap up the meal. Padraig raised a glass, toasting our engagement.

Williams, Hendrix, and Harry had chatted about old cases during dinner. Hendrix teased Harry about the bets in the office that he would only marry if the woman crunched numbers all day. "How he got a stone fox like you to even look at him twice is amazing."

"It was fate. We saw each other across a crowded room and I assumed he was looking at my cousin. When he called the next day, I was so surprised I agreed to a date, thinking he'd be shocked when he saw what someone palmed off on him when he expected Agnes. Turned out, he really was insane and wanted to date me and not her. Of course, trying to get some time together while I was getting ready for the fashion show, showing Dillon and whelping a litter of puppies was a challenge, but we pulled it off."

I refused to look at Harry during my weaving of this story, but he'd set up this fantasy. We returned to the drawing room, where Niall had opened the cabinet doors, revealing a television. I returned to my seat. Harry pulled up a chair beside me and reached for my hands which I'd curled into white-knuckled fists.

The dog show began with the hound group. Bill was first out, and Ashraf looked magnificent. As they moved to their positions, I asked Manny if they'd made any progress on Sonja Kunar's murder. He said they had a lot of evidence but they weren't getting any closer to identifying the killer.

Hendrix spoke up, showing interest in the discussion, "Why would anybody murder a dog groomer?"

"Well, perhaps because she wasn't just a dog groomer—Wait, here goes Bill. That dog is really in amazing condition. Of course, Bill is no slouch as a handler either. Notice the length of the dog's gait. He floats. And the perfect stop. It's going to take a lot for one of the others hounds to top that performance."

Hendrix was looking at me. "What do you mean she wasn't just a dog groomer?"

I pulled my attention from the screen. "She was the royal bodyguard for the dog. Her job was to protect the dog, which belongs to the Prince of Zanifra. Apparently, they feared that if the prince were distracted by anything happening to his favorite dog—which according to the catalog, he bred—it could upset the peace talks later this week.

"I found out she had been nasty to the people who were involved in the fashion show, so I took her aside and we talked. This assignment was her test case before she would be allowed to guard members of the royal household. She'd been upset with playing what she considered a demeaning role as groomer. I stressed the importance of undercover work and how the prince had trusted her to guard something he holds dear. It seemed to change her mind about the operation. Maybe she found out someone was trying to harm the dog and, rather than calling in help, tried to stop it herself. It's only a theory."

"No worse than the ones we've got." Manny grumbled stretching his legs and plunging his hands into his pockets.

"Kate, tell them about the note Agnes sent you. Wasn't that about some plot?" Harry realized he wasn't an academy award winning actor and looked back at the screen. "God, a lot of these breeds I've never even heard of."

"Well, Agnes was only guessing." I began the account, my eyes constantly returning to the screen. "She found a thumb drive in her bag after she left a party at the Zanifra Consulate. She thought, because everyone had been talking about the fashion show at the event and since the prince's dog was involved, someone had given her the drive to deliver to someone involved with the show but had forgotten to tell her. On her way home, as she and her escort were crossing the street some driver chased them right up onto the curb. He was probably drunk, but she reported it anyway. Considering what's happened since, I think it was someone trying to kill her. But, back to the thumb drive.... After that scare, she got suspicious and checked to see what was on it. She found a document that was in code. Now Agnes is a puzzle nut; hell, she does the *Times* crossword in ink. So she recognized in the nonsense way the letters were arranged, that it was some coded message. Of course growing up around Maeve, we all know that a code needs a key. She was able to tell that it had something to do with Zanifra. The obvious thing was to bring it to you, Maeve, since she knows you've done so many codes for MI-5, so she hid the drive in her jewelry box, planning to bring it up after work the next day. However, while she was working, someone broke into her place, tore it apart, and found the thumb drive. What really freaked her out was that on her way home from work, someone tried to push her in front of a subway train."

"She didn't tell us that!" Padraig grabbed Maeve's hand.

"She didn't want you worried. For a few days, she went around disguising herself as me and was able to get things done safely. Someone must have caught on and she spotted them following her. That was when she really went into hiding. Unfortunately, the timing was bad because that's when I showed up. Whoever was after her decided I was Agnes and tried to kill me. Harry got the idea of having us both appear at the fashion show together to let whomever this idiot is see there are two of us. Unfortunately, when the fashion show ended, she went to spend time with Mr. Connolly's son, Sean, to recover from this madness, only to have the bad guys blow Sean's house up. And we don't know where either of them is hiding now." I stared at the dog show playing on the television for a moment.

"I've been thinking about Sonja's murder," I said finally. "I know Sonja spoke to Agnes early on the morning I arrived because someone saw her. And I'm wondering; could there have been a connection? When I spoke to Sonja, she seemed very angry at Agnes. I wonder if she was the one who was the contact for the thumb drive." I kept my eye on the screen and left my story hanging.

Williams picked it up. "Could it be possible for our victim to have been involved in the attack planned against the dog? If what was on that drive was something she was to get from your cousin…"

Manny pointed to the screen. "The dog's now at the front of the line." We all turned to see Bill and Ashraf win the group. "Hey, he won. What does that mean?"

"Well," I looked at the group on the couch, "if I were you I'd think about setting up a way to protect that dog. He'll be at the Garden again tomorrow night. That would be their last chance to get at him. I'm sure that tonight, as soon as his photo is taken, Huey, Dewey and Louie will have him whisked back to the consulate and safety."

"Huey, Dewey and Louie?" Williams looked at me while Manny snorted.

"They're the bodyguards who were brought in to protect Ashraf after Sonja's murder. It seems the powers that be in Zanifra are taking the possibility of a threat seriously. Mr. Hendrix, have you heard anything through your channels of a threat on either the dog or someone related to Zanifra?" I watched as he inched forward on the sofa. He looked decidedly uncomfortable.

"No, I haven't, but if what I've heard here is true, it looks like I need to check into it now." He stood and turned to Maeve and Padraig. "I want to thank you for including me this evening, Mrs. Donovan, Sir. Congratulations, Harry. Seems she's not just a looker, but, is smart, too. However, I think I'll go see why nothing has been done about this threat."

Harry walked him to the door, and I sat back, turning to the screen in time to watch Spike eat up the ring. It was obvious why he won so often.

When Harry got back, Maeve and I were applauding as Spike took the toy group. Harry sat on the sofa, looking toward the fire, and balled his hands into fists. "I don't think that Hendrix believes you. He hinted that you have a vivid imagination."

"He's right I do, but not where this is concerned."

CHAPTER THIRTY

The party broke up with Manny and Williams arranging we'd meet us in the morning at the piers. Harry decided he'd hitch a ride back to the hotel with them and bring the crate and grooming table to the piers in the morning. Running up, I got his pass and saw them out. Then I went back to staring at the television as Lucy got a group four, and finally Jimmy won the herding group. Connelly left, and Padraig said good-night. I clicked off the set and the room filled with silence. Maeve sat with me.

I stared at the fire, reflecting on the consistency of my life. I'd had twenty-four years without a relationship and it now looked like I might make that twenty-five. Harry was good at what he did. He had certainly convinced everyone he was my fiancé. I should be grateful for that. Hell, he'd had *me* convinced that there was something between us. However, I knew that what I had to do was going to blow this relationship to pieces.

"I think this may be a record for shortest Killoy engagement ever." I told Maeve with a sigh. "Of course, Mom will be disappointed because he's a mathematician. You know what I've got to do, Maeve...and no man's ego is going to weather that."

"You're writing him off rather quickly." Maeve watched my face, which stayed blank.

"Did you talk to AIC Billings as I asked you to?"

Maeve nodded. "I told him everything you wrote in your note. He's agreed not to act unless needed."

"If it happens the way I suspect, Harry will be justified in hating me." I stood, Dillon at my side. Maeve looked toward me and I turned toward the fire, not wanting to see the pity in her eyes. "I've got a show to do tomorrow, so Dillon and I need sleep." I leaned down to kiss her on the cheek and she took hold of my hand to stop me.

"You smile and show people your public face, and then crawl into a dark hole filled with hurt and resentment. You've been doing it for years. This week you let someone bring light into that black little corner. I saw the dark cloud lifting and hoped you would let in the sunshine and joy. You're right; what you're doing will cause a problem between you two. Maybe it will be a big a problem. But Kate, no problem is so big it can't be overcome."

"There's something else, I don't know."

"What?"

I stood in silence as her eyes still held mine in a vise grip. "How do I know whether he wants this persona that Agnes created or me? He doesn't really know me, and when I let little bits of me peek out, like I did today at the precinct or tonight, he runs away. All the hoping in the world isn't going to make this happen if it's not meant to be, so for now, the only thing I can do is show a dog."

She released my hand, and leaning in I kissed her cheek. Dillon and I headed up to bed.

In the half-glow of dawn the next morning, Sally was three steps ahead of me when I emerged from the shower. Cocoa was on the night stand and my clothes were laid out. Dillon had been gone when I awoke, so I assumed he was outside. Once again, I silently thanked Agnes' makeup experts for teaching me the skill I needed to hide my lack of sleep and the ravages of tears. Maeve's blue jacket was the only jaunty thing I brought to breakfast. I opted for the substance of oatmeal with raisins, walnuts and cranberries with my tea. Maeve was dressed and sitting at the end of the table, finishing her tea and scones.

Niall stepped in from the laundry room, his normal sartorial splendor marred with white dog hair. "If there is a loose hair left on this dog, it's not my fault."

Dillon pushed past him to greet me, looking absolutely magnificent. I jumped up from my seat and hugged the old man, who immediately grabbed a lint brush to take the hair off my jacket. "Sit and finish your breakfast. We leave in fifteen minutes."

Maeve stood, "I always liked that jacket when I wore it in the ring. It sets off the white coat so well." She headed toward the powder room as I put my empty bowl in the sink to soak. Then I checked the entry paperwork for the show. When Maeve came out, I ducked in, knowing there'd be little time later to waste on standing in line for the ladies' room.

When I emerged, Niall, now devoid of dog hair and having donned his parka, was helping Maeve into hers. I smiled in surprise and took her arm after Niall hustled me into my parka.

Maeve scooped up my tote and handed me the picnic basket. "I'm neither John nor Tom," she said with a grin, "but today I think you could use a Killoy in your corner. Let's go. We don't want to be late."

Traffic was back to normal today as we cut across town and then headed down, eventually joining the line waiting to unload at the piers. My emotions may have been scattered, but the sun peeking up over the Hudson gave the day a glow of hope. Veterans of this game that we were, Maeve and I transitioned from van to building without fuss. I pulled out my paperwork and noticed Maeve waving to the show executive waiting by the check-in area. We were through in two seconds with several of the old guard now in tow, happily chatting away with her. I steered her to the right, and we went to check the booth. Jen and Heather were busy tending to customers, but smiled and gave a thumbs-up. I turned back toward the benching and promptly bumped into Manny.

"I see you brought a bodyguard, Kate." He grinned and went on to shake Maeve's hand thanking her again for dinner.

Our movement through the aisles was impeded by everyone who wanted to greet Maeve, but we finally located our spot. Harry already had the crate in place and the grooming table set up. He'd even magically snagged two chairs, which Maeve and Manny immediately claimed. I shed my parka and jacket, slipping into my lab coat for the final grooming. I wished Harry good morning then pulled out the combs, scissors, towels and water bottle. Dillon put his front feet on the table, and Harry boosted him up. I started at the bottom, trimming any stray hairs that marred the neat look of his feet. I checked that his paw pads were clear of hair to afford him good traction. Opening my thinning sheers, I combed his hocks, getting a smooth, clean line and taking out any loose hairs Niall might have missed. I worked up his body, brushing his pants, underbelly and chest, removing any trace of mud he might have picked up outside. Finally, my muscles were getting warmed up.

When a cup of tea appeared before me, I looked up. Green eyes looked back, unsure. The smile I managed barely reached half mast, but it was the best I could do. Maeve pushed me back and took over, back combing from the base of Dillon's tail up to his withers.

Lily Peters tapped me on the shoulder then introduced herself to the group. She told everyone that she'd traveled all the way from Texas just for me to see her bitch. She wanted to remind me so I would be sure to watch for Katja in the ring. Then she dashed off.

I explained to Maeve that Lily wanted to breed her bitch to Dillon. On the face of it, the pedigree looked quite good, but I'd value her opinion since, if I agreed to the breeding, I was considering taking a stud puppy instead of a stud fee. I finished my tea and began brushing Dillon's tail as Maeve finished his ears, ruff and cheeks.

Finished now, I reached for him, only to have Harry lift him to the floor and tell him, "Shake." The physics of centripetal force in the form of a white blur finished the work we'd done, and Dillon was ready. He jumped into his crate to rest.

Maeve sat and accepted one of the scones that Manny passed out. I spotted a hand on her shoulder and looked up to see Padraig had arrived and was holding my armband. Harry picked up my jacket as I took off the lab coat and held it for me. He turned me to button it, laying his hand on my cheek when he finished. Warmth flooded me. Closing my eyes, I leaned into it. The familiarity in that rough palm drew me in and left me unprepared when his mouth lightly took my lips.

"I care." The words were so soft I wasn't sure I'd heard them. Padraig stepped forward, clearing his throat and slipped my armband over my sleeve. We then joined the flow of dogs and bodies heading for the ring.

When we got there, I saw that friends had saved Maeve and Padraig seats in the front row, and Padraig was checking his camera. I passed into the exhibitor's-only section, followed by Manny a few minutes later. It seems a badge trumps an entry form any day.

As happens at any breed gathering, it was old home week. Breed friends stay connected even if you only see them once every few years. I relaxed and chatted as the Boxer judging concluded.

Next, we watched the class dogs do their thing. I was pleased with the judge's placements. Moving in closer to the ring, I watched the class bitches. Katja only needed a single point to finish her championship. I could tell she was not in full coat, as I'd seen photos of her at her best, but bitches often shed their coats prior to coming in season. I was glad since it made it easier to observe her structure in motion. Both her front and rear movement were excellent. I noticed that when the judge moved her in the triangle she didn't get quite the extension I expected, but when he asked the two bitches to circle the ring, it showed up in spades. She obviously liked a little competition. Even though the other bitch was in full coat, her rear was close and her shoulder layback threw off the front-leg extension and made her movement choppy. Solid structure won over hair, finishing Katja's championship.

Then it was show time. We entered in numerical order, which put Dillon third. As the judge marked his book and checked our armband numbers, I chatted with Dillon, a routine I'd begun with his great-grandfather. By the time we moved, Dillon was totally focused. I lowered my hand, allowing no tension on the lead, and he responded by flowing around the ring. When the judge asked for a halt, I clicked my tongue, and Dillon slowed to a square stance, ready to relax while the others did their thing.

When the judge finished the dog in front of us, we stepped up, ready to show. I had been keeping Dillon focused with poetry recitations from Robert Louis Stevenson's *A Child's Garden of Verses.* These, along with quoted passages from *Winnie the Pooh,* had been a staple of our ring-focus exercises. Even in a quiet voice, the rhythm and cadence of these poems would hold his attention, no matter how long we had to stand around. When the judge turned to get his first look, I made sure Dillon and I were at least two feet apart, and the lead formed a relaxed U from my fingers to his collar. I stepped in when he approached Dillon's head, but the judge got Mr. D's seal of approval as soon as his hand was offered to be sniffed. The gesture sent Dillon's tail wagging to beat the band.

The judge's hands worked slowly down his body as though he were performing a tactile CAT scan of Dillon's structure. After stepping back to survey the dog, he gave him a pat and asked me to move him in a triangle. I took a breath, turned Dillon to set up his line of movement with the judge's position and gave the lead a tiny flick. Dillon trotted smoothly across the ring with every bone and tendon singing joyfully. As we turned to go back to the judge, I aligned our approach and gave my boy his head. Three steps before we reached the judge, I flicked the lead, and Dillon stepped right into a four-square stop with each foot placed perfectly. I vaguely heard applause from ringside, but what caught my eye was the half smile the judge tried to hide. We then circled the ring to the end of the line and I relaxed and switched my recitations from Stevenson to A. A. Milne.

Twenty-two champions were competing along with the winner's dog and bitch, but both Dillon and I were used to the "hurry up and wait" life of the ring. The judge worked quickly and soon finished the last dog. He had a good poker face as he stood in the center of the ring studying the full line of dogs one final time. As he strode down the line, he pulled out those he would choose the winner from and dismissed the rest of the class with his thanks.

When he returned to those left, he moved us around once without rearranging the line. Finally he turned and pointed to Dillon for breed, my friend John's bitch for best opposite and Katja for best of winners. Next, he chose his select dog and bitch and the awards of merit. I smiled accepting congratulations and hugged Dillon. Then, I turned to smile at my family. Both Maeve and Padraig were on their feet, cheering. Harry was at the end of the top row of bleachers. He'd also been cheering, but, catching my eye, he smiled and nodded. My attention returned to the ring for ribbons, photos and a compliment from the judge under whom I'd never shown, but definitely would again.

I exited to more congratulations, including those from Manny, who shadowed us back to the lobby. While Maeve and I hugged, Padraig offered to take Dillon out to relieve himself. Once back at the benching, Lily arrived with Katja. Two seconds later, Maeve had her up on the grooming table and was running her hands over the bitch. When she finished, Maeve asked to see the pedigree. Conversation for the next ten minutes dealt mostly with genetic contributions from each ancestor and what each could possibly deliver to a potential litter. Finally, amid smiles, handshakes, and a nod from Maeve, we agreed to the breeding. Since her season was still six weeks away, we agreed Lily would bring Katja to Connecticut then. Lily had relatives in northern New York State, and she'd accumulated a lot of unused vacation time in her job as assistant district attorney, so she and her husband were planning on turning the breeding trip into a family reunion.

Jen and Heather ran by with congratulations. Cathy Santos and Heather's boyfriend were covering the booth so the girls could watch the judging. Jen told me she had shot video, which she would send me.

After Padraig returned Dillon, he went with Harry to buy lunches. When they returned, he and Maeve headed out, taking the picnic basket and Dad's grooming bag. Maeve wanted to nap so she'd be in good shape for the group judging tonight at the Garden.

Manny had joined Harry and me, and we ate while chatting about what would happen this evening. Since we had taken breed, we were free to leave early. The extra sets of hands helped with getting everything packed up and into Manny's own station wagon for the trip across town. He stressed that since Williams was directing tonight's operation, he wouldn't be able to be with me all the time. He and Harry shared looks, which again required a Y chromosome to read.

Once back in the hotel, we headed for our room and sent Dillon to his crate for a nap. I took a hot shower and lay down. Harry turned on the television and found an old black-and-white mystery movie to watch. Not able to sleep, I studied Harry. I memorized the angles of his face which, after tonight, I probably would not see again. He must have felt my gaze because his green eyes turned to lock on mine. We stayed that way, not speaking, as the movie score performed a background to our silent drama.

Then awake and ready to go, Dillon gave me a big sloppy kiss breaking the mood. The clock declared it was the end of our intermission. Act two was about to begin.

CHAPTER THIRTY-ONE

A doorway big enough to let in an eighteen wheeler gave access to the benching area tucked away under the stand's seating which would later be filled with thousands of dog enthusiasts. The line moved quickly, leaving us to follow the signs arranged by group to our benching area. The benching was alphabetical, so we were between the Saint Bernard, who had yet to arrive, and the Siberian Husky, whose handler I knew because she also handled Sams.

Harry set up the crate and lifted it into the slot labeled Samoyed. He shed his topcoat, folding it neatly and placing it with his hat on the crate, which he opened to let Dillon leap in. The grooming table came next, and I slipped off my parka and jacket in favor of my lab coat. Now came the waiting. It occurred to me, that we hadn't had supper. I was about to say something when Manny earned Angel status by walking in with a bag from Nathan's. Hot dogs and fries, plus onion rings all topped off with slices of Lindy's cheesecake. It was a meal definitely sent from heaven.

We were just polishing off the last crumbs when a woman appeared, teetering on four-inch heels and struggling to keep from being pulled over by the tug of her Saint Bernard. The dog was lunging at every canine he passed, and, though she made a valiant effort to stop him, she was losing the battle. As he leapt toward Dillon, I grabbed the massive lead from her hand, did a quick about turn, waved to stop people about to step into his path and halted.

Reaching into my bag, I grabbed a training lead, slid it over his head and gave it a quick snap. "Sit." I commanded.

The bruiser may have outweighed me, but I had at least five hundred pounds of experience on my side. Half way into the sit, he spotted a Dobie and lunged, becoming almost airborne, as I used all my force to snap a correction and execute another about turn. He landed in a sit.

"Heel!" I ordered.

I took advantage of his momentary obedience by moving the beast four steps forward then demanding another sit. We repeated the routine of heel, four more steps, and an about turn. I saw that Harry had the woman's crate in place with the door open, and, the panicked dog was delighted when our next move was to the crate. He jumped right in and when told and lay down, seemed content with the familiar. I looked at the much-chewed, stuffed elephant sticking out of the woman's tote, grabbed it and gave it to the dog slipping the training lead off. I closed the crate door. Once again, peace reigned.

Two men rushed up. Konner Montgomery, a handler I'd seen now and again but didn't know, began yelling at the woman about her having taken the dog from the room. It turned out he and the woman's husband were in the bar when they realized they were late. They saw the dog was gone and panicked.

"You said he had to be here by five," the distraught woman explained. "When I couldn't find you, and you didn't answer your phone, I just took him. I didn't realize he'd become Cujo when he saw other dogs. He's such a pussycat at home." Tears followed.

As the handler opened his mouth for a second rant, I stepped up to the woman. "You did your best. You couldn't help it if these irresponsible clods were off getting soused. Why don't you go fix your face and then get yourself some coffee?" The woman scooted off, and I turned to stare into Montgomery's thunderous face.

"Who the hell…" he began with a snarl until I stuck my hand in front of his face.

"*I'm* the person who saved your asses. If that dog had bitten someone, not only would *he* be out of the show, but both of *you* would be facing lawsuits...not to mention, the AKC would be looking plenty hard at whether to let you keep your license since you were off drinking instead of taking care of your dog. Oh, and the next words out of your mouth will be 'Thank you.'"

Shouts of approval and agreement followed from the crowd. Without a word, Montgomery stomped off. The husband, who happened to be a lawyer and could add two and two together, uttered a quick thank you and went to find his wife, leaving their dog unattended.

I leaned on the grooming table and looked at Harry. He stared at me, white faced. "He could have...."

"Bitten me? Yeah, I know. I had to do that in the group ring when I was twelve, and I've got the scars to prove it. You'd think I'd learn, but I never do. It was stupid, but the alternative could have been worse. The dog was terrified and panicked. He needed the security of a firm hand, though my arm is going to ache something fierce tomorrow from hefting him. But you're right. It was stupid. Boy, I sure could use a cup of tea."

Harry grabbed Manny's shoulder, muttered something, and staggered off. I watched his back, feeling the hammer work yet another nail into the coffin of this relationship. I glanced over at the cop, who was smiling, and raised my brows.

"He wants me to use the handcuffs on you."

I nodded, smiling, and looked up as Jimmy strolled by. "Hear you've been throwing Saints around just for fun."

"You know me, Jimmy, a pushy bitch, never satisfied with the status quo. A girl's got to get some exercise."

"Your fiancé looks a little the worse for wear. I think you scared the guy."

"I did. He's probably checking train schedules back to Boston."

"He just needs to get to know you. If he bails now, he's not worth keeping." His arms came around me in a quick hug. I mumbled my thanks, patted Alexa and then, hearing the announcer call the Non-Sporting Group into the ring, laid out brushes, combs, towels and water. Dillon got up on the table, and I mentally blessed Niall. Dillon's coat was good to go as soon as the snow spatter was off his feet and belly hair. I still brushed him head to toe, but more to calm myself than anything else.

Listening again to the announcer, I took off the lab coat, put on my jacket, fished out my armband, slipped it into place, and stuffed everything else back into my bag. I grabbed a little bit of bait, just in case. Tossing everything into the crate, I locked it and headed out with Manny at my side. We'd almost reached the staging area when a hand slid into mine, and Harry walked me to the check-in.

"You scared me, Kate. If anything happened to you…."

"Harry, this is my world. It's the same as I'd worry about you in a shootout. Life is messy. I use the tools I have. I'm sorry I scared you, but I can't tell you I'd never do it again under the same circumstances." I glanced over my shoulder then back at him, feeling my tenuous hold on this thing we had disappearing. "I've got a dog to show. If you're still here when I come out, we can talk." I walked with Dillon up to the steward and checked in.

When I looked back toward the entrance, Harry was gone. Retreating to the edge of the group I closed my eyes so I could pray for help, but, instead, I heard Gramps' voice saying in my head, *Pray for help all you want kiddo, but God expects you to work your fanny off, so focus on the job at hand and get in the ring and do it.* Applause brought me back in focus, and as the Non-Sporting dogs filed out, I shook off my pity party. There was work to do, everything else could wait. I stood up tall, and smiled. With an imaginary hat tip to Gramps and Dad, I gave Dillon a pat and we walked into the ring.

Dillon signaled me he wanted to show as we circled to our spot. I apologized for being distracted and focused on him, sparing only quick glances to check out the competition. This was a good group, and it was going to require a great performance. I stared at Dillon as each burst of applause sounded, and he beat out a happy dance. Ego has never been lacking in my boy. The judge, Mrs. Mabel Coggeshall, signaled the first half of the group to move around the ring and then, one at a time, she examined those dogs.

Then it was time for the second half of the group, including us. I'd been pointedly ignoring Montgomery's Saint Bernard while we were waiting, but when we began to move as a group, I noticed him begin to purposely swing his dog toward Dillon. I'd seen this trick pulled in the ring in the past and knew what to do. I stepped in front of Dillon just as the big dog would have hit him and took the blow myself, staggering perhaps slightly more than necessary.

"Control your dog," the judge ordered Montgomery. I noticed that the Saint was shaken by the encounter and had gotten off to a rough start. Dillon, on the other hand, slid into his Joe Cool mode. With the extra space we'd gained as a result of the encounter, he was able to stretch out and fly. He sailed around the ring to cheers, and I got the distinct impression he was so 'on' tonight I could have gone out for tea and scones and he would have shown himself.

When Mrs. Coggeshall began her individual examinations of the second half of the group, I slipped into my poetry recitations, but Dillon only gave me half an ear. Rather, he focused on the other dogs and the crowd. Instinct told me not to cramp his style, so I let him choose the music for this dance. The judge finished her examination of the Saint Bernard, and it moved down the ring as I stepped out into the examination area giving Dillon every inch of lead I had.

When the judge turned toward us, Dillon stood frozen, head up, muzzle parallel to the floor, tail firm over the back, every bone and muscle sorted, cataloged, and filed. *Perfection!* Then Mrs. Coggeshall approached, and my flirt's tail went into motion. She gave Dillon her hand to sniff, which is the ritual handshake, then she checked his bite, his eyes, head shape, ears, neck, shoulders, upper arm, depth of chest and worked back to the rear legs, hocks and, of course, the family jewels. That tail only stopped moving when the she took hold to check it out. When she was finished, she stepped back, and Dillon gave a little shake, flashing a brilliant smile as she whistled. She chuckled.

She asked us to move, and following a turn to line him up with her position, I gave him his head. He built to the perfect speed to show those bones and muscles doing their work. The crowd loved it as we flew to the end of the ring, whereupon he swung into a perfect return without breaking stride and headed straight for his new friend. He was smiling every step of the way. When I flicked his lead, giving the signal to stop, he slowed to align his body and landed, four square, then turned his glorious smile on her. I was sure I heard him say, "Ta-da." She smiled back, and, had us circle around to our place.

Noticing Montgomery's stormy expression, I made sure my body was constantly blocking my dog from any other tricks.

A few minutes later, the judge began her last look at each dog, walking slowly from one to another, doing her whistle to check their expressions. When Dillon saw her coming, he turned up the wattage and sparkled. There was definitely a love affair going on here. When she finished, her review, she began pulling out her choices. Group judges usually pull out all the dogs worthy of recognition for their performance on that day. She had pulled out eight when she pointed to Dillon telling me to take him to the number-two position. When she finished her last look, she asked the other dogs to step back and had the line of those pulled out circle the ring. We moved once around and then she went one, two, three, four. The Dobie was first, Dillon second, the Bernese Mountain Dog third, and the Portuguese Water Dog fourth. I whooped, hugged Dillon, congratulated Watt Thorington, the Dobie's handler, and when given the ribbon, thanked the judge. She commented that my dog was a real charmer. I exited with the others to make room for the terrier group to come in. Friends with dogs in that group shouted congratulations.

Still walking on my own personal cloud, I looked around for Harry, but saw neither him nor Manny—nor any police presence. I stepped over to wait to have my photo taken with the judge, keeping my eyes peeled for any sign of security in the area.

I spotted Richard and Spike heading toward the check-in steward. Seeing the ribbon he congratulated me. Jimmy appeared, patting me on the back and said he'd heard. I watched as the judge arrived for the photos and when she'd finished the other placements, I took my place on the podium. Dillon stepped into place before me but wouldn't take his eyes off the judge long enough to make it a good shot. Jimmy finally let out a whistle, and as Dillon looked, the photographer took the photo. The judge then said that it had been a mighty difficult choice between first and second. I was delighted.

When I came out, Richard said that I should probably stay where I was because there was a big dust-up going on with cops and a bunch of people in the lobby. They weren't letting anyone go up there or come down to the grooming area. I turned and saw Bill and the Afghan hurrying toward the staging area with a young boy at his heels, carrying brushes and water. He didn't have his entourage with him, which worried me. He paused to get his breath, and I asked what was going on.

"Some idiot set off a smoke bomb near the box where the Zanifra delegation was seated. Security cleared the area. Then some people pulled guns, and police were everywhere. I was barely able to get through the barricade around them to get Ashraf down here to show."

We stepped over to the corner. "Catch your breath and get calm so you don't throw Ashraf off." I advised. I turned to the boy, who had a hand on the dog's back and was watching our interchange.

"Perhaps you might want to brush Ashraf. I'm sure it would calm him so he will show in the ring at his best." The boy was startled, but immediately complied. Bill went to say something, but I saw the boy shake his head. Suddenly it dawned on me. The prince who was in danger stood right next to me, a twelve-year-old, wearing blue jeans and a Yankees sweatshirt. Only his keffiyeh and regal bearing gave a hint of the truth.

"How convenient it is to find you both together." Agent Hendrix appeared out of nowhere, wearing an

NYPD jacket with his hand in his pocket, holding something. He blocked our exit. His disguise had let him slip by security, unnoticed. "We're going for a little ride. With all the excitement going on in the lobby, we'll just use the service door. This close to the end of the show, they won't be checking for paperwork. Just leave the dogs behind. You can tie the leashes to that post; first you, Your Highness, and then you, Kate. I'd hate to have to shoot such beautiful creatures." He pulled out a gun with a silencer attached that made the barrel seem a mile long.

"No." The prince held himself still, showing no fear. His bearing seemed to increase his five-foot six-inch height. Seeing a momentary distraction and using the large second-place rosette for cover, I slid my hand down Dillon's lead and flipped open the clasp. The dog's focus was on Hendrix and his hackles were up. I needed either time for help to arrive or a good distraction. Taking a breath, I stood tall, looking Hendrix right in the eye.

"His Highness is correct. We're not going anywhere. But since we're here, tell me, Hendrix, why did you kill Sonja? I can understand your trying to stop Agnes after you stupidly gave your plans to a code breaker, but Sonja?"

His lip curled in a snarl. "She was a good little traitor until she talked to you and developed a conscience. It's your fault she'd dead."

A sudden movement came from my left. Harry raced around the corner, heading straight for Hendrix at a dead run.

"Hold it right there, Foyle." Hendrix raised the gun, pointing it directly at me. "Don't come any closer. Take your gun out and put it on the floor, Harry, or your lady love dies right here. And don't pull any lame-brained stunts; I won't miss at this range." He watched as Harry slowly pulled his gun from his back holster and, holding it with two fingers, bent forward to lay it on the floor.

Hendrix's gaze followed Harry's hand which was what I needed. I whispered "Stick!" and Dillon shot forward, tore the gun from Hendrix's hand, circled our group and came to sit at my feet, his "flag" in salute. Hendrix dove toward us.

Harry, his gun now in his hand, pointed it at Hendrix and yelled, "Freeze, Hendrix, or I will kill you."

Agents flooded into the area from behind pillars and curtains. I took the slobber-covered gun from Dillon. Hugging him I told him what a super dog he was, gave him a treat, and told him to heel. Manny ran in, spotted me holding the gun and took it.

Other exhibitors who had become pantomime players frozen by this drama, came to life, and, everyone talked at once. I turned to the young prince and suggested that now, more than ever a brushing might, calm both him and Ashraf. With a slight smile, he stepped over to Bill's side and started stroking the brush over the dog's coat.

Harry spun me around, lifting me off the floor in a hug. Flinging caution to the wind, I threw my arms around him. I could feel his heart racing. He kissed me and hugged me again. For the second time this evening, I was filled with joy.

Then he set me down, took me by my shoulders and held me at arm's length. "You have aged me at least ten years today. When I saw Padraig leaning over the stand waving, saying you were in trouble and he couldn't get to you....When I realized I'd left you unprotected.... Kate, I...." He couldn't complete a sentence if his life depended on it. My hands reached to stroke his face sliding around his neck to hold him close.

I momentarily looked aside as the announcer gave the winners of the terrier class, I saw my friends get ready to enter the ring for best in show competition. The prince, water and brush in hand, moved to watch, accompanied now by Huey, Dewey and Louie. Halting, he turned back for a minute and bowed to me then left to get a good view of the judging.

Harry's arms were still holding me when AIC Billings walked up. "You're a lucky man to have this woman, Foyle. Miss Killoy, I want to thank you for the heads up. Maeve said that you suspected there would be a kidnapping attempt here right before Best in Show and you suspected who would be involved. We got it all on film, though I must say you surprised us with that trick of the dog grabbing the gun. It saved the day, so thanks."

Harry looked from Billings to me and back. I could read his thoughts and they weren't happy ones. Maeve and Padraig rushed up, full of hugs and congratulations on the win and praise that Billings had said Dillon saved the day. I stepped back from Maeve's hug to return to Harry, but he'd vanished...and with him went my hope.

Now came the questions, the paperwork, the requests for fingerprints and more. I answered on autopilot not caring. I heard the announcement that Jimmy had taken Reserve Best in Show and that Bill and Ashraf had won it all.

I was glad for the prince's sake, but I just wanted this day to be over. Aware of Harry's leaving, Maeve agreed when I claimed exhaustion and asked Padraig if we could leave. We gathered up my gear. Harry's hat and coat were gone. We left through the big work doors out into the city night. Manny was waiting with a vehicle to get us safely home. Thanking him, I slipped in next to Maeve with Dillon at my feet while the men loaded the gear. I just wanted to get home to my tiny house, my dogs and puppies and our routine. After today, cleaning up dog poop would look good to me.

CHAPTER THIRTY-TWO

I may have slept some, but I was up and dressed when Sally came to wake me. Dillon had slept in the kitchen with his grandma and was out romping in the snow. I packed my tote, carefully folding the blue jacket and sliding it in next to my ribbons before walking down to breakfast.

Niall was hanging up the phone as I entered. He pulled out my chair. "Mr. Mondigliani will be waiting in front of the hotel at eleven-thirty sharp. But before that, Detective Williams will meet with you at the precinct at nine o'clock. Mrs. Sarah has checked out of the hotel and is spending the morning with someone named Carolyn. She will meet you in the lobby at eleven-twenty. Due to the fullness of this time line, I shall be accompanying you to the hotel to facilitate the packing. We leave in twenty minutes, so I suggest you have breakfast. Mr. Dillon has been fed and exercised and is ready to go."

My seven-year-old's, "Yes, Niall" response left my lips, and, for a few seconds, I found myself back in the security of those early years. I looked at the man, who had shown little visible change in all those years. This morning, his clipped recitation of what would happen while brooking no disagreement was a balm to my soul. I longed for any sign of order after my week of chaos.

I ate quickly, adding Sally's travel snacks to my tote. It was quiet because nobody wanted to mention the call that hadn't come. When Dillon came in from the yard, I pulled his travel collar from the tote's pocket and slipped it over his head, pulling his matching lead from the hook by the door. Niall and I headed up the stairs to the front hall. Maeve and Padraig waited there with quick hugs and news that Sean and Agnes were returning from Texas where they'd been visiting a designer friend of hers. She would see me next week.

When we arrived downtown, the exodus was in full swing. We threaded our way through the masses of humans and canines. Once at the room, a quick glance told me no trace of Harry would be found. Niall tended to the suitcase packing while I dismantled the dog setup. The stack of luggage was loaded on the luggage carts and the room was returned to its normal state in nineteen minutes flat. I asked the bell captain to arrange for it to be brought to the lobby by eleven-fifteen so Sal wouldn't be delayed. Then I checked out.

We took a cab that would drop me at the precinct before taking Niall back home. Much to my surprise, Niall said he wanted to offer me advice. "Miss Kathleen, I have known you all your life and have watched you grow from an eager child to a strong and beautiful woman. You have worked hard to become exceptionally good at your design career and at your dog career. What you haven't done is actually worked at love. People talk about falling in love being wonderful, and it is. It is also fragile. Love easily withers if care and hard work are not put into helping it grow. If there's one thing I know, you are not afraid of hard work." The cab pulled to a stop in front of the precinct. "Don't lose something of value because you don't think you can succeed. Success isn't given to you, my dear. It's earned. Good luck, Miss Kate, and come back soon."

I watched the cab disappear as Niall's words filled my mind. They would have to be filed away for now then taken out and examined later. For what I hoped was the last time, I opened the precinct door.

Dillon led the way as we approached the desk to let them know I'd arrived. The desk officer nodded for someone to escort me up; Dillon's reputation apparently gave him carte blanche.

When we got to the conference room, it was full. I was introduced to those I didn't know in the NYPD, FBI, the State Department and members of the Zanifra delegation, who were there along with Huey, Dewey and Louie. Hands reached to pull out an empty chair in front of me so I could sit. I turned to express my thanks and looked into the beautiful green eyes I thought I'd never see again. Harry slid into the chair next to mine, and Dillon snuggled between us, sharing his love.

AIC Billings called upon Harry to begin, but Harry deferred, saying it was my story to tell. So I began once again with the November day when Agnes arrived and drew me into this adventure, and finished up with the events of last night—Hendrix's unsuccessful attempt to kidnap both the prince and me, his threat to kill me, and his confession that he had killed Sonja Kunar. I occasionally glanced at the stenographer in the corner of the room, taking the whole story down.

For forty minutes, I was peppered with questions from every part of the alphabet soup of agencies before me. I spoke of my conversation with Sonja Kunar, and one of the Zanifra gentlemen asked about her behavior, what she had done, what she had said, and why there was a knitting needle available to kill her since she had no knitting skills.

Williams nodded to me, and I explained it was a tool that she would have used to untangle Ashraf's coat and would probably have had in her pocket.

They asked Harry about the attacks on me, and he and Manny described the men who had carried out the attacks.

Apparently, because of my recall of the van's license plate, they'd found the vehicle and eventually the driver, who gave up the shooter. Billings revealed they had found a connection between the shooters in the van and the operation in Massachusetts last year in which Harry had been involved.

The entire session was a grinding exercise of give and take. We gave, and they took. Nothing was volunteered about Hendrix or the others involved. When I asked, I was told that, since it was an open case, they couldn't discuss the details. So I asked if I could safely walk the streets without guarding my back from attacks from the FBI, which got me dirty looks from most of the men in the room, but a reassurance from Billings.

At that point, I checked my watch, stood, informing the group I had to leave to meet my ride back home to Connecticut. "If you have any further questions," I said, you know where to reach me."

Manny, Harry, and Williams stood when I did; slowly, the other men in the room did as well. Williams thanked me on behalf of the NYPD for my help in solving the murder and, in preventing the kidnapping. His bosses and the rest of the suits muttered their agreement. As Harry held my coat, a man stepped forward from the Zanifra delegation. He handed me a jeweler's box.

"Personally and on behalf of the people of Zanifra, I wish to thank you for saving my son's life. I have been advised"— he bent and placed a ribbon with a medal hanging from it around Dillon's neck—"that I must, also convey my thanks to this dog as well and that you would understand." He nodded and returned to his delegation at the end of the room.

Harry slipped into his coat, took my arm, and we left. On the sidewalk, he put on his hat and took Dillon's lead. He slid his arm once more through mine, and we walked toward the hotel. Silence swirled between us until we approached a Dunkin' Donuts. I stopped. "I need a cup of tea."

We turned in, snagged a table by the door, and Harry stepped up to the counter. He returned in a couple of minutes with tea, croissants, and marmalade.

I sipped my tea and began on the food, knowing I needed to say something. "Why did you bail on me last night?"

Harry, slowly organized our trash into the molded carrier box that had held our order. "I needed to think, and I couldn't do that with you in my arms."

"And *were* you able to think once I wasn't around? Did you come to any conclusions?"

"Actually, I spent most of the night sitting in on the questioning of Hendrix. Billings felt I'd earned that."

"What did you learn? I know you might not be able to tell me because of all that mumbo jumbo just now, but I'd like to know what you learned."

"Well, my friend Hendrix was a bastard from first to last, as I suspect you already knew."

"Dillon didn't like him."

Harry laughed, reaching down to pet Dillon who was hiding under the table so we wouldn't get tossed out the door. "I've learned to respect his judgment in all things.

"Anyway, it turned out Bill Hendrix was building his retirement portfolio working both sides of the law. Remember I told you there had been a mole in the office that blew my cover in Springfield? Hendrix passed the information in exchange for a cut of the action. Conveniently, he was able to make some contacts with the group that shot me, and when he needed some out-of-town muscle and gunmen, he had a ready source."

I looked down at my hands, which had on their own, grabbed his. When I went to pull away, he tightened his clasp.

"Why did they give Agnes the drive?"

"He knew about her work with the state department and figured they could use her as a mule then take her out. Apparently, her work at getting your handler friend's daughter out of Zanifra uncovered a covert smuggling operation that was hiding behind the cover of the school. The teachers didn't know about it because it was run by a local leader who was trying to overthrow the standing government. When the State Department people went in, they uncovered the truth, and the government of Zanifra was more than happy to pay for the woman and her daughter to return to the US."

"So his attacks on Agnes were not just to protect the plan, but to exact revenge. I suppose that he was getting money from that as well."

"He was being paid to keep the rebel group informed. They were also behind yesterday's kidnapping attempt, and after they collected the ransom, the plan was to murder the young prince and you. Hendrix would get to keep the ransom money."

"Harry, you need to choose better friends." He looked up to see my smile and nodded. The moment passed quickly, and a glance at my watch told me we had to go. I grabbed my tote and put it on the table. When I stood, it fell open and the box the prince had handed me slipped onto the table. Harry picked it up to put it back in my bag.

"What's in this? Do you know?"

"Probably a medal; open it."

He found the tiny catch on the front of the box and opened the clamshell lid. We both sat again, blinking at the display sparkling within. Lying on the box's satin lining was a necklace dripping in diamonds, rubies and emeralds with earrings to match. Harry quickly snapped the lid down so nobody passing by could see it.

"Wow!" I exclaimed in a hush as he carefully tucked the box back into my tote bag.

Harry stopped me as I started to rise. "Before we go, I've got a couple of things to say. If I don't get them out now, I might never have the nerve. You're right about my needing to choose better friends—especially one friend who is immensely important to me." He pulled a small box from his pocket. "After that king's ransom, this is going to look pretty paltry. We never got to go shopping for an engagement ring and, considering the circumstances, it might have been a little premature. But while I was at the show, Monday, I found something I'd like to give you."

He opened the box. Inside lay an exquisitely designed gold ring. It had a flat band into which had been carved a design of two Samoyeds running beside three reindeer. I was familiar with the artist and I'd always wanted a piece he'd designed, but I'd never consider buying it for myself.

Harry took my hand and slipped the ring onto my finger. "I don't think we are ready to be officially engaged, Kate. But I would like this to be a promise ring between us. I need to get used to being in love with a woman who cares so much about people, animals and what is right she's fearless when challenged. And I hope you care enough about me to explore where this thing between us could go."

My hand sought his face and rested on his cheek. "You are more than a friend, Harry. I love you. But as I was reminded today, falling in love is the easy part. Creating a lifetime of love takes a lot of work, and maybe that's what we need to do. But don't worry, I was also reminded I've never been afraid of hard work."

Harry picked up my hand and kissed it, then leaning in kissed my lips, just to seal the bargain.

"Well, it's certainly not the most valuable piece of jewelry you got today," he said as he stood to shepherd me to the door.

"Yes, Harry, it is. I only wish I had something to give you so you'd remember me."

"Believe me, Kate, I don't need a token to remember you." He pushed open the door and stood aside to let me exit.

I chuckled and danced away from him as we regained the sidewalk. "Oh, that's right. All you have to do is look at the scar from the bullet you took for me, and you'll say, 'Ah yes, that Kate Killoy. What a piece of work she is.'"

Dillon barked and jumped up, catching my silly mood. Harry took my hand, and with our time running out, we raced to cover the blocks to the hotel. We arrived in the lobby with five minutes to spare.

Standing with Ajax, Sarah was talking to Carolyn and Jimmy. I spotted the carts holding my stuff just as Sal pulled up in front. I signaled the bellhops while Sarah shouted her goodbyes and moved toward the van. Harry and I pushed back out through the door to the sidewalk. I put my hand up and stopped.

"Wait a second I do have a gift for you that is truly equal to diamonds, rubies, and emeralds." I dug down into the bottom of my bag and came up with a red-plaid tin. I held it out to Harry, who took it and popped open the lid. The smell of Sally's scones filled the air.

Smiling, he closed the lid. "You're absolutely right about that. It's perfect." After shaking hands with Sal and putting Dillon into his crate, Harry opened the passenger door. He pulled me into his arms and kissed me in a way that chased away all my doubts.

Finally, as though handling something precious, he tucked me into the front seat, fastened my seatbelt, and reminded Sal to drive carefully. With one last kiss, he shut the door, slapping his hand onto the roof. I looked back to see him one last time, as he watched Sal ease the van out into Manhattan traffic.

Here is a sneak peak
at Peggy Gaffney's next
installment in the

Kate Killoy Mystery Series:

Suspense for the Dog Lover

PUPPY PURSUIT

Learn more by visiting
www.peggygaffney.com.

CHAPTER ONE

"Kate, I don't understand how you managed to live in the twenty-first century and travel all over the country showing dogs when you've never flown." Sal Mondigliani, my kennel manager settled deeper into the second of my two kitchen chairs and I knew another fear-of-flying lecture was about to descend on me.

"We drove. Gramps, Dad and I were always taking a bunch of dogs somewhere. We'd load up the van and hit the road. Plus, that way we got to see the country."

"Wait. Are you afraid of flying?"

Bam. There it was right on schedule. "Sal, I'm not having this discussion. In the last twenty-four hours, every Killoy possessed of a Y chromosome has weighed in on the subject. Seamus has been inundating me with statistical information on car versus plane crashes, Tim with the aeronautical data on lift forces, Tom on time versus cost ratios and

Will has forwarded me forty-one online articles about overcoming the fear of flying. In spite of—or maybe because of—this, I will admit I'm not looking forward to flying to Denver alone this afternoon."

"Didn't Foyle say that he had to be in Denver tomorrow? Weren't you two going together?"

"Apparently not." The hurt I was struggling to keep out of my voice crept in. Harry Foyle, my sort-of fiancé, and I had planned weeks ago to take this flight together. We'd been so busy lately that a day spent together, even flying, was going to be a treat. He was going to hold my hand so I wouldn't be afraid. He'd referred to himself as my security blanket. However, it had only taken a ten word text message this morning to yank that blanket away.

"I still think I should drive to Texas to get the puppy rather than bringing it back on the plane," I proposed once more in my struggle to stay on *terra firma.*

"You don't have time. You have to be back by Tuesday to cover for my vacation. You do remember I'm taking Pete, Sarah and little Emma to spend the rest of the month at the Cape."

"How'd you manage to score a beach rental this time of the year?"

"We'll be using a friend's cabin while he's in California for his first grandchild's birth. Just think—three weeks on the beach avoiding the August heat. It's perfect, plus I'll get to spend some time with my new granddaughter."

He's right, I'm a selfish bitch. And I've got a tee shirt to prove it. All because I don't want to strap on metal wings, defy gravity, and take to the sky. I would not only be depriving Sal of his first time off in a year, but also his son, just back from serving in Afghanistan, his daughter-in-law, who's a brand-new mother, and Pete and Sarah's three-month old daughter. This was to be their perfect vacation together.

I finished packing, stepping carefully around the block of guilt the size of an elephant he'd dropped right in the middle of my kitchen.

"Look, Kate. Being afraid to fly is nothing to be ashamed of if you've never done it before. I was scared stiff the first time I flew."

"Where were you going?"

"Nam."

The guilt in the room just took on blue-whale proportions. Leaning my whole weight on the suitcase, I managed to zip it closed, yank it off the table, and roll it over to the space by the door that already held my oversized purse with my ticket, wallet, and Kindle.

On the table lay my phone, programmed with everyone's number I could possibly need. I picked it up to check my texts again then set it down. I was disappointed, yes, but that wasn't what had me in such a purple funk.

I switched on the kettle to heat water for tea. I didn't feel like eating lunch, but Seamus had texted me this morning, reminding me to eat and take the air-sickness pills he'd left on the counter because airlines no longer fed you. I brewed the tea, made some toast, downed the pills, and sat at the table, trying to decide whether to share my fears. Then I jumped up and grabbed an apple off the counter, thinking I might get hungry later and dropped it into my purse.

"Okay, I know you, girl. You're nervous as a cat. What's going on? As much fun as it is to tease you, this jumpiness is not just a fear of flying."

Looking out the window at the dogs in the exercise yard, I saw each had claimed a shady spot, and all were sleeping. Dillon was asleep at my feet. Being without him for a week was going to be difficult. Sal's stare finally got to me. Maybe what I needed was for him to laugh at my suspicious mind and point out the holes in my misgivings.

"Last night, Harry called to talk as he does every night." I smiled at the thought. "Before he hung up, he sang the Beatles' song *I Want To Hold Your Hand* to me in his elegant baritone. He told me he was going to hold my hand all the way to Denver so I wouldn't be afraid. I slept like a log, reassured he would be there. Then, at ten-thirty this morning, I got a text saying, 'Flying out of Boston. See you when I get back. H.'"

"So Harry won't be meeting you at the airport? A text, you say, not a call," he mused, a frown settling on his face. "He didn't tell you why. That doesn't sound like him."

"I tried calling him when I got it, but the call went to voicemail. I pulled out my phone and opened the text. "The message was signed 'H.'"

"Yeah, I would imagine that Harry wouldn't bother writing out his name."

"Except since February, he's signed all his texts with 'F' for fiancé." Of course, something could have come up or he could have gotten an emergency job and been distracted, but it didn't feel right. "Sal, do you have Sadie's number?"

I had never spoken to the wondrous Sadie who was the other love of Harry's life. I remembered being jealous the first time I heard about her. Of course, that was before I discovered that this amazing woman who managed Harry's business was a former FBI agent and a grandmother five times over. "Something doesn't feel right about it to me. For my peace of mind, I need to know I'm wrong. That all my worrying is for nothing, just a combination of my disappointment and my fear of flying."

Sal pushed up the brim of his Red Sox cap and stared at me. Reaching into his back pocket, he pulled out his phone, plucked mine off the table, and loaded the number. Dropping mine back where I'd left it, he reeled in his lanky, time-worn, six-foot four-inch frame and pressed 'dial.'

"Sadie, how are you doing? It's Sal. I was trying to get a hold of our boy and his phone keeps going to voicemail. Do you know where he is? Right. They are. I must have forgotten it was today. Yeah. No, I'll wait and talk to him later. Thanks, Sadie." He shoved the phone back into his pocket and pulled out his keys. Then, not looking at me, he stood.

"It's time to hit the road, girl. You have a puppy to go get."

Dillon stood, knowing something was happening, and licked my face as I hugged my new-daddy dog. Telling him I would be bringing his kid back, I let him out into the yard with the others. Silently, I followed Sal out to the van. The quiet lasted until we turned onto I-84, heading toward Hartford.

"She talked to him at eight this morning. He was packed and couldn't wait to head out to meet you. She thought he might have turned off his phone so you two could have some alone time without interruption. She said she'd let him know when he calls in that I wanted him. But she told me since you two have so little time together, we shouldn't bother you. Kate, why do you suppose he would change his mind between eight this morning and when you got the text?"

"It was ten-thirty, and I'm not sure we even know for sure he did change his mind." I stared through the windshield, my head playing with the possibilities that kept bouncing up in my brain like a game of whack-a-mole. It was still early enough in the day that the descent through the tunnel and the climb up the flyover in Hartford moved easily. We transitioned onto I-91, heading north. My mind tried to play hide-and-seek with possible answers, but I came up with zilch. I didn't want Sadie to worry, but if I didn't hear from him by tomorrow; I'd have to give her a call and fill her in.

"I'm worried he's in trouble. What I want to do is drive to Boston and find him, but I haven't any idea where he is. So I've got no choice but to get on that plane and fly to Denver. Sal, it'll be late here when my flight gets in, so I won't call you, but if I don't hear from him, I'm calling Sadie tomorrow. She would know who he was supposed to be meeting and where he was scheduled to stay. Maybe she can call those places and see if he's there." I glanced again at my phone, and then, defeated, jammed it into my pocket. I turned toward Sal. "Look, I'll be staying with Joyce Marks tonight, along with Cathy Harrison. Their numbers are by the phone. We're scheduled to hit the road by five tomorrow morning for the drive to Lubbock. I'll call and let you know if I find anything out."

"Why are these women driving you all the way to Texas to see the litter?"

"Well, Joyce is thinking about using Dillon as stud to her new champion bitch, who is a half sister of Katja, the puppies' dam. She and Cathy were already planning to go see the litter, so when she heard I'd be coming out to choose my stud puppy, she suggested I join them. Since it's a direct flight between Hartford and Denver, it worked out well for me. This way, I won't have to change planes with the puppy on the way home and it will be a much shorter flight.

"Joyce is an old friend who began showing and breeding just a few years after Gramps did. Cathy bred Katja and wants to see what her next generation is producing. Both Joyce and Cathy are judges as well as breeders. Both have judged at the Samoyed National Specialty Show. Since this is Lily Peters' first litter, she wanted them to use their expertise to critique the puppies. Lily's bringing the litter up to Lubbock, a couple of hours north of her home, to make our drive shorter.

"It's a quick trip for all of us. Cathy's flying down to Denver from Utah to ride with us and visit, but she's got a judging assignment to get to next week. Joyce works for the Denver Sheriff's Office, so she's got to be at work on Monday, and I've got to be back here, so we won't waste time. We'll drive down tomorrow, which will give us a chance to chat and catch up with each other. We'll spend all day Saturday with the puppies. We'll drive back to Denver Sunday with my stud puppy, so Cathy can make her connection home Sunday night. On Monday, I'll get my direct flight back with the puppy."

The highway had begun to get congested with people heading north of Hartford, homeward bound after the early shift. I was glad when we pulled onto the connecting road that headed directly to Bradley International Airport. As the terminal came into view, my stomach clenched. Ready or not, I was going. Since I had only one small suitcase, I didn't need to check my luggage. I hopped out at the Southwest entrance, waved goodbye to Sal, and strode quickly through the automatic doors before I could change my mind.

My younger brother Tim, who of the twins was the bigger pain in the butt, made me put up with a gallon of mockery in exchange for guiding me through the steps to get my boarding pass online and to double check that the return reservation said I'd be traveling with a puppy in the cabin. It was worth the grief, though, not to be standing in that long line at the ticket counter.

Turning left, I followed the signs to an open area where security was set up. Hefting my carry-on bag, I put it on the conveyor and took a bin, which I loaded with my shoes, phone, and keys, and purse. I watched them slide out of sight into the x-ray machine. Next I stepped into the little cubicle for my TSA colonoscopy.

"You need to stand with your feet on the marks on the floor, miss, and extend your arms over your head."

I heard a beep and thought I was done, but, no, it seemed I had set off their alarm and was now considered a threat to my country. I knew that, except for my watch, my earrings and the ring on my finger, there was nothing metal on me. The agent had me step to one side, where she waved a wand over me, front and back, then between my legs and over each arm. My watch set it off. I'd forgotten it had a steel band. I'd gotten it after countless generations of Shannon Samoyeds had dined on a menu of leather bands. In the end, the security guard decided that I wasn't a danger and I was released. Sitting, I put on my shoes and asked directions to my gate.

The flight had seemed an ideal time for me to be alone with Harry, my sort-of fiancé, especially since our unusual engagement was still a work in progress. Instead, this trip was becoming more like the first level of Hell, and flunking my first-ever security check certainly qualified as Limbo.

Ten minutes later, the trip reached the second level when the announcement came that our flight, which was scheduled to take off in twenty minutes, was still in Baltimore, so that there would be a delay of at least an hour.

Now rapidly twisting itself into a knot, my stomach warned that if we weren't taking off for another hour, I should eat. By instinct, my feet carried me to Dunkin' Donuts. Five minutes later, I emerged with some toasted croissants, marmalade, and cocoa—strictly comfort food. I settled into a seat nearest my gate's check-in area to satisfy my now-real hunger and prepared to wait. While discarding my empty cup and the rest of my trash in the bin was next to the check-in desk, I noticed what looked like an irate would-be passenger haranguing a tight-lipped boarding attendant.

"Look, just page him, lady," the man growled.

I hurried back to my seat as she picked up the microphone and announced, "Would passenger Harry Foyle please report to the Southwest check-in at gate eight?"

I froze, waited and slowly looked around. *Was Harry here after all? Who was this guy? He didn't look like one of Harry's usual corporate clients.* I turned toward the desk again as he made her repeat the call. That's when I got an insane idea.

I pulled my phone from my pocket, and, waving it around as though I were having trouble getting a signal, I snapped two photos of the man's face. Then I casually returned to my seat. Before I could talk myself out of it, I sent the photos to Sadie, telling her Harry wasn't with me and asking whether she knew who this man was; he was angry and looking for Harry.

A minute later, my pocket buzzed. I reached in and read the text from Sadie. *I'll try to locate Harry. Continue your trip. At all costs, stay away from this man. He's dangerous.*

Note:

Anyone wishing to knit some of the designs described in the

Kate Killoy Mystery Series,

visit

www.kanineknits.com,

where the designs are available for purchase as patterns or in books.

A NOTE FROM PEGGY

Dear Reader,

As a lifelong mystery reader, who often reads a book a day when I can squeeze it in around my writing, I find that my favorite mysteries are those that not only solve a problem but introduce me to characters with whom I want to spend time. So when I began to write this series, I knew I wanted to share with you, not only a world of showing dogs. but also the life of a knitting designer who caters to dog lovers, a role I've played for the last twenty years.

Kate's world is inhabited by a large Irish family, an extended family of dog breeders and trainers, mathematicians, members of the "long arm of the law club", and, of course, Harry, who along with Kate, always seems to have a knack for finding adventure.

If you enjoyed this book, I'd love to hear from you. You can find me at my website, **www.PeggyGaffney.com** and learn all about The Kate Killoy Mysteries. While you're there, sign up for my newsletter to keep posted about when the next books will be available in the series. You can also join me and Kate on our Facebook page **Kate Killoy Mysteries** where others have talked about their reaction to the book. You might want to add yours.

I look forward to bringing you further adventures with Kate, Harry and all the dogs.

Peggy Gaffney

www.ingramcontent.com/pod-product-compliance
Lightning Source LLC
Chambersburg PA
CBHW030421310726
48979CB00009B/1559/J

* 9 7 8 0 9 9 6 4 5 3 1 5 8 *